7º

the taxi driver's daughter

Crocodile Soup
Bloodlines (short stories)
Sudden Collapses in Public Places (poetry)

julia darling

the taxi driver's daughter

VIKING

an imprint of

PENGUIN BOOKS

VIKING

Published by the Penguin Group
Penguin Books Ltd, 80 Strand, London wc2r orl, England
Penguin Putnam Inc., 375 Hudson Street, New York, New York 10014, USA
Penguin Books Australia Ltd, 250 Camberwell Road, Camberwell, Victoria 3124, Australia
Penguin Books Canada Ltd, 10 Alcorn Avenue, Toronto, Ontario, Canada m4v 3b2
Penguin Books India (P) Ltd, 11 Community Centre,
Panchsheel Park, New Delhi – 110 017, India
Penguin Books (NZ) Ltd, Cnr Rosedale and Airborne Roads,
Albany, Auckland, New Zealand
Penguin Books (South Africa) (Pty) Ltd, 24 Sturdee Avenue,
Rosebank 2196, South Africa

Penguin Books Ltd, Registered Offices: 80 Strand, London wc2r orl, England

www.penguin.com

www.juliadarling.co.uk

First published 2003
1

Copyright © Julia Darling, 2003

Set in 10/13pt Sabon
Typeset by Intype Libra Ltd
Printed in Great Britain by Clays Ltd, St Ives plc

A CIP catalogue record for this book is available from the British Library

isbn 0–670–91419–3

To Bev, Scarlet and Florrie

acknowledgements

Thanks to:

The drivers of Five Star Taxis, with whom I have had many discussions.

Avril Joy, who talked to me about her work in women's prisons.

Charlie Hardwick and the women at Melmerby Hall, for reading and listening.

Scarlet and Florrie, for their thoughts on adolescence.

Bev, for her careful corrections.

The film-maker Ian Cottage, for his help at the beginning.

Andrea Badenoch, Debbie Taylor, Gerry Wardle, Wendy Robertson and Linda France, who have been my writing companions on various retreats.

My mother, Vicky Darling, and sister, Josie Darling, for reading and helpful thoughts.

My agent, Hannah Griffiths, for her clarity and support.

Mary Mount, for her skilful editorial work.

The English School of the University of Newcastle upon Tyne, for letting me write in peace.

New Writing North, for making things easier.

I would also like to acknowledge financial support from both the Royal Literary Fund and Northern Rock.

mac

Mac drives like a man in a pot of treacle. His hands rest heavily on the steering wheel; his big back is encased in the warm curve of the driver's seat. He indicates slowly, sighing as he waits for the traffic lights to change. The blue polished taxi smells of his days: of slowly chewed Extra Strong Mints, of coat linings, used five-pound notes and other people's shower gel.

The city infuriates him, with its roadworks and changing one-way systems. He knows every part of it, each cul-de-sac, terrace, avenue and estate. Mac shakes his head at flimsy cyclists who don't indicate, at overcautious drivers who always seem to wear hats. He watches the city with his weary taxi-driver's eyes; the demolitions and the beginnings of new buildings appearing like skeletons on his skyline. He thinks about concrete and football scores, and what he would do if he ran the country. He half listens to his radio. He answers quiz questions out loud. Like all taxi drivers, he longs for trips to the airport. He craves acceleration. So when a woman dressed like a meringue gets into his taxi and tells him she's going to southern Spain, he smiles like a child, his big mouth stretching his face into creases, and he doesn't mind when she laughs a scratchy laugh and tells him she always goes to Spain at this time of year, and then talks for the whole journey about her daughter's divorce. He agrees with everything she says about her son-in-law, and drives to Newcastle airport affably, piling her creamy-coloured cases on a trolley when they reach the terminal, and then watching her disappearing into the crowd. He wraps her ten-pound note around the others with a rubber band holding them in a tight coil, and roars out of the airport, on to the fast ring road, with the sky ahead of him turning bright pink, and the trees sticking up in fierce black fingers, and he delights in the almost empty dual carriageway, and in the feeling that he can swerve into any lane he chooses. His car gallops along like a horse let loose on an endless beach, and there are no traffic jams, no plastic cones, no warnings of unavoidable delays. He drives at eighty miles an hour, recklessly, the photographs of his wife, Louise, and his two daughters, Caris and Stella, dangling from the mirror in a fluffy frame, with sparkling eyes, approving of him. The city ahead is a heap of twinkling jewels.

Mac sings. He opens his mouth and sings 'Jerusalem', feeling his rusty voice gather strength.

And did those feet in ancient times!

And then his mobile rings, cutting into his euphoria, and he must search for the jangling phone in the inner pocket of his leather jacket and swerve into the slow lane. It's his eldest daughter, Stella, her voice sharp and nervous.

'Dad, you've got to come home.'

In the background he can hear his younger daughter, Caris: 'What? What's going on? Tell me!'

'Speak up, will you!' he says to Stella. 'Tell Caris to shut up.'

'It's Mum,' Stella whispers, her voice breaking. 'She's been arrested.'

decorating the tree

Caris stands in the middle of an over-decorated sitting room holding a plastic angel by the waist. She's fifteen years old. Around her bare, purposeful feet there are ragged piles of tinsel, squashed crackers, tangled fairy-lights, broken shepherds and wise men from various Nativities pulled from a dented cardboard box marked 'Xmas'. The television is on, but the volume is turned down, and the screen is filled with wide-eyed celebrities with pink necks and glossy hair who peer out at Caris as she squeezes the small angel in her hand. Caris hums, filling the room with her strong young body. She loves the glitter and trash of Christmas. It makes her heart beat and her cheeks turn red.

In the corner of the room there's a gawky artificial tree. It's the same tinsel Christmas tree that the family have used for the last five years, and it looks depressed, as if it has been in the dark too long and can't work up much enthusiasm for the festive season. Caris would have preferred a real tree but her mother, Louise, wasn't having it. 'The needles drop off and stick in the carpet,' she'd said briskly earlier that day. 'Don't they, Mac?' and her father had looked up from his newspaper with a loose dreamy expression. 'I'm not bothered,' he'd grunted.

If it was up to Caris, she would hang lights from the chimney pots and have an illuminated Santa and sleigh galloping across the roof. She would wear a dress made from tinsel, and glass slippers on her feet.

3

Her sister, Stella, is upstairs learning lines from *Macbeth*. It's getting on Caris's nerves; she can't hear the words, just squeaks and growls as her sister paces up and down, shoulders stiff, script outstretched. Stella is always learning things. *By the time she leaves school she won't have any space left in her brain* thinks Caris. Then she thinks of her own brain, as a new, unused sponge, whereas Stella's would be all grey, and waterlogged with words.

Caris smirks and sticks the angel on the top of the tree.

'Stay there!' she says firmly. She wishes it would stand straight and not dangle sideways. The angel's eyes are flaking off, which makes her look cross-eyed. Caris steps backwards and treads on a glass bauble, feeling it crunch.

'Oh, fuck it,' says Caris. 'Fuck, fuck,' inspecting her foot, which bleeds slightly from the heel. She flops down on to the sofa and stares at the blood that gathers itself into a shining bead, and dabs at the cut with a brown cushion, then picks up the remote control and waves it at the television, ignoring the broken glass on the floor. The room fills with raucous celebrity laughter.

Her sister stalks into the room, still haughty from her acting, and stares down at Caris on the sofa.

'What art thou doing?' she asks, pushing her black hair from her face.

Caris looks lazily at the television. Stella leans over the sofa back and pulls Caris's ear.

'Where's Mum?' says Stella. 'She should have been back ages ago.'

Caris pushes her away and changes channel. She likes annoying Stella; it's like scratching an itch.

'You've broken a bauble,' snaps Stella. 'That's a hazard.'

Stella often uses health-and-safety vocabulary in conversation; words like 'harmful' and 'unhygienic'.

'Go poison yourself,' sneers Caris.

Then the doorbell rings. Stella sighs loudly and goes to open it. Caris shuts her eyes and listens. She is always hoping that there might be a surprise caller, someone who asks for her, someone with an urgent message.

The voices in the hall are male, and thick as soup. Caris limps to the sitting-room door and squints through the crack. There are two policemen. They look immense in the narrow hallway, with blue beefy shoulders, daunting hats and meaty jaws. One of them glances up and sees Caris.

'Is that your sister?' he says.

'Yes, that's Caris,' says Stella, as if Caris is a stain she hasn't got round to removing. Stella is pale. Her voice has a catch in it, and she looks tiny and white next to the blue policemen. Suddenly Caris feels protective.

'What's going on?' she asks loudly, stepping into the hallway.

'It's your dad we're after,' says the younger policeman, who has a schoolboy circle of pinkness on each cheek.

'What for?' asks Caris.

'He needs to come to the police station.'

'What's he done?'

'He hasn't done anything,' says Stella. 'It's Mum.'

'What about her?'

'She's been caught . . .' Stella stops and turns to the policemen for help. There is a pause then one of them cuts in.

'Does your father have a mobile?'

Stella nods.

'You might like to phone him, to ask him to come home.'

'Why?' badgers Caris.

No one answers her.

'I'll phone him,' says Stella.

'He'll be driving,' snaps Caris. 'It's dangerous. What's happened to Mum?'

Stella dials Mac's number, ignoring Caris's indignant questioning.

'Dad,' she says, 'you've got to come home.'

'What?' cries Caris. 'What's going on? Tell me!'

'Dad says shut up,' says Stella.

The policemen step outside and stand on the pavement with their legs slightly apart, making a great business of breathing in and out, their car parked in the middle of the road with the lights on and the doors open. *They act as if they own the bloody street*, thinks Caris. She can hear her father's voice asking questions down the phone. She pictures him, plump as a cushion, as he steers his taxi through the teatime traffic, drumming his fingers on the steering wheel, filling the driver's seat with his heavy body.

'It's Mum,' Stella tells her father, in a melodramatic whisper. 'She's been arrested. The police are here, and they say she's distressed.'

'What?' shouts Caris. 'Did you say she's been arrested?'

Stella puts the phone down.

'Be quiet, Caris,' she says. 'People will hear.'

The policemen plod back into the house. Their radios keep on squawking and bleeping, and Caris can't think straight. It's as if the house is filled with a flock of large birds. Stella herds everyone into the sitting room, and the four of them stand awkwardly around the broken bauble on the carpet.

'Christmas, eh!' says one of the policemen.

'I wish someone would explain,' cries Caris, who feels as if she is in a television programme but has been given an inadequate script.

'Let's just wait until your father comes home,' says the older policeman, who has a bit of crisp hanging in his moustache.

'He'll be here in a minute,' Stella says. 'He was on the way back from the airport.'

The pink-faced policeman goes to the mantelpiece and peers at a family photograph. In it the family cluster together in summer T-shirts and bikini tops, Stella and Louise in the middle, more like sisters than mother and daughter, with thin faces and identical long hair, and Caris on the left with her strong bright features, and Mac with his shaved head, brown as a conker, on the right.

'Holidays?' says the policeman.

'Tenerife,' says Stella.

'Lovely.'

'Has my mother killed someone?' asks Caris.

'Of course she hasn't,' says Stella.

6

'I'm only asking,' says Caris. 'I've got a right to know.'

No one speaks. Caris stares at the policemen's chests. She wonders if they're wearing bulletproof vests.

The two girls recognise the sound of their father driving round the corner, changing gear, parking, and slamming the door of his taxi.

'That's him,' mumbles Stella nervously.

Mac charges in wearing his worn leather jacket, pushing through the door, stroking his neatly shaved head. Stella grabs his hand. Caris folds her arms over her chest.

'Well,' says Mac, 'what a business. It must be a mistake.'

'Your wife was arrested for shoplifting in Fenwick's department store at . . .' The policeman reaches into his breast pocket for his notebook, and turns the pages authoritatively. 'Five twenty-five p.m.'

'What did she steal?' asks Caris.

'She was apprehended with, er . . . footwear.' The policeman coughs gently, embarrassed.

'What kind of footwear?' says Caris.

'Luxury footwear.'

Caris stands on her toes, trying to reach their level.

'Excuse me!' she says. 'I think you've got the wrong woman.'

'Can you come with us now, sir?' they ask Mac, who is shaking his head, over and over again, like the ornamental dog on his dashboard.

'She was probably about to pay for them,' says Caris.

'She'd left the store,' says the policeman. 'She was arrested in the street.'

Stella says nothing. She turns and goes into the kitchen and fetches a dustpan and brush and kneels in the centre of the circle of legs, sweeping up the broken bauble. A tear runs down her nose and slides into the corner of her mouth.

Caris feels as if the inside of her head is a slide show, an endless series of images of her mother running down a street, chased by a policeman, wearing a pair of beautiful shoes.

'I'd better get down the station, then,' says Mac.

The policemen nod sympathetically and start to escort Mac out of the room.

'Can I come?' calls Caris.

'No,' says Mac.

'You'll just make things worse,' Stella says, wielding her dustpan as if it's a dagger.

'I'll wait in the car,' says Caris.

'It will take a while,' mutters the older policeman. 'We haven't charged her yet.'

The two policemen exchange glances then herd Mac out of the room, leaving Caris with her mouth open and her green eyes blazing. Stella trudges into the kitchen and starts clattering and wiping.

Caris begins to hurl decorations at the tree, bunging things any place where there's a gap, all the time imagining her mother wandering through the fine-smelling floors of Fenwick's, surrounded by forests of tempting shoes, their toes pointing at her, their soles arched, their high heels posturing. She sees her with a furtive, criminal expression on her face, eyes darting about, a glistening layer of sweat on her forehead. But it doesn't fit in. The last time Caris saw her mother she was hoovering the bathroom wearing a pair of bedroom slippers. Caris had noticed how old the skin on her hands looked, even though the rest of her looked so young. Now Caris feels as if she hardly knows her at all.

Caris might explode with curiosity. She stands by the sitting-room curtains, looking out hungrily into the street, biting the edge of her little fingernail until it bleeds. She can picture her father saying, 'Why, Louise, why? Don't I work night and day to buy you anything you want? Didn't I recently get you a new saucepan set?'

My mother is a robber, thinks Caris. *The robber mother. Other people's mothers get things like depression and have hysterectomies, but my mother is a thief.*

It's late when Mac finally returns in his taxi. Caris runs to the door and stands there framed in light, her chin jutting out, her hands on her hips. Mac climbs out of the car and walks round to the passenger door, opening it to reveal Caris's mother.

Louise looks diminished; huddled in her raincoat, her girlish hair undone and falling either side of her face, staring straight ahead, then turning to blink up at Mac, her face shuttered.

The couple walk slowly to the door.

'Hallo, Caris,' says Louise. Caris can sense Stella, standing behind her on the stairs.

'So,' says Caris loudly, 'did you do it?'

'That's enough,' says Mac, pushing past her. Louise makes a run for the stairs, slithering past Stella.

'Tea's ready,' says Stella in a prim voice. She walks into the kitchen and begins to drag the dried-up casserole out of the oven.

Caris follows Mac into the sitting room.

'She's not herself,' he says finally. 'She didn't know what she was doing.' He looks helpless. 'Monthlies,' he murmurs, and picks up a newspaper.

'Have they charged her, or what?' asks Caris.

'Yes. Let's not talk about it now, pet,' he says. 'Let's watch the news.'

Caris can hardly contain herself. She stamps up to her room, ignoring weak calls of 'Tea!'

Her mother's door is closed. Caris sits on her bed and considers things and how much they cost. She wonders if a stolen thing looks different to something you've bought. She wonders if any of the birthday presents her mother gave her were stolen. *Perhaps she stole me*, she thinks.

brussels sprouts and toasts

By Christmas morning Caris is swollen with questions that no one
will answer. She feels as if her head is about to burst open.

As usual, Louise's mother, Nana Price, sashays into the house
with her sagging handbag, her bunions, and a brown bottle of
sweet sherry. She lands on the sofa and stays there all day, her straw
hair becoming gradually more dishevelled, her jokes more lewd,
and her cigarettes more frequent. Caris sits next to her, nibbling
peanuts, while in the kitchen Stella and Louise baste the dead bird
in the oven, and rip small green leaves off Brussels sprouts and etch
deep crosses into their stalks. Caris can hear the quiet music of
their conversation. It makes her feel left out. Stella and her mother
have always been close, like birds on a perch. Caris suspects that
Stella and Louise have talked about the crime behind her back, and
that Louise has confided in Stella, telling her everything.

Unwrapped presents are piled on the floor, and shreds of
wrapping paper and ribbon spill out of the waste-paper basket.
Gifts were particular lavish this year, as if Mac and Louise were
trying too hard, Caris thinks. She got new jeans, a stereo, make-
up, and Louise gave her a brightly beaded purse with a twenty-
pound note in it. But Caris found it hard to gasp with surprise
and be grateful. Her mouth ached, and she hardly looked up.
Somehow, nothing felt like a surprise any more. *It's all just stuff,*
she thinks, *and they probably got in debt to buy it. We're skint.*

Nana Price thinks that Louise needs a holiday, and she says so, over and over again, to Caris, who is the only one who appears to be listening.

'It's stress, pet lamb,' she rasps, inhaling loudly on her cigarette. 'It's your father and them taxis. Teenagers. Christmas.'

'I still don't get it,' says Caris loudly.

Nana Price purses her blurred lips, shakily topping up her sherry glass. Caris looks at the crumpled brown skin on her hands, the loose rings on her twig fingers.

'She wasn't right in the head,' Nana Price mutters. 'I've read about it in magazines. It's like a disease. Stress, syndrome, somethin'.'

'So what will happen?'

Caris feels that all she does is ask this question, and that no one ever answers.

At least Nana Price tries to communicate.

'Well, Caris, sweetheart,' she sighs, 'I expect she'll get put on probation, or somethin' like that, and mebbes pay some sort of fine.' She frowns, confused.

'Did you ever steal?' asks Caris.

'I think I might have had that postnatal thingy when Louise was born. I liked to nick the odd thing, perfume and that, but nothing serious, like.'

'Did you get caught?' asks Caris.

'Never.' Nana Price looks smug.

'Perhaps she's going off her head,' says Caris.

'She just needs a holiday, that's all. Louise, d'you hear me? What you need is a holiday somewhere nice, pet. Do you want a hand?'

There is no reply from the kitchen. Just stirrings, bubblings and the chink of glass. Then, when the dinner is cooked, the four women sit waiting for Mac to come home from work, staring at the TV, eating crisps and cracking nuts. Caris loathes the way they chew, their jaws moving in a synchronised rhythm, and the sound the food makes as it slumps down their throats. She can't stand it any more.

'Why are we here?' she says, waving a pair of nutcrackers. 'What's the point of anything?'

'Shut up, Caris,' says Stella, without even turning her head.

'It's Christmas,' slurs Nana in a furry voice, raising her glass. 'All the best!'

Just then Mac appears, eyebrows raised, carrying a large box of cheap crackers. Since the incident Mac has developed a sideways walk, and he bends his head as if expecting to be hit when he walks into rooms.

'I'm back,' he announces. 'Here I am!'

'Ho, ho, ho!' says Caris, with a mean, thin expression.

'It's dinnertime, then,' says Louise, grimly.

The meal is lengthy, the room filled with steam. Caris looks round the table at her preposterous family in lopsided bright paper hats, unrolling jokes from crackers.

Louise speaks plaintively about the turkey: 'Is it a bit pink, d'you think, love? On the bottom? Shall I pop it back in?'

Stella spoons out Brussels sprouts with a look of pleased pain on her face. There are more toasts.

'May our troubles soon be over!' says Nana dreamily, looking as if she might fall into the gravy.

As Louise holds a match to the Christmas pudding Caris can't control herself any longer.

'Do you realise we are now a criminal family?' she says.

'This is not a criminal family!' exclaims Nana Price.

'I have driven taxis for eighteen years, and I earn my living by hard graft!' shouts Mac as the brandy flames subside into a glowering blue shadow.

'Taxis?' snorts Caris. 'It's not hard, driving about, is it?'

'That's enough,' whimpers Louise. 'I'm sorry, I shouldn't have done it.' And the flame goes out.

'But why did you? I just want to know?' asks Caris. 'I'm interested.'

'Because . . . because . . .' Louise stares at the Christmas pudding, trying but unable to form words.

'It's stress!' trumpets Nana Price. 'She hasn't robbed a flaming bank! What's all the bloody fuss about? Eh?'

'Let's not spoil the day!' says Mac, holding a small glass in the air with his large hand.

'Shut up, Caris,' says Stella. 'Why don't you keep your stupid mouth shut?'

'Don't, Stella,' says Louise.

'I just want an explanation!' yells Caris. 'What's wrong with that?'

'I don't know, Caris,' whimpers Louise. 'It was like I was dreaming.'

'You see!' croaks Nana. 'She was just confused, weren't you, love. Just a bit out of sorts.'

Caris stands up, rips her hat from her head and lets it float to the carpet, and stalks out of the hot, impossible room and out of the door into the street.

'Help!' she shouts at the closed doors of Christmas Day. 'Save me!'

She sits on the doorstep, her head in her hands, and senses the door opening behind her, knowing it will be her mother.

'Go away,' she groans.

'Come back in, Caris. It's Christmas,' whispers Louise.

She feels her mother's hand on her shoulder, light as a bird.

Caris tenses and shakes her head. Mac stamps up behind them.

'Get back inside!' he shouts.

A small girl in a blue woollen hat wobbles past on a new bike, staring at Caris framed in the doorway. Her mother waddles behind her with her hands outstretched and shaking.

'I'm sorry, Caris. I was stupid. I don't know why I did it,' mumbles Louise, her fingers pressing into Caris's neck.

'Leave her!' shouts Mac. 'Shut the door. Ignore her!'

'Stop shouting, Mac,' Louise says. 'Please stop shouting.'

Caris feels Mac pulling Louise back, and then hears the door locking behind her. She shivers. She looks at the street she's grown up in, at the closed windows, the symmetrical front doors, each with an identical porch. She sees herself, sitting there, entangled in a web of identical redbrick streets and terraces surrounding the city. From where she sits she can see the hollow of the park, a pool of ink in the middle of the suburbs, its grey trees reaching up into the sky.

A flock of birds fly above her like black rags.

Caris waits for Louise to come out again and beg her to come back, but she doesn't come. Caris sits there until her fingers are numb, eventually going to the window and looking through at her family, who sit in a row on the sofa. They look like waxworks. She can see the oblong shape of the television reflected in their eyes. Mac glances up and sees her, nudges Louise, and smiles victoriously, as if he was right all along. He nods to Stella, who comes and opens the door with a prim, ironed mouth.

'You can come in now,' she says. 'We're watching the Queen.'

lovely girls

Jeannie's insistent voice echoes over Mac's radio. 'Mr Kawoto. The Willow Hotel, Jesmond. He's going to Team Valley industrial estate. There's been an accident on the Tyne Bridge. You'd better go round by the Redheugh. How's your back?'

Jeannie always asks about Mac's back, as if it's a member of his family. She's got aspirations to leave the taxi business and become an aromatherapist. She's done an evening course, but she can't make the break. She sits like a prisoner in the booking office behind the station, with a pock-marked computer, and a grubby telephone, drinking coffee from polystyrene cups, smoking herbal cigarettes. There is a faint smell of lavender, like a memory, behind the smells of body odour, plastic and old carpet. Mac has never even seen Jeannie's legs.

He doesn't bother answering.

He drives carefully over sleeping policemen in the suburbs of Newcastle. An eager Japanese businessman crouches behind him, his sharp spectacles glinting, his hair oiled. The taxi smells of Mac's lunch, a coronation-chicken buttie that he picks up every day from Filler's snack bar.

'You got a family?' says Mac, affably, lifting his eyes to the mirror slowly, as he indicates left. At least, he tries to sound friendly. Lately he finds himself trying to fill the silences, afraid that at any moment he will fall into the morose pit that Louise has dug

15

for him, with its accusing voices and hot rushes of lava-like shame.

'Excuse me?' says the businessman, brushing the lapel of his smart suit.

'A family? Children? A wife?'

'Yes,' says the businessman.

'Kids, eh!' says Mac, tapping the steering wheel, then reaching out to adjust the photographs of his daughters. He wishes the Japanese man would ask him a question. 'That's Caris. She's fifteen.' He makes a dog-like expression, which is lost on the businessman, who hears only a series of friendly barks coming from the front seat. 'It's a Welsh name, Caris. After my grandmother. She was Welsh, see. And that's Stella, my eldest. She's into drama, like. Shakespeare.'

'Yes,' says the businessman.

'Lovely girls, both of them,' muses Mac. 'Caris is a bit wild. She just says what she feels. Just like that. Her sister, she's the clever one.'

He turns into the industrial estate. The grass verges look new, as if they've been placed there overnight.

'Caris is difficult. Don't get me wrong; I love Caris. Well, you do, don't you?'

'Yes,' nods the businessman enthusiastically.

'You should see her room. Stuff everywhere. Loud music. You can't ignore her. She stamps about.' Mac chuckles, although he finds that Caris makes him uncomfortable these days. 'But her sister,' he goes on, 'she's into that Lady Macbeth. Out damn spot! You know that one?'

'Lady Macbeth?' echoes the businessman.

'Shakespeare.'

'Ah, Shakespeare!' The businessman nods and nods, wondering what Shakespeare has to do with anything.

'Caris, she's a lovely girl. Very striking. Stella, too, but Caris is really noticeable. You worry about your daughters. D'you have daughters?'

'No.'

'Christ, do I worry. You have to put your foot down. To set boundaries. It's hard, y'know. I mean, it's a bloody forest out there.'

Mac gestures towards the flat car parks of the industrial estate, and the businessman assumes that the trading estate was once a forest and nods sympathetically.

'Drugs, sex. You have to have eyes in the back of your head.'

Mac pulls up next to a square clean building with 'PLASTICS INC.' written in large letters above the door. The businessman is uncertain what to do next. He leans nervously over the seat, holding a twenty-pound note.

'This is I,' he announces brightly. 'I am in plastic.'

Mac is still thinking about drugs and sex. He imagines a wolfish stranger beckoning Caris into an alley.

'I worry, see,' he says to the twenty-pound note. 'Christ, do I worry. It's Caris. She gets carried away, y'know, she gets . . .' He searches for a word, switching off the engine. 'Overexcited,' he says eventually. 'And then she gets disappointed. How do you deal with your daughters in Japan?' He turns to look at the businessman, and sees his blank expression.

'Oh, yes,' says the businessman.

Mac sighs and takes the money, then unwraps a plastic bag full of change and begins to count out coins.

'Nice talking to you,' he says. 'I hope your plastics go well today.'

'Thank you,' says the businessman, beginning to open the door.

'You don't want your kids to be disappointed,' says Mac, turning to look at the man who is no longer there.

'No, you don't,' says Mac, feeling the wad of anxiety in his chest tighten.

'Temple Grove Rest Home!' squawks Jeannie. 'Mrs Ernest. She says she's been waiting for half an hour, and she's foaming. She's going to the crematorium.' There's a short pause. 'Again!' cackles Jeannie, making the radio rattle with her hoarse, herbal laughter.

'I'm coming,' says Mac, working out a route in his head, like a well-oiled machine.

'You working late?' splutters Jeannie.

'Yeah, I expect so,' says Mac, knowing that he would rather be working than sitting at home, with Louise guiltily stirring a pan of soup in the kitchen, and Caris sucking her hair and looking at him as if he's a wall she'd like to demolish, and Stella frightening him with her long words. *Home is complicated*, thinks Mac, *whereas driving taxis is simple, like doing a jigsaw over and over again.*

cheap shoes

Caris lies with her arms outstretched on the bed in her room with her red hair fanned out on the pillow. The room is cluttered and full of torn magazine pictures, loose compact discs, pots of make-up with no lids, dried-out mascara brushes, crumpled clothes and felt-tips that no longer work. Caris considers her lampshade with pictures of rabbits around it. *I need a new one*, she thinks. *I'm too old for rabbits.* Her friend Margaret sits cross-legged on the floor, reading an article in a magazine about leg waxing. Margaret has flannel skin and beige-coloured hair. Caris is trying to persuade Margaret to cut it off.

'I'll cut mine off,' she says. 'I'll do it now. Chop, chop, chop!' Lately Caris has felt extremely *urgent*. It seems to her that everyone else moves along far too slowly. She feels like a young horse tied up in a stable, kicking at the walls.

'I like long hair,' says Margaret.

'It would be good. You could dye it. It only takes half an hour. You could dye it green.'

'I don't want to, and anyway, my mum wouldn't let me.'

'Why should she have anything to do with it? It's your hair!' says Caris, pushing herself up from the bed and glaring at Margaret.

'I said I didn't want to.'

'Do you think I should change mine?'

'I dunno,' says Margaret. 'That's your decision.'

'Everyone's got long hair,' sneers Caris. 'Everyone looks the same round here; hair in bobbles, blue coats, black shoes.'

'What's wrong with that?' says Margaret. 'I don't like standing out.'

'I do,' says Caris, not sure if this is true.

'Does waxing hurt?' says Margaret, turning the pages of the magazine.

'What's wrong with body hair?' says Caris.

'It's not nice,' says Margaret. 'It increases body odour.'

'I like sweat!' snaps Caris.

'It's disgusting,' says Margaret.

Caris yawns.

'I'm bored,' she says crossly, but in fact it is Margaret who is boring her. Margaret is as predictable as a school day. She feels as if she is a yawning drain sucking away her energy.

'I might shave my head, though,' says Caris, getting off the bed and walking over to the window, watching an Alsatian shitting on the pavement while its owner smokes lazily and gazes up at the moon.

'You couldn't do that!' exclaims Margaret.

'Yes, I could,' says Caris. 'I might pierce my clitoris, too.'

'Oh, God,' says Margaret. 'You're just trying to be shocking.'

'It's good for sex,' says Caris.

Downstairs someone shouts, and something crashes. Caris knows it is her mother, arguing with Mac. Their arguments have become increasingly frequent. They swell up like fragile quivering bubbles, then pop back into damp nothings.

'What's going on down there?' asks Margaret.

'Nothing,' says Caris.

'Is your mother fighting again?'

Caris doesn't like the way Margaret says 'again'. She suddenly feels furious, and trapped in the small room.

'So what?' she snaps. 'What's wrong with fighting? At least fighting is exciting.'

'Is it about her stealing?' says Margaret.

Caris has confided in Margaret about the shoplifting. Actually

20

she had been rather proud. It had been a bit of dramatic gossip that had brightened up a lunchbreak sat on a concrete bench, producing expressions of shock and surprise from other girls. Caris had embroidered the incident, too, telling them that Louise had been chased through the town centre wearing a pair of stolen stilettos. But now she feels some regret. Her friends have cooled towards her, despite their initial expressions of sympathy. She wishes that she had said her mother was having a hysterectomy.

'It must be weird,' says Margaret smugly, 'to have a mother like that. My mum says it's a cry for help.'

The idea of Margaret talking to her tracksuited, fat-shinned mother about Caris's family makes Caris kick her legs in the air.

'Lots of people steal,' says Caris. 'Anyway, it wasn't much. I got it wrong. She only took one shoe.'

'Why would she take one shoe?'

Caris falters. 'It was on the display.'

'That's even more mental,' says Margaret.

Caris frowns. It bothers her, too. Why would her mother steal a single shoe, even if it was half of a pair of elegant Italian leather sandals, with jewelled straps? She'd overheard Louise talking to Mac. She was saying, 'I just wasn't thinking. I tried it on, then I must have put it in my bag', and he'd yelled, 'What were you going to do with one shoe, for Christ's sake?' and she'd sobbed, 'It was beautiful. A beautiful thing. It had tiny glass beads sewn on to the straps. It was made in Milan!' and he'd said, 'You're a nut. You're a fucking fruitcake', and then the door had slammed.

'She's quite normal, you know,' says Caris, not really knowing what 'normal' means. Louise certainly was normal, in that she didn't stand out from other girls' mothers. Meat and vegetables appeared on plates, bathrooms got hoovered, there were holidays, arguments. Her mother's purse bulged like any other mother's purse, bulky, fingered and packed with supermarket vouchers and spare change. But now everything is different, even the normal things are abnormal.

'She just got carried away,' mutters Caris. 'Perhaps she just wanted some excitement.'

'I see,' says Margaret, as if excitement is a disease.

Caris picks up a round magnifying mirror and plays with a spot on her chin, trying to ignore Margaret.

'She probably needs counselling,' Margaret says knowledgeably.

Margaret's face looms behind Caris in the mirror. Caris considers Margaret's watery eyes, her pale lashes, and her insubstantial chin. 'I'm going to bed,' says Caris, as a door slams downstairs. 'Why don't you go home?'

'What, now?'

'Yeah.'

Margaret sighs and pulls on her hooded coat.

'I thought you wanted me to stay for the evening.'

Caris farts.

'I'll see you tomorrow, then.'

Not if I can help it, thinks Caris. She feels the net of friendship slipping away from her.

'Yeah, maybe,' she says, and doesn't see Margaret out, just stands at the window watching her plodding back along the street with her slack shoulders and corned-beef calves.

She is plain, thinks Caris, *as plain as a classroom, as plain as a cheap pair of shoes.*

judgement day

It's February; the month that everyone dreads. The naked trees in the Vale rattle together and the sky is a grey blanket. The dogs shiver. The paths that snake across the park are slimy and wet. Mac's taxi is iced up every morning and he has to spend ages carefully de-icing with an aerosol and a scraper.

Stella slices ham sandwiches in the kitchen. Everything about her is tight. The buckles on her schoolbag are stretched over a bundle of exercise books and her hair is wrenched back firmly from her face. She has rubbed concealer on the spots on her forehead so that it glistens. Caris spoons cornflakes into her mouth.

It's the day of their mother's court case.

'What about me?' yells Caris, slapping her spoon into the bowl, splashing milk on to Stella's bag. Louise stands at the doorway in an obedient navy-blue jacket, her long hair tightly pinned in a plait, gripping a respectable handbag. She feels in her pocket to check she has some cigarettes. She knows it's going to be a long day.

'What about you?' Louise asks in a moist voice.

'What am I supposed to do when you're in court?' shouts Caris, scraping her chair, her forehead hot.

'Go to school.'

'I won't be able to concentrate.'

'That's enough,' says Mac, stamping in, slapping his big red hands together. 'Go to school! We'll be back later.'

Caris glares at her parents.

'Please, Caris,' mouths her mother, 'don't be difficult.'

They look innocent standing there, as if they are going to a civic event, or posing for a wedding photograph.

'It will all be over soon,' says Louise. 'Then we'll get back to normal.'

'Normal,' states Mac, as if it's a holiday destination.

Caris loathes her parents so much at this point that she has to shut her eyes. In her darkness she hears them making a run for it, and her sister calling from the hallway, 'Good luck, Mum!' in a plaintive voice.

She listens to the taxi revving up outside, and then opens her eyes and runs out of the house into the slippery street, and watches Mac's taxi bumping along the road, her parents' heads bobbing like puppets as they lurch over the sleeping policemen.

'Fuck you!' she shouts.

'Be quiet. People can hear!' says Stella, appearing beside her, blushing. 'There's nothing you can do anyway. Stop being selfish.'

'Oh, piss off!' snaps Caris bitterly. Stella stalks off down the street, trying to be older and dignified, but slips on the ice, making Caris snigger nastily.

And then it's quiet. There's just Caris and the open front door, the frosty street, and inside the spilt milk, the muttering radio, the crumbs on the sideboard, a white cat tiptoeing along the wall outside, avoiding lumps of ice.

Caris has no intention of going to school. She pulls off her school jersey, and leaves it hanging over the banisters. Without it she feels lighter, as if she could float anywhere, do anything. She shakes her red hair out of its ponytail, and strokes her eyelashes with gummy mascara. She puts on jeans and a hooded top, leaves her bag in her bedroom, picks up her dinner money from the hall table, and runs out of the house to the bus stop, past plodding parents ushering their children to the local primary school.

The yellow number 1 bus appears on the brow of the hill like a wish. When she climbs on the female driver grins at her, as if she is complicit in her escape. The seats are full of university students carrying files and smelling of shampoo. Caris stands in the middle of the aisle, chewing. A man with grey hair looks up from his newspaper and stares at her breasts. She yawns and mentally tells him to fuck off. She often feels like spitting or swearing these days. Words rise up in her throat like phlegm.

She gets off in the centre of town, pushing past a woman who laboriously lifts her buggy on to the pavement, and heads straight for Fenwick's. As she walks into the store the warmth encloses her like a mohair wrap. She inhales the scent of luxury goods like she's breathing in oxygen.

She slowly wanders through the store, stopping to finger cobweb scarves, buttery leather gloves, silk handkerchiefs, stockings and lingerie. She hovers by a Chanel stand and is ignored by a beautician who gives everyone else a leaflet on moisturisers. She imagines herself in Louise's shoes, the smarter black ones that she wears to town, her feet on the hoovered carpets and beneath her the trembling foundations of the city. She sees her as a ghost, her eyes feverish, her long hair nearly reaching her waist, her daughters at school, her fat, earthy husband rolling down his driver's window to chat to another driver, with a whole day on her hands, a day like this one that Caris inhabits: empty, unplanned and dangerous. A day when a woman has no structure, no scaffolding, only the feeling of wanting something that she can't name, and that in this department store, beneath the counters and behind the packaging, there is something forbidden, something that she deserves to have for nothing. Caris looks at the faces of other early shoppers and wonders if any of them are plainclothes detectives. She glides up the escalator to the shoe department, where rows of pointed shoes are placed on stands, and classical music tinkles in the background and the air is heavy with the smell of finely stitched leather. Caris glances at the price tags, astonished at the cost of a flimsy pair of sandals. She picks up a narrow court shoe with a golden buckle and marvels at its lightness. She buries her nose in a velvet slipper and smells castles. She watches a woman in a smart camel coat trying on a selection of fur-lined boots, standing before the mirror and twisting her feet this way and that, then making a sudden decision, unfastening her purse and throwing down a gold credit card. She pictures the silky sheets on her bed, the silver in her cutlery drawer.

Until Louise was arrested, Caris had never really thought about what she didn't have, about the world outside her street and her school, and the fact that most of the things she owns cost less than nine ninety-nine. Now she feels invisible, as if she hardly exists, as if she is filling up the cracks between people. She hears the clunk and tinkle of tills, filled with cash. She wants to tell Louise that she understands. She's there for at least an hour, and only leaves when a crying baby begins to scream, splitting open the atmosphere. Afterwards she stands in the pedestrian precinct of Northumberland Street. A morose busker plucks an electric guitar, the notes twanging sadly down the street. It starts to snow in large weightless flakes that disappear as soon as they land on the pavement.

Caris pulls up her hood and walks down Grey Street to the quayside, where the new law courts are. The town is smart and icy, with tight little men clipping along with efficient steps, and people urgently cleaning the shop windows, and sweeping the pavements. She walks past cafés and the warm smell of coffee, and then on down Dean Street where a girl with a cold sore tries to sell her the *Big Issue*. Down by the quayside the river is ominous and deep, and Caris hurries under the thick girders of the Tyne Bridge where it stinks of pigeon shit. Everywhere things are being built; new hotels, restaurants, galleries. Builders shout to one another from scaffolding. There are hoardings with pictures of new apartments on them, urging people to come and view show flats. Mac is always talking about the quayside developments. He speaks about 'the developers' as if they are gods pulling strings from high above Newcastle. He's proud of Newcastle's transformation from coal to art. He thinks it means more money for everyone. Lately his taxi has been full of foreigners. 'I could do a town tour,' he boasts. 'I know that much about the buildings of Newcastle, I could run a tourist bus.' Caris feels like a child among these huge edifices. *There's nothing here for me*, she thinks. *What am I supposed to*

26

do down here? It's all for middle-aged people with comfortable coats and handbags.

She gets to the new law courts. She knows that Mac and Louise are somewhere in this aloof redstone building, with its wide steps and glassy-eyed frontage. Caris strides on to the new bridge, hoping that they'll see her, standing alone on the bridge, waiting like a waif. She wonders if anyone is defending Louise, and if so what they might say. 'She's been upset, she gets period trouble, she's had depression.' All these things could be true, but Caris hadn't noticed them. *There had been a lot of silence*, she thinks. They would all be in the house, but no one would speak. Stella would be doing her homework. Caris would be listening to music, or drawing pictures of thin, long-eyelashed women, or watching television, or sitting with Margaret. Louise would be in her bedroom having a rest, or wiping something, or chopping something up, and Mac would be behind a newspaper, or, more likely, not there. Now it seems to Caris that the silence was filled with something poisonous, like the murky river that flows beneath her feet.

At home she waits for her parents to return, not turning on the lights, just lying on the floor in the twilight. It's teatime when she hears the clunk of the front door and her father taking off his coat and hanging it up. Immediately Caris knows that he is alone. There are no rustles, no small sighs, no nervous hands fluttering to undo buttons, just him, placing the car keys on the hall table, and then coming into the sitting room. Mac sees Caris and looks ashamed.

'What?' says Caris.

'You're back early,' he says.

'What?' she says again.

'She's gone.'

'Where?'

'She's been sent away.' Mac looks at the floor. 'To prison.'

The word is precarious and difficult. Caris sees her mother, shackled and behind bars in her blue jacket. Her mouth opens and won't close. Mac sits down in a slump. He puts his head in his hands. Caris watches with horror as he sobs. She has never seen him cry before. She doesn't know what to say or do.

'How long?' she croaks.

'Three months,' he moans.

'What, for stealing a fucking shoe?'

Mac stops crying and frowns at her, unblinking, his face wet with tears.

'Sorry,' says Caris. 'But three months!'

'She hit a police officer with the shoe. She hurt his eye,' wails Mac.

'No one told me that.'

'No.'

'Do you mean when they caught her?'

'Yes. It was a stiletto. It was sharp. She didn't realise.'

'What, in the street?'

Mac nods.

'So she got done for that too?' Caris tries to imagine it; her mother holding a sharp shoe like a weapon, blood dripping down a policeman's face.

'Yes,' says Mac desperately. 'For assault.'

'Assault.' Caris repeats the word uncertainly. She shivers, even though her face is hot and red. 'Is she ill or something?'

'I don't know. I don't understand.'

'Did she hurt him?'

'Not really.'

There is a wounded pause.

'But she's got responsibilities. What's the point of locking her up? What good will that do?' says Caris, suddenly feeling a current of anger looping round her young heart.

'Don't start shouting, Caris,' mutters Mac, who is stuck on a replay of the moment when Louise said goodbye, squeezing his hand, then turning into what appeared to Mac to be a dark tunnel into an underground dungeon.

'What will we do?' says Caris. 'We can't manage.'

Mac wishes Caris wasn't there. All day he's been hanging about in the waiting rooms of the law courts, fetching cups of tea, looking on the bright side. Not far away from the room in which they waited, the optimistic River Tyne glittered, and the new bridge arched itself in a yawn of delight. He and Louise had sat there, along with a collection of car thieves and petty criminals wearing borrowed suits and staring sulkily at the 'NO SMOKING' signs, waiting to be called, and all the time Mac was thinking, *I shouldn't be here with these losers; and what if someone recognises me – what do I say?* He watched barristers and solicitors pacing along the corridors in urgent discussions, looking as if they knew everything, while he, Mac, knew nothing. He sat next to sober drunks, pulling at their too-tight collars and trying to look innocent. And still Mac had believed that it would all turn out right in the end. But the bright side never happened. From the moment they stepped inside the courtroom everything became gloomy. It was all so confusing and unexplained, with clerks whispering into one another's ears, and a sense of emptiness, as if they were performing in a theatre with no audience. Even the judge seemed to have been marinated in melancholy, holding papers in his hands as if they were lead weights. When he spoke about Louise he made her sound like a criminal, with a previous conviction from when she was eighteen and she and a friend were caught giggling with a bottle of perfume, and now this, the theft of a very expensive shoe combined with an assault upon a police officer. Mac was ashamed. Ashamed of being there, ashamed of his wife, and afraid of the future. This was not how it was supposed to be. Now Mac wishes he could just be by himself for a bit, to think things through, to stop the images of Louise being ushered from the court by a frog-faced policewoman, and feeling a rush of pain that he couldn't control and doesn't know how to stop.

'It will pass in no time,' he tells Caris.

'My mother has gone to prison!'

'We're going to have to pull together, love.'

'We should appeal,' says Caris, hating the way her father sits there, cowed, as if nothing can be done.

'It won't do any good,' says Mac.

'Don't you think she must have had a reason to go out stealing stuff?'

Mac wants to shake Caris. Does she think he hasn't thought these things? That he hasn't asked Louise again and again? He can think of men who might have hit out, or taken to drink with the thoughts he's had. He thinks about the other taxi drivers, laughing at him, huddled around their cabs. These thoughts taste so bitter that they make the veins stand up in his head.

He turns on the television, hoping to shut Caris up.

Then Caris bursts out laughing. Her laughter fills the room. It sounds awful, like a series of barks, like a mad person's laughter. Mac looks at her grimacing face, and for a moment he hates his daughter. He wishes that he had never had children, nor met Louise. He thinks, *My daughter is wicked*. Caris abruptly stops laughing, shocked by the shine in his brown eyes, by the dislike that flickers across his mouth.

Inside Mac's chest it feels as if a large building has collapsed, leaving a pile of dust and rubble. He gets up and walks out of the room. Caris can hear him putting his coat back on, picking up his keys, and going back to the safety of the taxi with its warm velvet seats, and turning on the engine.

'They've stolen my mother,' she says to herself. 'The bastards.'

She doesn't know what to do. She wishes he would come back. She wants to have the conversation again. She wants it to be different. She wishes she hadn't laughed. She goes upstairs to her parents' bedroom and looks at her mother's clothes in the cold wardrobe, at her creams and lipsticks and brushes on the dresser. She wonders what her mother will do without her things. *Her hair will get greasy, her skin will dry out, and her nails will crack*, she thinks. She sees her sitting in front of the mirror, brushing her long hair with endless sweeping movements, even when it didn't need brushing. Caris remembers leaning against her, watching her dip her fingers into ointment jars and slowly rub her face with circling fingers, and the room filling with a sweet, creamy smell.

Caris takes a pair of her mother's shoes from under the bed and puts them on to her feet. They fit her well, but she's not used to heels and wobbles about on them. She picks up a photo in a frame and a blue coral necklace, and carries the things to her untidy room. She clears a space in the corner, then goes downstairs and roots through the cupboard under the stairs until she finds the Christmas box. She pulls out fairy-lights and tinsel, and baubles. Upstairs she arranges all these things into a kind of shrine, with her mother's photograph in the middle, hanging the fairy-lights around the edge. She gets so absorbed in making this altar that she almost forgets about her mother, who is simultaneously being checked in, and who has just had a conversation with a very pleasant murderer called Carol. Louise shows Carol a photograph of Caris and Stella, and Carol shows Louise a picture of her adolescent son. The two women peer at the faces in these photographs as if hoping to communicate with the children who look back at them.

Caris doesn't even hear Mac coming back, feeling too depressed to continue working, nor Stella and her gasp of horror as she hears the news, and then the sound of her sister and father reassuring one another that 'things will be all right'. Neither does she hear Mac phoning Nana Price, who makes a long whistling sound rather like a distant train. By the time Caris finishes her shrine-making and goes downstairs the house has reassembled itself and Stella and her father sit side by side on the settee watching *Star Trek* as if nothing has happened.

the vale

When Caris opens her eyes everything is different. The house
doesn't sound the same. You could always hear the radio when
Louise got up, and the sound of running water as she got into a
shower. Now, there is no smell of toast and no knock on her
bedroom door. Caris can't remember a time when her mother has
been away alone like this. Stella calls up the stairs, telling her that
she's got to go, and that it's time Caris got up. 'Dad went ages ago,'
she calls. 'You're on your own.' Then the front door slams, and
there's a delightful silence.

Caris eats rice pudding spooned from the tin for breakfast, uses
her mother's deodorant and nicks a pair of Stella's ironed knickers
from her chest of drawers.

Louise always told Caris not to walk through the Vale on the way
to school. She said it was filled with paedophiles, drug addicts
and gangs of neglected children and that Caris should go round
the long way, by the shops, next to the high wall that surrounds
the park. But Louise is gone, and thieves don't have authority, so
Caris strides through the wrought-iron gates with their benevolent
stone lions and down the foggy winding path towards the woods.
The ground around her is sludgy with dead leaves and mossy
stones, and the air smells brackish, of drains and damp. She passes
men in black donkey jackets walking their dogs; they turn to look

at her, but Caris isn't afraid. She feels reckless, as if something inside her has come undone.

She hears a voice calling her through the trees and turns to see Margaret plodding along the path, followed by a girl called Layla Tumility. Caris stands there, not certain that she wants to wait. She's never liked Layla, who has a neat, spiteful face and who wants to be a model, and whose father is a bouncer in a club down on the quayside.

'What are you doing, Caris?' asks Layla in a sing-song voice.

'Walking to school, I suppose,' says Caris.

'Your mum's in the paper. She got sent down, didn't she? Is she nuts or something?'

'No.'

'Fancy your mum being a thief.'

Layla comes closer. Caris smells her minty breath, her body spray, her malice. Margaret lurks in the background, a striped knitted hat pulled over her blonde hair, playing with her mobile phone.

'Leave her, Layla,' Margaret says. 'She's probably upset, aren't you, Caris?'

'No,' says Caris. 'I don't give a shit.'

'That's not very nice,' says Margaret. 'I'd never talk like that about my mother.'

Caris shrugs, and starts to walk away.

'Wait,' says Layla. 'Tell us about it, Caris. How's she getting on in prison? She'll be with prostitutes and all sorts.'

Caris blushes. It feels like her head is filling with boiling water.

'She's only just gone in,' she says. 'How should I know?'

'You're red,' says Layla.

'I'm hot.'

'Oh, come on, Layla,' whines Margaret.

Layla's mouth tightens. *It looks like a bum*, thinks Caris. *Full of shit*.

'Got any money?' snaps Layla.

'What for?' asks Caris.

'Because I haven't.'

33

'You can't have mine.'

'Yes I can.'

Layla reaches out and grabs Caris's bag from her shoulder. Caris clutches the straps and the two girls pull against each other, until Layla wins. Caris feels sick.

'So,' says Layla, 'let's have a look.'

She holds the bag upside down, and lets everything fall into the mud. There's a school maths book, a comb, a torn school timetable, a cigarette lighter, a pencilcase in the shap of a fish. Layla picks up the beaded purse that Louise gave Caris for Christmas and stuffs it into her pocket.

'Thanks,' says Layla.

Caris runs towards Layla and shoves her against a tree. Layla squawks like a trapped cat, and then slaps the side of Caris's face with her hard hand. Caris falls backwards, her hands landing in the cold, gritty mud.

'Aw, no,' protests Margaret weakly. 'Leave it. It's really late.'

'Hold her!' says Layla.

'What for?'

'Keep her still.'

Caris can hardly believe it as Margaret obediently climbs on to her chest, pushing her even further into the mud, saying as she does so, 'I don't believe in violence, Layla.'

She wonders why she ever liked Margaret. Once she'd found her quite a laugh. Now she would rather be friends with a black mamba.

'What the fuck are you doing?' shrieks Caris as she feels Layla undoing her shoes.

'Oh, come on, Layla,' says Margaret, her warm lardy buttocks pressing down on Caris's ribcage. Layla hoots with laughter and Caris hears her jumping up and down in the mud, hurling her shoes in the air.

'Can I get up now?' says Margaret. 'My legs are aching.'

'Hang on,' says Layla. She straps the shoes together and throws them again. This time they don't return.

Margaret heaves herself up. Caris lies there, not moving. Mud has seeped through her coat. Now Margaret's weight has gone it's almost comfortable. Caris considers pretending to be dead.

'We'll be late,' says Margaret. 'I've got Mr Fortoba.'

'Oh, come on, then,' says Layla. 'Nice to see you, Caris. Thanks for lendin' us the cash. You look a bit dirty, like you could do with a wash.'

And then the two girls run off into the woods, their tinny laughter echoing through the misty trees, leaving Caris gazing at the shapes of twigs against the sky and the hard outlines of two large sombre crows.

degna

After listening to the details of a bowel operation all the way from Consett, Mac is exhausted. The patient, a withered man with very large hands and feet, had left the cab with the cheery words, 'Don't ever get old, son,' a phrase that Mac hears several times a day. Afterwards Mac stopped at a garage and bought a pine air-freshener. Now he's outside an Italian restaurant waiting for his fare. He's trying to think positively. He's trying to understand. He thinks of everything he likes about Louise. Her mouth, for instance, her clean straight teeth and the skin of her belly. Her stroking the back of his neck while they watch a film. That time in Tenerife. And he likes to think of her dancing, confidently moving her body, and clicking her fingers. He remembers the way she glances at him sometimes and winks. On the other hand, there hasn't been much winking lately. As Mac sits there he tries to wink and finds he can't. It's as if his winking muscle has finally worn out.

He's suddenly aware of a woman's face peering through the window at him with her eyebrows raised, and realises he's been twitching. She opens the door and steps in, seeing a large, smooth-faced driver, and smelling valeted seats, and car deodorant.

'Where to?' says Mac, embarrassed.

The woman pulls down the passenger mirror and touches her lips. *She looks nice*, thinks Mac, *and she smells of something sweet, maybe icing sugar, or chocolate mousse. Thank God.*

'Home,' she says. 'Jesmond.'

'Where abouts?' asks Mac.

She gives the address, and Mac pulls away. He starts to hum, then feels stupid.

'Been for a meal, have you?' he asks.

'I work there,' she says. 'I cook.'

'A chef?' says Mac. 'Spaghetti and stuff?'

'That's right.'

For the first time in days Mac feels hungry. He thinks of a plate of spaghetti, cooked by this woman whose hands look smooth and agile. He sees her chopping up onions on a large wooden board.

'Do you get much business?' he says, aware that he's asking the same questions that drive him mad.

'Not bad,' she says. 'I haven't been there long.'

'Where are you from?'

'London.'

'I see.'

'I fancied a change,' she says.

'I see.'

'You should come and have a meal,' she says.

Mac drives up a leafy avenue. He feels hot, a little self-conscious. *It's strange*, he thinks, *how some people fill the cab, and others might not even be there at all.*

'My wife used to like cooking,' he says.

'Is she dead?'

'No!'

'It's just you said she used to like cooking.'

'She's away.'

'What did she cook?' she asks.

Mac considers, trying to forget the image of his now-empty fridge.

'Traditional,' he says. 'Stews and that, casseroles, dumplings.'

The word 'dumplings' brings a lump to his throat which he swallows immediately.

'I'm no good at dumplings,' she says. 'I'm better at Mediterranean.'

'I like Greek salad,' says Mac. 'Olives.'

'Well, you should come down,' she tells him. 'Bring your wife.'

'I will,' says Mac, 'when she gets back.'

Other people in his cab don't really listen to anything he's saying, he realises. But she's listening. She's all ears.

Mac drums the steering wheel wildly with his index finger and accelerates round a corner.

'She won't be back for a few weeks.'

'That's a long time.' The woman gazes calmly out of the window. Mac is suddenly filled with an urge to confess.

'My wife,' he says wildly, 'she's gone to prison.'

The woman doesn't even look surprised.

'Shoplifting!' snorts Mac. 'I ask you?'

The dumpling in his chest rises up into his throat. They slow down at a zebra crossing and watch an antique woman with a short-legged dog hobbling over the road.

The woman in his cab laughs.

'Oh dear,' she says.

'Exactly,' says Mac.

'But everyone steals sometimes!'

'I don't.'

'I had a phase of it. It was something about not wanting to go through a transaction, you know, with the money and everything. And the stores filled with all that unnecessary stuff, and wanting to just take it.'

'But it's not yours to take, is it?' says Mac.

'No, I suppose not. Still, it can seem so easy.'

'Not if you get caught it isn't.'

'It's bad luck.'

'She didn't need to steal. I would have bought her what she wanted.'

The woman stares at Mac. He feels one side of his face get hot.

'So, have you got kids?'

'Yes,' says Mac glumly. 'Two. Teenagers.' He flicks the side of the photograph dangling from the mirror. 'I'm doing everything,' he tells her. 'Shopping, washing, driving.'

'Oh dear,' she says. 'Can't they do it?'

38

'They don't, especially the younger one. She's being really sarky.'

The woman laughs. Mac joins in. Suddenly Caris is just an ordinary teenager.

Mac draws up outside a terraced house. The front door is painted red. He wishes he could talk to her longer. That's the trouble with the nice fares: you have to cut the conversations short. She gives him a ten-pound note and he pulls his plastic bag of change out of his pocket and counts out golden pound coins slowly.

'I need a regular pick-up,' she says. 'Late.'

Mac knows he should tell her to phone Jeannie at the switchboard, but he doesn't.

'From the restaurant,' she says. 'Fridays. Midnight.'

'No problem,' he says, feeling simultaneously cheerful and disloyal.

'My name's Degna,' she says. 'Will you remember?'

'Oh yes,' says Mac, and she opens the door.

'Thanks,' she says.

'No problem,' says Mac, and then, to his horror, he winks at her.

tree-climbing

Caris lies in the mud, staring up at her shoes hanging in the heavy branches of the oak tree. They look like gnarled fruit. Tears run down her cheeks. Slowly, she unclenches her fists and sits up. Her back is coated with thick mud. The park feels huge and empty. She could be anywhere, in the middle of a forest, miles from home. She staggers to her feet, and wetness oozes through her socks. She limps to the base of the tree and touches its solid trunk. Its bark is etched with signatures, rough hearts and symbols, like old battle scars. The first foothold is several feet up, and she can't see how to reach it. She tiptoes round the tree then sees a lichen-covered log, which she rolls to the base of the tree and uses as a step, pulling herself upwards into the generous arms of the oak.

She climbs up easily, tears drying on her streaked cheeks, and tries to reach the first of her shoes, but it's too far away and the branch is too fragile. So she gives up, and sits with her wet feet dangling, aware of the view around her – her school, with its Victorian roof, and the newer, prefabricated buildings around it, the chimneys of the terraces, the rolling hill of the Vale, and the dirty river. She would like to hang Layla upside down in the tree, and leave her there, with her tongue lolling and her hair hanging down. And if Layla's read about her mother in the paper, then that means that everyone knows.

Then she hears someone below her, and looks down.

A boy with lanky blond hair is standing there, wearing a cotton jacket. He stares at Caris with blue eyes.

Like a prince, she thinks.

'What are you doing?' he calls up to Caris.

Caris examines the boy, and then, without really thinking, she spits. Her aim is horribly accurate, and a drop of spittle lands on his forehead. He doesn't even move, or try to wipe it away. Instead he smiles.

'What did you do that for?' he says.

'I just did,' says Caris crossly.

'You look like an angel,' he tells her. 'Like an angel in a tree.'

'Me, an angel? I don't think so!' Caris laughs. The sound reverberates through the branches. Birds startle from their nests. She lifts up her head and laughs with her mouth wide open, shoeless, high above it all.

When she looks back down the boy has gone, leaving footprints in the February mud. Caris is disappointed. She wanted to know who he was. She wanted to tell him to get lost.

She clambers down from the tree, back to the cold mud, and picks up her things, stuffing them into her bag, and walks back along the narrow path to the street and then to her house.

As soon as she opens the door she knows that Nana Price is there, with her woody cigarettes and her rasping breaths. Nana Price is talking on the phone to one of her friends, with long breathy 'oooh's and 'aaah's.

'She's having a terrible time with her Filipino tubes,' she says knowledgeably. Then, 'All right, lovey, all right, yes, uhuh, uhuh.'

The television is on. The gas fire blazes, and in the kitchen the radio is on full volume. Caris waits for her grandmother to finish the conversation, noting her yellow teeth and charity-shop jewels, and the varicose vein that snakes up her shin.

'I must go, darlin'. Caris has just come in all covered in mud. She must be . . .' Nana Price squints at Caris, 'poorly, I think.'

'I'm not,' says Caris. 'I've got no shoes.'

Nana replaces the receiver.

'Why's that, petal?'

'I lost them.'

'You're a bit dirty, like. Shall we put you in the bath? Were you in a fight, love?'

Nana chuckles, remembering countless fights, involving shoes, hair, nail files, black eyes, some of them fairly recent.

'Oh, sort of. What are you doing here, anyway?'

'I've come to help!' says Nana brightly. 'Thought I'd move in for a bit, now that Louise is, you know, well, I thought it was my duty.'

'Have you told Dad?'

'Not yet. Tell you the truth, I'm having the front room decorated.'

Nana Price lives in a festering bungalow up on the coast, alone, since her husband, Walter, left. The house is chaotic. Her garden is a mass of nettles, thorn bushes, and cow-parsley. The walls feel damp when you touch them, and there are odd mushrooms growing around the pipes in the toilet, piles of yellow newspapers in the corners, and the remains of a model train set in the back room. Caris has overheard several conversations lately about Nana Price not managing. She's heard Louise pleading with Mac to let her mother move in, and Mac refusing.

'He won't mind, will he, pet?' says Nana Price, squeezing a teabag into a cup.

Caris doesn't answer. She grimaces.

'But where will you sleep?'

'I thought I could sleep in your bed and you could move in with Stella.'

'No!' exclaims Caris.

'Why not, lovey?'

'I hate her.'

'Don't be like that!'

Nana gets a dishcloth and starts to rub at Caris's cheek.

'Geroff,' snaps Caris.

'Look at you. What would you have done if I wasn't here!'

'Give it here. I can wash my own face.'

Nana makes a face, then shoves the dishcloth under Caris's chin.

'You have a wash, then you an' me will have a cup of tea and a nap, then watch a bit of telly. We could have a game of crib if you like.'

'If you're moving in, you'll have to sleep in the boxroom,' says Caris. 'I'm not going in with Stella. We're incompatible.'

'That's a long word, that. Things they teach you! Well, that's sorted, then,' beams Nana, opening a cupboard and rooting through it, finding a packet of digestive biscuits, humming wildly.

'Dad will have to find you a bed,' says Caris, knowing that Mac will be furious.

'Go on, then, wash yourself!' Nana Price says. 'I'll get the telly pages. We'll have a lovely day.'

Nana pulls a local newspaper out of her bag and leafs through it, suddenly freezing as she reads the headline 'Woman attacks police officer with stolen shoe'.

'It's all right,' says Caris, 'I know all about it.'

'Tomorrow's chip paper,' says Nana, scrumpling up the page and chucking it across the room.

'Yeah,' says Caris, and runs upstairs to lock herself in the bathroom.

stella

As Stella sits in the library doing her history homework, she senses
a kind of silence around her. The school is full of noise – running
feet, staccato voices, bells, scraping chairs and shrill teachers – but
no one speaks to her. She feels abandoned. Stella writes down
dates in different-coloured felt-tips, and glances out of the window
at the playing field with bright figures running up and down it.
The librarian sits at the end of the room, guarding the quietness.
Stella catches her eye and smiles. She packs up her pencilcase, and
puts her books into her bag and walks down to asks her if she can
order a book. The librarian writes down the title carefully on a
small card.

'How are you, Stella?' she asks in a voice that she doesn't usually
use.

'Fine,' says Stella, looking at her feet.

'Good,' says the woman. 'I'll get that ordered for you straight
away.'

Stella nods gracefully and leaves the green room, with its quiet
computers and thoughtful chairs. She goes down to the drama
room, where there's a meeting about the play. The corridors are
almost empty, but it seems to her that the people she passes
are looking at her. The drama department is in a new building. It
has a polished wooden floor and wide windows. It's where the
parents are taken on tours. When she goes into the room there's a
circle of people sitting in the centre of the room.

'Stella!' calls Mrs Capes, the drama teacher. 'Come over!'

Stella pulls up a chair. Mrs Capes, who has foundation spread over her face as if it's margarine, leans over and gives her a piece of paper, and at the same time touches Stella's knee in a protective way. Stella squirms, and focuses on the list of rehearsal dates in front of her. *Louise won't be able to come*, she thinks, *and Mac will be working, and I don't want Caris and Nana.* She feels like tearing up the paper and leaving the room, but she doesn't. She sits there listening to Mrs Capes, who has a voice like an underground pipe, telling them what they need to wear, asking them to decide whether they want recorded music or the school band to play live. Macbeth, who is a dark-eyed, overweight boy with enormous confidence, winks at Stella. She sucks in her cheeks and doesn't respond.

'I think it should be pre-recorded,' she says, 'so that it can't go wrong.'

Mrs Capes gurgles in reply. Stella looks at her watch, given to her by Mac on her last birthday. It has a narrow, ladylike face.

'I have to go to English,' she says, and stands up.

'I think we're finished here,' croaks the teacher. 'See you Monday night.'

Stella walks out of the room, aware of two of the witches leaning towards each other to whisper into each other's ears. *They're talking about me*, she thinks. She starts to run, feeling like shouting. Mr Fortoba comes round the corner carrying a pile of orange books, and nearly drops them all.

'What's the matter with you, Stella?' he yells. 'Running isn't allowed.'

But Stella ignores him, and disappears off down the corridor. Mr Fortoba doesn't know about Louise. He doesn't read the local paper, and rarely gossips in the staff room. He decides that Stella must be running to the toilet and plods on towards his classroom, where his pupils will be wild-eyed and bored as caged beasts.

sprung mattresses

The next day, Mac wakes up in the middle of a dream about spaghetti. In it Degna is feeding him with a long silver fork, and he is sucking it up into his kiss-shaped mouth. Mac looks at the photograph of Louise by his bed and feels guilty. It annoys him, this guilt. He wants to bottle it and throw it in the Tyne.

Downstairs the sitting room is blue with smoke, and Nana sits in her chenille dressing-gown stirring a pot of tea, looking like a hag out of a fairy story. Mac doesn't speak. He looks at his mother-in-law with distaste. He's already tried to persuade her to go home, but the old lady just giggles and rolls her eyes as if he's a difficult child. Even Stella didn't back him up. Caris had said, 'But she's old,' as if being old was a passport to anything.

So he grabs his coat and leaves, stopping for a bacon buttie at Filler's. Increasingly Mac feels that his home is his taxi, and that the home he had no longer exists.

He pulls up outside Sleep Tight, a bedding shop in the middle of town, and a woman with owlish spectacles and a briefcase clips out and angrily sits down beside him. She smells of hairspray.

'Where to, love?' asks Mac.

'Crow Valley,' she says. 'Here!' And she passes him a neat white card with the address printed on it.

Mac pulls out into the stream of traffic. Someone has fingered the words 'FUCK OFF YOU CUNT' on the back of a dirty van door in front of them. Mac feels embarrassed.

'You work in beds, then?' he asks, then feels stupid.

'Mattresses,' she snaps. 'Sprung mattresses.'

'Plenty of business?'

'Yes, plenty.'

'I could do with a new mattress,' says Mac. 'Got any good offers on? The mother-in-law's just moved herself in. Just like that.'

'Depends on if you want quality. It's worth it in the long run.'

'Just a cheap one would do,' says Mac.

'It's not advisable to have a mattress without proper support,' she says wearily. 'We deal in futons too,' she adds.

Mac isn't sure what a futon is. He indicates left, then says, 'Aye. Mebbes a futon.'

'Sleep is crucial,' states the mattress expert, rubbing the side of her head as if to ward off insomnia. 'You get what you pay for.'

'The mother-in-law, she's pushing seventy. She doesn't have any trouble sleeping. Sleeps all day. She doesn't do anything else but smoke and drink, and eat. I don't want her, tell you the truth; I says to her last night, "You can't stay", but she's stubborn.'

The mattress saleswoman yawns.

'It would be different if it was my mother.'

'Yes.'

'My mother's dead,' says Mac.

'I see.'

'She never drank a drop, my mother,' Mac goes on pompously. 'She was a church woman. Made us say our prayers every morning and night.'

The woman takes some papers out of her briefcase and studies them, but Mac can't stop talking.

'I mean, I'd rather go into a home than depend on people. She's creating unnecessary stress. That's the trouble with old people. They think you owe them something.'

He can feel rage flickering in his throat like a small fire.

'She's inconsiderate. She's only thinks about herself. Says she's come to help. Help, my arse! I'm all for euthanasia like.'

'Isn't she a bit young for that?'

'Oh, aye, but I mean in theory. Old people shouldn't make other people's lives a misery. She's causing distress.'

'Can't your wife deal with it?'

'She's away. No, it's all up to me. I tell you, it's bedlam at home.'

Mac speeds along the ring road, growling at a passing Lada.

'There's too many old people, if you ask me,' he says. 'They need pruning out; just leave the healthy independent ones!'

'I don't agree.'

'She's a bad influence, with her drinking and all. She hogs the telly and the bathroom. She lets my youngest stay off school. I tell you, it's a nightmare and it's going to get worse.'

They scream to a halt outside a factory. The woman pays quickly, without giving him a tip. Mac is giddy and confused.

'Don't get me wrong. I'm not a fascist,' he says. 'Voted labour all me life.'

The door slams. Mac rubs the surface of Louise's photograph and wishes things were different.

'Mac, have you cleared?' says Jeannie anxiously. 'Mad Betty's waiting at the end of her street.'

'*No,*' says Mac.

'It's your turn. She wants you to take her to the police station. She says the neighbours are conspiring. She sounds worse.'

'Please!' Mac groans as Jeannie chuckles mirthlessly.

'She's waiting, Mac,' sings Jeannie.

more shoes

Stella flings open the door of Caris's bedroom and throws a letter at her.

'It's time to get up!' she says loudly, and strides off leaving the door wide open.

Caris looks at the letter. It's old fashioned, with a prison stamp in the corner. It's from her mother. Her careful handwriting fills Caris with dread and hope. She tears it open, and finds a home-made card made of pressed flowers, stuck down childishly in the shape of a cat with petal ears.

'*I made this myself in the art room,*' it says on the inside.

I want you to know, Caris, that I love you very much, and that we will soon be together again. I am fine in here. It's not what you think. There are some lovely people. I am going to an art class. Please keep me in your heart, as I keep you in mine. Help Dad with the housework, and do your homework. With lots of hugs and kisses,
   Mum.

Caris reads it over and over again. It is as if her mother has been invaded by sentimental aliens. Louise is not generally given to such endearments; she is usually quite down to earth. Caris is also disturbed by the contented tone of her words. Louise sounds quite happy. Shouldn't she be suffering from guilt and remorse? She wishes that she had told her more detail. For instance, she would like to know about the other women, particularly the murderers, and what crimes they have committed. She would like to know about the meals, and the bathrooms, and what time the lights are turned out. She places the card in the centre of her tableau, but the new voice of her incarcerated mother has disturbed her, and spoilt the magic of the shrine.

Stella locks the bathroom door and stares at her chin in the mirror. She thinks it looks like the surface of the moon, with its pimples and ridges. She wipes it carefully with a heated flannel that she keeps in a plastic bag in her bedroom. Then she dabs each pimple carefully with blue lotion from a bottle. Her skin looks enraged, and Stella tries to calm it down with small amounts of concealer. By the time she's finished her skin is flat and nervous. She carefully dresses in her ironed school shirt and skirt, flattening the pleats with her hands, and walks slowly downstairs, aware of the smells of her sleeping family as they grunt and doze in their beds.

Mac opens his eyes and sees his wife's pink dressing-gown hanging on the back of the door. A man on the radio is talking about drug abuse. He can hear Stella downstairs, running taps and boiling kettles. His back aches and he gets out of bed stiffly.

Stella shouts again from downstairs, and Caris gets up and goes to the bathroom, where her nana's false teeth and eau-de-Cologne clutter the shelves. She breathes in the sharp smells of Stella's spot lotions and creams. She pulls off her pyjamas and looks at her naked body critically: her breasts that seem too large; her uneven nipples; the erupting spot on her shoulderblade; the blotchiness of her neck. There's a bruise on her upper arm, like a map, where Layla grabbed her.

She ignores the perfection of her belly, the smooth curve of her hips, the peachy glow of her skin. Hating herself, she drags on dirty knickers, a crumpled shirt and her navy-blue school trousers. She puts on her trainers, knowing that she will get told off for not wearing school shoes.

'Bring us a cup of tea, will you,' whines her nana from the boxroom.

Nana Price has moved her things into the windowless boxroom at the back of the house. She sleeps surrounded by boxes and bags of jumble, on a camp-bed dug out by Mac. She looks like an old crone in a cave, with her lined face peering out of the small room, which is lit only by a dim lamp.

Downstairs Stella is buttering toast. Next to her is another, identical card.

'What did she say to you?' asks Caris.

'Nothing much, just that she misses us.' Stella looks sensible and understanding.

'Do you think she'll become a drug addict?' asks Caris.

'Of course not.'

'People do, in prison. You get a lot of prostitutes, too.'

'It sounds as if she's coping quite well,' says Stella, clearing up her plate.

I hate the word 'coping', thinks Caris.

'Take Nana a cup of tea,' says Stella, 'and don't forget to go to school.'

'Yeah, yeah,' says Caris.

They hear Mac coming down the stairs. He's already wearing his leather coat.

'See you later,' he says gruffly.

'Dinner money,' says Stella.

Mac pulls some coins from his pocket and lets them roll on to the table.

'That's not enough,' says Caris.

'Make some sandwiches,' he grunts.

'There's no more bread,' Stella tells him. For a moment the two girls are united, looking at him with neglected expressions. He grudgingly takes a five-pound note from his wallet and gives it to Stella.

'See you later,' he says again, and then he's gone.

'He doesn't eat anything,' says Caris. 'He just works.'

Stella doesn't answer.

She gives Caris the change. Caris considers arguing, but doesn't. She eats cereal watching television. Stella leaves next, without saying goodbye, her footsteps brisk and efficient. Caris wonders if anyone has said anything to Stella at school. *People don't tease Stella*, she thinks. *She looks too dignified. She hides in libraries, behind books. She looks like a book.*

As Caris ties up her laces she realises that her hands are trembling. She's afraid of the outside, of what will happen. She's seen other girls forced into corners by Layla. Caris tells herself she's bigger than Layla, that she isn't afraid. She makes herself leave the house, and walks down towards the park. Her body complains, still bruised from the fight the day before. Woodpigeons making low warning 'coo's in the distance. The Vale is filled with the sounds of trickling water, dripping through moss, and oozing into every crack.

She turns the corner and sees the tree, bare and stark against the sky. There's a figure in the branches, silhouetted against the light, like a huge bird. She slows down and tries to see. It's the boy from the day before, dressed in a billowing T-shirt, his coat in a bundle at the base of the tree. He's hanging a pair of red shoes up in the branches: a pair of expensive women's shoes. For a moment Caris feels jealous. *That's my tree*, she thinks. *Get out of it. Who do you think you are?*

She stands, then, in the shadows of a laurel bush and watches the boy moving about like a dancer. Then he sits down and looks around, proudly, the shoes glowing red against the grey landscape.

Caris steps out and shouts up at him: 'What are you doing?'

He's startled, glancing about, trying to locate the sound. Caris strides to the base of the tree, and he looks down at her as if he has been waiting for her to arrive.

'Decorating the tree!' he tells her. 'I was hoping you'd come.'

'Why?'

Caris is hot. She feels herself blushing.

'I wanted to see you again.'

'Who are you, anyway?'

'D'you mean, what's my name?'

'Yeah, what's your name?'

'George.'

'George!' She laughs.

'Why are you laughing?'

'I don't know anyone called George,' she says. 'What's your other name.'

'You don't need to know my other name.'

Caris walks towards the tree. She doesn't like being below him. 'Whose shoes are those?'

'Why don't you come up?' he says.

Without taking her eyes off the boy she circles the tree, looking for a foothold, and steps up using the same log she used before. She is aware of George watching, blocking out the light. She tries to climb gracefully, but her feet keep slipping on the slimy branches.

As she gets closer George reaches out towards her. She sees that he bites his nails. She lets herself be pulled up to the wide branch where George sits. Once she's there he looks different. His eyelashes are long, and his hair is greasy and uncut; his face white and sharp. Caris feels nervous, and turns away. She looks again at the shoes.

'Whose are they?'

'My mother's,' says George.

'She'll be pleased.'

'She's away,' says George. 'She's got hundreds of pairs of shoes. She's got so many she keeps them in a room all by themselves. They've got numbers – look.' He pokes at the shoes so that they swing round, and Caris sees a small ticket with the number 113 written on it.

'Why are you hanging them in the tree?'

'It's something to do.'

Caris can't work him out. He doesn't sound like other boys she knows.

'I started it,' she says eventually.

'I know. I thought you could make a wish.'

'What are you on about?'

'When you hang a shoe in a tree, you make a wish. I read it somewhere.'

Caris frowns at him. 'Oh yeah?' she says cynically. 'So what are you wishing for?'

'That my mother will leave me alone.'

Caris likes the idea, but doesn't want to say so. She can think of quite a few wishes that she might like to make.

'Do you want me to get your shoes back?' he asks.

Caris shrugs. Next to the expensive shoes they look cheap and bedraggled.

'I might want my own wish,' she says.

'Go on, then.'

'I'm not going to tell you,' she says.

'You don't have to,' George takes a cigarette from his pocket and lights it.

Caris wishes for smaller breasts.

'We should hang up more shoes, don't you think?' says George.

'Maybe.'

'Who are you, anyway?'

'Caris.'

'Caris who?'

'None of your business,' she says automatically.

'All right,' he says, and swings his long legs.

'Look, I can't sit here all day,' says Caris.

'Why not?'

'School. Don't you go to school?'

'No. Not at the moment. I'm changing schools.'

'Where from?'

'None of your business. I'm school-phobic,' he adds. 'Meaning I don't like school.'

'Who does?' says Caris.

'Can I walk along with you?' asks George.

'If you like.'

They climb down. Caris grazes her elbow on the bark, leaving a smear of blood on her arm. George leans over and wipes it with his coat sleeve. Then they walk down the path. He's taller than Caris. George swipes at weeds with a stick.

'Who were the girls who took your shoes?' he asks.

'Fucking bitches,' answers Caris.

'Do you often get into fights?' asks George.

'Sometimes. Don't you?'

'No. Never.'

'I'll get them back,' growls Caris.

'Good,' says George.

A woman in a squishy anorak passes with a fat yellow Labrador.

'Are you rich?' Caris asks.

'My parents are. I'm not.'

Caris thinks of Mac, driving and driving, and his fat wallet that is always filled with cash.

'My mother's in prison,' she tells George.

'Really?' says George, stopping to stare at Caris, his eyes lighting up. 'What for?'

'Stealing.'

'Amazing,' says George. Caris feels rather pleased by his reaction. 'What did she steal?'

'A shoe.'

George bursts out laughing, and Caris begins to giggle. It's a relief to laugh about it. Caris suddenly feels lighter.

They arrive at the dead school gates. The building is quiet, filled with a thousand muted teenagers, standing in lines in assembly.

'I'd like to see you again,' says George.

'Would you?'

'A lot,' says George. 'We could find some more shoes.'

'You're weird,' says Caris. She smiles at George 'Where are you going now?'

'Home. The other side of the Vale.'

The other side of the Vale is where the big houses are, with ivy climbing up the drainpipes. Girls from there call girls like Caris 'charvers' and live in rooms with wide floors and large cushions, and have dancing lessons and go on holidays to villas in Mauritius.

'Oh,' says Caris.

'I don't know anyone round here. I was at school in Scotland. Meet me at the tree. After school.'

She doesn't answer, just watches George slope away, his hands in his pockets. Caris feels as if her landscape has opened out, like a pop-up book that makes something flat and ordinary into something three-dimensional.

Unwillingly she turns and walks towards the doors of the school and the smell of tedium and chips.

revenge

When Caris walks into the classroom everyone looks at her. The room smells of farts and old wood. Mr Fortoba looks up from the register and coughs. He runs his finger down the register, looking for Caris's name. A few weeks ago Caris fancied Mr Fortoba. She and Margaret had discussed him at length, and stood too close to his desk. Now Caris won't look at him. She strides to her seat and collapses into it. She can feel Layla's eyes on her back. Margaret is playing with her hair, winding it into a rat's tail.

'You're late, Caris,' says Mr Fortoba, who is a neat man with thick eyebrows, a self-conscious mouth, and pock-marked skin.

'I was sick,' says Caris.

'Where's your note?'

'My dad was out.'

There is a repressed giggle behind her. Caris watches Mr Fortoba writing something about her in the register. She looks around the square room, with its bland walls and oblong whiteboard, on which is written the words 'Of Mice and Men'. Mr Fortoba is talking about GCSEs. That's all they ever talk about. They talk about them as if they are vital, like a blood supply or oxygen. Caris thinks GCSEs are a waste of time. Her bag is full of pieces of scrumpled paper filled with instructions about coursework and careers.

A bell rings, and everyone jumps up, grabbing bags and coats. The first lesson is games. She thinks of the dull field where they must stand in lines waiting for the teacher's whistle. She sidles up to Mr Fortoba's desk and waits for him to finish ticking things, noticing how neat his handwriting is, and how his fingernails are cut into neat arcs. He's wearing a blue and orange patterned jersey. *Mr Fortoba thinks he's trendy,* thinks Caris, *but he's a cut-out, just like one of the men in Nana's knitting patterns.*

'What now, Caris?'

'I've got period pains, Mr Fortoba,' she says, and he winces.

'You'll have to go and sit in the library,' he says. 'You'll have to read something.'

'What?'

'What do you think, Caris? Read a book, for God's sake!'

'I know that. What book?'

'Haven't you got some homework to do? You don't seem to have done any lately.'

Caris imagines Mr Fortoba having sex, his face covered in sweat, his hands quivering. She smirks.

'Have you been ill?' he asks.

'Yes,' she lies. 'I'm on antibiotics.'

'You need to get a note.'

'I know.' Caris sighs.

'Are you all right, Caris?' he asks, more tenderly. Mr Fortoba is supposed to be somewhere else. He knows that down the corridor there's a class that is whirling out of control, like a room of unfed dogs. Caris suddenly wants to cry. She wants to show him the bruise on her arm.

'Dunno,' she whispers in a small voice. Blood rushes to her cheeks. She cringes with embarrassment.

This will take too long, thinks Mr Fortoba. *There will be tears, and long silences. It will take hours to find out what's the matter with this girl, and I haven't got hours. I haven't even got seconds.*

'I'll catch you later,' he says, grabbing a pile of photocopies from the desk.

Caris is relieved. She turns and wanders out into the corridor, pushed by the throng of bodies surging past her. Layla nips her arm.

'Fuck off,' says Caris.

'I'll see you later,' hisses Layla. Margaret acts as if Caris is invisible.

Instead of going to the library Caris follows the swarm of teenagers down the brown corridors to the tiled changing rooms lined with rusty lockers. She hovers outside while the other girls pull off their school uniforms and put on aertex blouses and shorts, pulling their hair back from their faces and rubbing deodorant under their arms before setting off for the games field.

Then, when the last straggler has limped off to the field and the empty room is full of the memory of their shrill voices, Caris creeps over to Layla and Margaret's unlocked lockers and pokes about inside. She takes Layla's smart patent shoes and puts them in her bag, then searches for Margaret's wide flat boots and takes them too. Then she pulls out Layla's clothes and kicks them on to the floor. She finds an extra pair of knickers neatly folded in a paper bag, and she hangs them on a pipe with the gusset showing.

She walks away, at first heading for the library; but then, halfway down a corridor, she changes her mind, and strides back to the front door, waiting behind a corner for the headmaster to finish a syrupy conversation with a visiting parent.

'It's really a very happy community here,' he's saying. 'We put young people first. We have an excellent anti-bullying policy. We listen, you see.' And the parent, a ripe-looking woman in a velvet tracksuit, is nodding vehemently. Caris watches them shaking hands, and wonders if the headmaster really believes what he's saying, or if he's just so used to lying he no longer knows what a lie is.

Then she slips out, back into the reckless windy morning, away from the distant whistles and bells, and down the magnetic lane that leads to the Vale.

The tree waits for her, lit by a brief ray of sunshine that licks the branches and makes them look garishly green. Caris climbs up the trunk easily now, recognising where the footholds are, and hangs Layla and Margaret's shoes in the highest place she can reach. Then, as a flock of seagulls fly across the park, crying for the sea, she maliciously wishes both girls bad luck. The wish tastes sweet in her mouth. Then she sits and waits for George, watching dust-coloured men moving around their allotments and park gardeners trundling by with wheelbarrows and rakes, and the dogs and their owners who pass by beneath her, sometimes looking up and seeing the strange apparition of a red-haired girl in a tree surrounded by shoes, like something in a dream.

confession

Mac sounds his horn outside a church. There is a large sign saying 'INVEST IN JESUS. IT PAYS'. After a few moments a fat-cheeked black man in a dog-collar runs out, wheeling a large and shabby suitcase, waving goodbye enthusiastically to a flock of elderly permed women who stand with faces like tea cosies seeing him off. He shakes their plump hands warmly and makes kissing movements with his mouth, while Mac wearily loads the case into the boot of the car, then ambles to the taxi and climbs in.

'Where to, Father?' asks Mac, rather deferentially. Mac is afraid of priests. He was brought up a Catholic and worries that they will tell him off for not attending.

'The airport!' says the priest enthusiastically. 'I am going home!'

'Where would that be?'

'Tanzania!'

Mac isn't at all sure where Tanzania is. He imagines it is full of skinny black children, lions and missionaries.

'Had a good trip, then?'

'Wonderful,' hoots the priest. 'Truly wonderful! And what about you? Have you had a good day so far?'

'Not so good,' Mac says. 'I've got a few worries.'

'Worries? How can you be worried on such a beautiful day!' demands the priest.

'Home trouble.'

'I'm sorry to hear that,' says the priest, his religious zeal filling the taxi like air-freshener. Mac sneezes.

'Bless you!' says the priest.

'I've got these two teenage daughters, see.'

'Good. Are these your daughters here in the photographs?'

'Yes, that's Caris, and that's Stella.'

'And this is your wife?'

'That's her. That's Louise.'

'Good, good. So what are your worries?'

They are on the dual carriageway now, speeding along in the fast lane. Mac thinks he might start to cry. He feels swamped by emotion.

'It's Louise,' he mumbles.

'Your wife,' states the priest.

'My wife has gone to prison.'

'Oh dear,' says the priest. 'You must be upset.'

Now tears start to cruise down Mac's large cheeks. The priest hands him a handkerchief.

'It was just shoplifting. Just a short sentence,' he sobs.

'And you're left looking after these sweet girls?'

'I don't know how to! It's the youngest one that's the trouble. The older one is doing all the cooking and the cleaning. My wife's mother has moved in, but she's no help.'

'Calm down. Think about the good things in your life. Do you pray?'

'Well, I used to, when I was little. I grew up in Walker, down by the river. My mother was Catholic. She used to make us pray.'

Mac has a horrible memory of his mother repeatedly slapping the back of his head and telling him to kneel down and pray that he would become a better person. He also remembers sucking a church pew and then feeling sick.

'That's good. So that's what you must do now. Pray for help with your daughter.'

Mac doesn't think it will do any good. It never worked when he prayed that his mother would be consumed by flames. His tears dry up rapidly.

'Yeah, that's a good idea,' he says in a dull voice.

'Young women need a lot of help.'

'Fathers do, too.'

'And fathers,' agrees the priest. 'You need to get yourselves down to church.'

Imagine it, thinks Mac. *Caris sulking, Stella exhausted, Nana drunk and me, on the end of the pew, all saying 'Hail Mary'.* He wishes he had never started this conversation. His thoughts drift again to Degna and her hands, chopping and snipping and rolling and stroking.

'What are you doing over here, like?' asks Mac, trying to change the subject.

'Spreading the faith, and raising funds for our church in Dar es Salaam.'

'Oh,' says Mac.

'At least you have enough to eat,' says the priest piously.

'That's true,' says Mac.

'You should tell your girls to be grateful that they have an education and food on their plates.'

'Oh, I do.'

Actually, Mac can't remember saying anything to either of them for some days. When he gets in at night they are upstairs in their rooms with the doors shut. In the mornings he leaves money on the hall table, and when he comes back it's gone. There is usually a plate covered with silver foil in the kitchen, left there by Stella. Nana Price is stretched out on the settee in a stupor, talking to characters on the television. Mac eats his tea and then says, 'I'll be going to bed, then. Time you went, isn't it?' and she waves her wrinkled hand at him, and he knows that she'll end up there half the night, with the heating on and the lights blazing.

They arrive at the new airport. Mac helps the priest with his suitcase, finding him a trolley.

'You can contribute to our fund if you like,' says the priest with a wide white smile. 'We would be very grateful.' He makes a feeble pretence of looking for some money.

'It's all right,' says Mac wearily, 'have a free ride, Father.'
Everyone else does, thinks Mac.

The priest shakes his hand and looks at him with sympathy.
'God sent you to me,' he says with a noble expression, 'and I shall
pray for you.'

fish and chips

Caris comes home disappointed. George never showed up, and she
got tired of waiting. In the end she walked up to the pet shop on
the Shields Road and spent a while staring at tropical fish and
sleeping snakes. Her bones are cold.

Nana is having trouble with her underwear. She is standing in
the middle of the sitting room fiddling with her corsets.

'Give us a hand with this suspender,' grunts Nana.

Caris untangles the twisted straps, while Nana plays with the
television remote, flicking from channel to channel.

'You're nice and early,' says Nana, arranging herself on the settee.

'Staff training,' says Caris carelessly, stalking into the kitchen
where she opens the empty fridge and stares at a rancid carton of
cottage cheese.

'There's no food,' she says.

'Have a toffee,' offers Nana in a fudgy voice. Caris joins her and
the two of them sit in silence, chewing, staring at a guinea pig
having a hysterectomy.

'I wonder what our Louise is doing now?' murmurs Nana
eventually.

Caris frowns. All her images of her mother come from television.
She sees her walking round and round a small yard in a prison
uniform, then sitting on a narrow bunk in a brick cell, or scrubbing
the tiled floor of a prison toilet.

'Dunno,' she says. 'Will she have to work?'

'I suppose,' says Nana. 'I think they sew sacks.'

'What for?'

'Well, I'm not sure.'

'I'm hungry,' says Caris.

'Shall we have fish and chips?' Nana says, dreamily. She rummages in her cardigan pocket for her brown purse, which is as wrinkled as her face. Inside there is a crumpled five-pound note, which she hands to Caris.

The front door clicks open.

'That will be Stella,' Nana says smugly.

When Stella walks into the room she notices that Caris's hair is tangled, that she's wearing trainers with no socks. Stella feels horribly tired. Lately she has taken to working in the library or going back to her friend Elli's house where there are usually biscuits and a table where the two girls can sit and revise. Her own home looks the same, but smells different. There is suddenly nowhere in it where Stella is comfortable.

'We're just saying we'll have fish and chips,' Nana tells her. 'Caris is going.'

Stella doesn't answer. She walks into the kitchen and looks at the sink, noticing how the seams around the taps are filled with sludge, and that the window is splashed with grease. The back yard is filled with crisp packets.

Caris comes up behind her and says, 'What do you want? Haddock, cod or sausage?' in a dull voice.

'You smell funny,' says Stella. 'Of earth.'

'Charming.'

'Mr Fortoba was asking about you.'

'Was he?'

'You weren't at school this afternoon.'

'Well, no, I wasn't. I went for a walk.'

'Where?'

'Just around.'

Stella would like to knock Caris unconscious with the washing-up brush but instead she holds it like a sceptre and looks superior.

'You have to go to school, Caris,' she says.

'Why?' asks Caris.

'Because it's the law. You never do any homework, either.'

'I do. I do it in the library.'

'Yeah, sure. I've never seen you in the library.'

Caris wishes Stella would stop acting like she knows everything. She's tidying up the knives and forks now.

'What are you doing that for?' snaps Caris.

'They're all wrong. They need to be put in the right compartments.'

'That's ridiculous,' sneers Caris, feeling a bit sick.

'It's unhygienic in here,' mutters Stella. 'There's germs everywhere.'

'Who cares?'

'I do.'

'Do you want fish and chips or not?'

'I suppose so.' Stella starts to make a cup of tea. 'We should wait until Dad gets back,' she says. 'What's he supposed to eat?'

'That's his problem,' snaps Caris. 'I'm hungry.'

'You're just making everything worse,' Stella tells her.

'Oh, shut up.'

'It's not fair on Dad,' says Stella. 'He can't manage.'

'He's not here,' says Caris. Then, 'I'm managing perfectly well by myself.'

'You're not. You're falling to bits.'

'No I'm not. I'm offering to go and get the tea.'

They can hear Nana Price singing in the front room, joining in with a song on the television. Then the front door opens and their father's bigness fills the house.

'I'm going to tell him you wagged off,' says Stella.

'Don't.'

'I am.' Stella runs to meet her father, and Caris can hear her voice rising and falling in the hallway. Caris feels like breaking something.

Then Mac comes into the kitchen carrying a loaf of sliced bread as if it's a dead rabbit that he's just caught. Caris tries to smile at him, but he looks at her with a hard, empty expression. The boiling water in the kettle sounds like a growing wail of despair.

'So!' he says.

'I just felt tired. I went to a café,' lies Caris.

'That's not good enough,' says Mac.

'I was just going to get fish and chips. D'you want sausage or fish?' says Caris.

'Why did you wag off school, Caris?'

Stella looms up behind him.

'You need to sort things out. Look at her,' she snaps. 'She's dirty.'

'What happened to your arm?'

'I fell over.'

Mac looks helplessly at Stella.

'And I've got period pains,' adds Caris. 'I want to speak to Mum.'

Mac reddens. He doesn't know what to say or do.

'You've got to phone Mr Fortoba, and then go and see him at the school,' Stella tells him.

'I will. It's no good, Caris!' he shouts. 'You can't just go off when you want!'

Nana Price appears in the small kitchen.

'What's going on?' she asks.

'Nothing,' says Mac. 'Give Nana a cup of tea, Stella.'

'What's Caris done?'

'I just took the afternoon off.'

'What's wrong with that?' says Nana. 'They work them too hard at that place. What does it matter? Exams! Come on, Caris, let's watch *Richard and Judy*.'

'No!' shouts Stella. 'You've got to do something, Dad.'

Mac is frightened of school. He thinks of the long corridors, and the way he felt when the teachers spoke to him. He remembers wagging off with his friend Joey; hanging about at Metro stations, so bored that they counted people getting on and off trains. Most of all he recalls being cold.

'All right, Stella, we'll see,' he mutters.

'Mr Fortoba doesn't care. It's just his job. You don't have to go anywhere, Dad,' says Caris.

Mac feels relieved.

'Yes you do. They'll think you don't care otherwise,' says Stella.

'Is that kettle boiled?' asks Nana.

At this point the phone rings. They all stand there listening to it, until Mac lumbers to the hallway and picks it up. He speaks in his puzzled voice; the voice he uses when he doesn't know the answer to something.

'It'll be that Mr Cortina,' says Nana. 'He phoned up before.'

Caris pushes out of the kitchen and runs upstairs, hearing Mac say, 'Monday, four o clock. I'll be there, Mr Fortoba.'

Caris goes into her mother's room and throws herself down on the quilted bedspread and tries to cry, but doesn't. She can hear Nana carrying a tray into the sitting room, and Stella talking to Mac in a confiding voice. She closes her eyes, and thinks of George. She imagines them stealing an expensive car and riding away together, with the music on loud. She pictures him turning to look at her, his hand on her knee, and the road stretching on and on.

Perhaps my mother felt like this, she thinks, lying here, with the voices downstairs, talking about things that didn't matter like school, and sausages, and cups of tea and all sitting in a room that felt too small. *Perhaps she wanted to steal away into the night, wearing fine gloves and Italian shoes and ride to a place where she could be someone else.*

prison visit

It's Saturday, and the day is wide awake and yellow. In the street people wash their cars, sweep the steps and trim their hedges. Mothers amble down the terrace with young children in raincoats, on their way to the climbing frames in the park. There are sounds of DIY in the air, hammering and sanding and sawing.

The family are going to visit Louise. There is an air of anxiety about all of them, even Nana Price, who has spent an hour touching up her make-up and arranging her wispy blonde hair and who now looks contained in a jersey and tight trousers, with her younger self glimpsing out from behind her lined features.

Stella wears jeans, a black jumper and a hairband. She looks like an intellectual, with her black hair and white face. Caris puts on the dirtiest clothes she can find, and refuses to change them. She won't brush her hair, either.

Mac wishes he was going alone. At ten o'clock they all appear in the hallway, and he puts down his newspaper and goes out to his taxi. Stella sits in the front, and Caris and Nana are in the back.

'Seatbelts,' says Mac to Nana and Caris, but they ignore him.

'I wish you'd get some new photos,' says Stella, grimacing at the portraits hanging from Mac's mirror.

'Put some music on,' says Caris.

Nana hums loudly as Mac drives up to the motorway. She leans forward and warns him whenever a car passes.

'I can see, Nana,' he says. 'I've got a mirror.'

'I'm just being helpful,' she bristles. 'We don't want to be in a pile-up.'

'Driving's my job,' he says.

'You can get too casual about driving,' she snipes.

Mac taps the steering wheel with his big thumbs. Stella has a map on her lap. She directs him in a monotone voice.

'It's miles,' says Caris.

'Poor Louise,' whimpers Nana, 'sent miles away from her family. What kind of justice is that?'

'Well, she shouldn't have got caught,' mutters Caris.

'She shouldn't have done it,' says Mac, then wishes he hadn't.

'I'm not surprised she did it. You're out all the time. She's not someone who likes being on her own. She's always been sensitive.' Nana Price looks satisfied, as if she's been wanting to say this for some time. Her head wobbles about righteously on her old shoulders. 'I think you've had it coming a long time, myself,' she adds. 'A long, long time.'

'Leave it, Nana,' says Stella, as the atmosphere in the taxi intensifies.

'And you girls, too, demanding things all the time. She must have been suffering, poor lamb.'

'And you didn't help, either,' says Mac, glancing grimly in the mirror.

'What do you mean?'

'Always drinking, always thinking of yourself.'

'Now hang on a minute. At least I know how to enjoy myself.' Nana slaps her hands down on her lap and mutters, 'Louise should never have married you. She should have gone with that what's-his-name. The one who bred dogs.'

'Donny,' says Caris in a bored voice. 'Donny the Dalmatian dealer.'

'Yes, he was kind, Donny was, and you don't go out much if you breed dogs.'

Caris imagines having a father called Donny, and pens of dogs barking in a back yard.

'Shut up, Nana,' she says.

71

'Don't tell me to shut up! Tell her, Mac!'

Mac doesn't speak. He turns up the radio and Caris stares out of the window at the hard shoulder, and the misty fields filled with dishcloth-grey sheep and huddles of morose cows. Nana Price dozes off, making a sound like a dog dreaming of chasing a rabbit. Stella bites her lip and mentally recites her lines.

'This is it,' announces Mac at last. The family look up at a high wire fence as Mac turns into a driveway that leads to an imposing entrance, watched by security cameras. 'Look at this place. She's not a danger to society, is she?'

'Poor Mum,' says Stella.

Caris finds it all extremely interesting. The buildings ahead are grey and flat. They seem to have no windows. There's a barred gate, through which she can see a flowerbed and a circular driveway. She feels as if she's in a film. There are official signs everywhere, directing goods vans, special deliveries, visitors.

'Where do I park?' says Mac, who feels exhausted already.

'There,' says Stella pointing him towards the visitors' car park.

'Oh, well, we got here alive at least!' says Nana opening the door and tottering out in her high heels.

Caris pushes out of the stuffy car, and looks over at a door with the word 'VISITORS' written in red letters. A few people are wandering towards it, joining a queue of timid relatives who all appear hunched and guilty. She feels as if they are in another universe. Mac won't stop stroking his head as he locks the taxi.

No one speaks as they shuffle through the door and allow their belongings to be searched and their pockets patted. Stella looks humiliated as a prison warder tells her to turn round with her legs apart. Caris feels bemused. Nana snorts and tuts, and Mac stands there with his hands in the air in a posture of surrender.

They are shown into a large room with plastic chairs, fixed to the floor around low tables. In one corner of the room there's a coffee machine, and Mac immediately busies himself with change and plastic cups, while the three women sit down nervously, Nana playing with her cigarettes and eyeing the 'NO SMOKING' sign with distaste.

*

Louise smiles stiffly as she approaches the table. Her family look so real, so incredibly defined, while she feels insubstantial, like a ghost moving through rooms. She worries that she might not be able to speak, and coughs into her handkerchief. They all look up as she nears. Louise sees that Caris's hair is tangled and unbrushed, that Stella looks frightened and over-controlled. Mac won't even look up, apart from a brief fleeting glance, and her mother leaps to her feet, arms outstretched, as if she is meeting Louise off a plane.

'Darlin'!' she shrieks. 'How ya doin'?'

'Great,' says Louise. 'Fine.'

'Do you want a coffee, love?' asks Mac.

'White, two sugars,' says Louise, as if Mac is a stranger. 'Well!' she says, looking at them all.

'Met any murderers?' asks Caris.

Louise stares at her youngest daughter. *She doesn't look at all well*, thinks Louise. *She looks like an unpruned plant; beautiful, but running wild*. She ignores the question.

'Your hair needs brushing,' she says. 'Shall I do it for you?'

'No thanks,' says Caris.

'Caris keeps on wagging off school,' interrupts Stella, 'Tell her, Dad.'

'Don't start on about that, dear!' says Nana. 'How are you keeping, Louise?'

'Oh, it's fine. I'm doing art. Well, it's boring a lot of the time. Every day is the same,' says Louise.

'Do people take drugs in here?' says Caris.

'Some of them do.'

Caris imagines Louise, moving with ease among junkies and prostitutes. *Perhaps she will become a prostitute*, she thinks. Louise sips her coffee and looks up at them all nervously.

'Your mother's moved in,' says Mac. 'I think she should go home.'

'I'm helping,' says Nana with tight lips.

'Where's she sleeping?' says Louise.

'In the boxroom,' says Caris. 'She's no trouble.'

'It hasn't got any windows,' says Louise.

'I'm not complaining,' Nana says nobly.

'I think she should go home,' says Mac again.

'Caris likes me being there, don't you, pet?' says Nana brightly. 'Someone's got to be there when the girls get in from school. He's not.'

Mac sucks the back of his hand, hoping Louise will say something to her mother, but she just rubs her eyes and glances at the large prison clock on the painted magnolia walls.

'Aye, I'm helping, like,' says Nana sweetly.

'That's nice,' says Louise vaguely. 'What about you, love?' Louise asks Stella.

Stella shrugs. 'I've got to do everything.'

'Caris, you should help,' says Louise.

'Stella won't let me.'

'Liar,' spits Stella.

'That's enough,' says Mac. They all look at him glumly. 'Anyone like another coffee? Or a biscuit?' he asks desperately.

Caris studies Louise. She looks greyer, and a little thinner, and she's not wearing her usual make-up. There is something abandoned about her, as if she has put some part of herself in Left Luggage.

'What's it like at nights?' asks Caris.

'Noisy. I'm sharing with someone called Carol. She's over there.'

They look over at a big blonde woman with a tattoo on her forearm who is talking to a younger woman with a toddler on her knee. She glances back at Louise, and waves. Louise waves back, and Caris feels left out, as if her mother has a new social life in which she is not included.

'What did she do?' asks Caris.

'It's rude to ask,' says Louise.

'Why?' asks Caris.

'Because you're just being nosy.'

'I'm interested,' snaps Caris.

'She killed her husband, if you must know,' says Louise softly.

Mac raises his eyebrows.

'How?' says Caris.

74

'I don't want to talk about it.'

There is a long resentful silence. Caris taps her fingers against her teeth, until Mac tells her to stop.

Nana gets up and mumbles about going to the toilet, although it's obvious that she's looking for somewhere to have a fag.

'They want me to go up the school,' Mac says. 'About Caris.'

Louise looks guilty.

'What have you been up to, Caris?' she asks wearily.

'Nothing,' says Caris.

'You have to go to school, love.'

'Why?' asks Caris.

'It's the law,' says Stella.

'What shall I say, at the school?' asks Mac.

'Perhaps she's unhappy,' says Louise.

'Are you unhappy?' asks Mac, surprised.

'No.'

'Well, what is it, then?'

'I haven't got any friends.'

'What about Margaret?'

'I don't like Margaret.'

They all gaze at her until Louise says sensibly, 'Well, try harder, love. Are you eating properly?'

'No,' says Stella.

'We eat a lot of takeaways and that,' says Mac mournfully.

'Not long now,' mumbles Louise.

'When are you coming out?' asks Caris.

'Oh, soon,' says Louise.

Nana Price returns. The toilets were full of cameras.

'Bloody justice. What's the point in keeping you cooped up in here?' Nana Price looks around crossly. 'With these losers,' she adds.

'Sssh,' Louise whimpers. 'Mam, please.'

'Anyone like a Mars bar?' asks Mac.

The rest of the visit is filled with awkward pauses, as the five people sip from plastic cups and fold Mars-bar wrappers into tiny parcels.

By the time the bell rings Louise is exhausted. She kisses each person in turn. Caris thinks she smells funny, of some kind of disinfectant. She watches her mother disappear into the curious world behind the door, while Mac stands waiting for her, and the dull room clears. She can hear the sound of heavy doors closing and keys turning.

'Come on now, Caris,' he says. 'It's time to go.'

For a moment, as he watches his younger daughter standing alone in the centre of the vacated room, Mac is filled with a terrible sorrow. Caris looks confused, with her wide-open eyes, standing there staring at a locked door. *How could Louise have done this to her?* he thinks.

He calls Caris again, and she ambles towards him. He tries to put his arm around her, but she steps away.

'Come on, love,' he says. 'Let's get some chips on the way home.' When she was a child this would have made her pleased, but now she just looks at him with a cold expression as if she doesn't care.

sunday morning

When Caris opens her eyes the next day the house is empty. Mac is working. Nana has gone to see her friend Mona, and Stella is at a *Macbeth* rehearsal. Caris enjoys walking around the house in her mother's dressing-gown, with music playing in every room.

Then the doorbell rings, and for a moment she thinks it might be George, but then remembers that he doesn't know where she lives. Suspiciously she opens the door to see Layla and Margaret standing there like two indignant goats with their chins jutting out.

'It's Sunday,' says Caris, and starts to close the door, but Layla steps forward with her looped earrings wobbling in her pink earlobes.

'You took our fucking shoes,' she snarls.

'You took mine,' says Caris.

'I've told my dad and Mr Fortoba about you.'

'You're a thief, like your thieving mam,' quips Margaret.

'And you're a slag,' adds Layla.

'I'm not a slag,' says Caris.

'We say you are,' says Margaret.

Caris tries to close the door again, but Layla pushes forward.

'We're watching you,' she says. 'We're round the corner.'

'We're going to smash your face in,' adds Margaret in a bored voice.

'Oh,' says Caris. 'Oh dear.'

She tries to sound sarcastic but the words come out too brittle. She pushes the door again. 'Go away,' she says.

'We're going,' says Layla, 'but we're not going away.'

Caris watches them through the window, swaggering off down the middle of the road. She wishes she had a gun, and could shoot them. She tells herself she doesn't care, but she knows that things will get worse. Layla, with her pointed face and thin mouth, is someone who starts wars, who makes enemies, who draws others to her, and Caris is her victim now. Layla will get more and more obsessed with making Caris's life miserable. Caris has seen other girls, so scared they pissed themselves when Layla spoke to them. *She'll never leave me alone*, thinks Caris. *I'm finished with school. What's the point of going to school to get your head kicked in?*

She spends the rest of the morning huddled on the sofa, wondering what to do. Caris knows that Layla's kingdom is tiny, encompassing the school and the park, and a few terraces around it. Outside this compact world Layla is a nobody. *I need to get out of here*, thinks Caris, and the only person she knows who is outside this boundary is George. She gets dressed and smokes one of Nana's cigarettes, telling herself to be brave she ties back her hair, pulls on a red hooded jacket, and steps out into the quiet Sunday street, with its churchy smells of roast meat and sound of distant bells, and runs into the Vale.

There is ice on the ground, and the air is sharp. When she gets to the tree it glistens with frost, and the shoes hanging from its branches are dusted with a layer of thin snow.

Caris waits nervously for a while, wondering if George will appear, looking over her shoulder. Then, impatiently, she runs through the park, past the square bowling green that's dusted with white flecks, and over the Victorian iron bridge, to where the big houses are, and where she knows George lives. She passes vague families with snuffling dogs and prams with mittened, hatted babies who stare at her with large unblinking eyes. She reaches West Avenue, an opulent street, with gardens filled with rhododendron and laurel bushes, and languorous houses with balconies set back from the road behind high walls. Caris tries to imagine what it would be like to live in such a house, with too many rooms, and with so many doors to lock. She stops outside a house called The Conservatory and peers inside the wrought-iron gates.

The front door opens and a blonde woman steps out, fiddling with her handbag. Caris watches her climb into a polished car and start up the engine, examining her face in the mirror, and pushing her springy hair from her face.

Then she hears a low whistle behind her and turns to see George in a black coat, standing on the other side of the avenue, fingers in his mouth.

'Caris,' he calls.

She walks over. George grins, his face animated. He's smoking a cigarette, wearing fingerless gloves.

'What are you doing?' he says. 'Are you spying on me?'

'Looking,' says Caris.

'I've been looking for you, too,' he says.

'I waited for you. You didn't turn up.'

'I couldn't get away.' He scowls.

'What from?'

'Them.'

He puts his thin arm round Caris's waist as if she's an old friend and walks her into an even grander driveway.

'They're having lunch,' he says.

'Who?'

'My parents.'

George leads her to a window through which she can see the shadowy shapes of two people sitting at a table. Caris hides behind a bush and watches. They move their knives and forks slowly and sit there like two stones. The mother's hair is coiffured, and the father has a bald round head. They look tiny. Caris would like to reach in and pick them out and hold them in the palm of her hand.

'How many rooms have you got?'

'I don't know,' he says. 'I've never counted.'

'What do they do?'

79

'She's in cosmetics, anti-ageing cream, stuff like that. He's in electrics. Come on.'

'Where are we going?'

'Away from here. You don't want to meet them.'

Caris would love to see the inside of George's house. She wants to pee in his bathroom, to look at the ornaments on his mantelpiece, and touch the clothes that his mother wears. She wants to open the fridge and see what's inside, and feel the quality of his sheets.

'I do,' she says, not budging.

'You can come back when they're away.'

'Are you ashamed of me, or what?'

'No, I'm ashamed of them.'

He grimaces. Caris understands. She knows what it would be like with George on her settee, the agony she would feel with her family devouring him, asking him questions.

'What shall we do?'

'I've got more shoes.'

George slips into the porch and comes out with a carrier bag.

'There's a lot of people about,' says Caris. 'It's Sunday.'

'We'll get a coffee, then, and wait until it gets dark.'

Together they walk towards the Vale. Caris is jumpy, expecting Layla and Margaret to appear around every corner. It's getting misty and the yellow street lamps are lit even though it's mid-afternoon. George reaches out and takes Caris's hand. She feels the scratchy wool of his gloves against her palm.

God, she thinks, *I'm holding hands with a posh boy*. She hopes that someone from school sees her, walking along with George in the mist.

When they reach a clearing in the park George stops and lights another cigarette, offering Caris one. They stand there, looking at each other, smoking. Caris wonders what George would look like naked. She feels as if she's opening a door into another universe, as if all the walls that she's always imagined are there are collapsing one by one. George strokes her neck and his fingers are silky and cool. Caris shivers. Just as George stubs out his fag, leaving a smear of ash on the tarmac, and leans towards her, about to kiss her on the lips, she hears a loud call behind her.

'Caris? Lovey? Is that you?'

Caris turns, her heart beating, and peers down the path through the fog. Nana Price is staggering back after a day of drinking sherry with her friend Mona. She looms towards them with an uneven, bleary face.

'What are you doing, pet lamb? Who's this?'

'George,' says Caris.

'Nice to meet you, George,' says Nana. 'Can you give me a help home, love. I'm a bit lost. Me heel's dropped off.'

She lifts her foot and shows them her shoe, the heel hanging off like a child's milk tooth.

'George might have a pair of shoes you can have,' says Caris.

'Of course,' says George graciously. 'What size are you?'

Nana is confused. She watches George tip out a bag of assorted shoes on to the ground.

'Where are these from?' she says, leaning over to pick up a bony sandal.

'We were taking them to the charity shop,' says Caris.

Nana picks out a pair of fur-lined boots.

'These are nice,' she says. 'Put these on for us, will you, Caris, pet lamb?'

Caris kneels at her grandmother's feet, struggling to pull the boots over her bunions.

'Fancy that!' says Nana when the boots are firmly strapped up.

'They suit you,' says George, picking up shoes and putting them back into the bag.

'This is my grandmother,' Caris tells him.

'Call me Irene,' Nana adds proudly. 'I've moved in while they've got the trouble.'

'Trouble?' says George, taking Nana's arm.

'Family trouble.' Nana leans against George. Caris looks on with horror. George winks at Caris, who turns away.

'Oh, yeah, Caris told me,' says George.

'So, George, where do you live?' asks Nana as the three of them begin to shamble together along the path.

'Up there,' says George.

Nana steadies herself and studies George, then looks up towards the valley where he lives.

She looks suspicious.

'Have you got a fag?'

George lights a cigarette for Nana, who inhales dramatically then coughs.

'You're quite a girl,' says George.

'Who, me? That's right! They call me Irene,' she says again. 'What are you doing with a bag of shoes?'

'I told you. We're taking them to the charity shop for George's mam.'

Caris thinks that Nana might collapse. She keeps on smiling an unruly smile at George, and winking at Caris.

George sniggers. Nana Price drops her cigarette into the mud and stumbles.

'Whoah!' says George.

Caris steps in. There is something she doesn't like about the way George speaks to Nana Price. She doesn't like the sneer that flickers across his face.

'Leave it. I'll take her home,' she says, and grasps Nana Price's arm.

'Let Georgie come!' whoops Nana. 'Bring him home to meet us. Come on, Georgie!'

'No,' says Caris. 'Leave us. I'll take her.'

George steps back, annoyed.

'See you later, then,' he says crossly and slips away between trees into the wet dark, while Caris drags Nana back along the path, singing her sherry-fuelled songs.

eating pizza

They are all eating ham and pineapple pizza round the kitchen table when the phone rings. Mac gets up slowly, wiping a trickle of tomato sauce from the corner of his mouth. Stella doesn't lift her eyes from the book that is beside her plate. They hear Mac saying, 'Louise?' and everyone sits up, as if Louise is on holiday somewhere, calling to make sure they are all right.

'We're eating pizza,' says Mac, 'from that place on Heaton Road. How are you doing?'

Caris plunges her fork into a shrunken mushroom.

'Stella's done her Lady Macbeth. She said it went very well,' says Mac. 'No, we couldn't go. I told you, I was working. Course I wanted to go, but I couldn't.' There is a long pause. The two girls hear Mac breathing crossly. 'Caris? She's here now. Do you want to speak to her?'

Caris stands up, wanting to be first. Mac holds the phone out towards her.

'Mum?' says Caris.

Louise's voice sounds as if it comes from an underground cave.

'What are you up to?' she asks.

'Eating pizza,' says Caris.

'How's school?' asks Louise.

'All right.'

'Do you miss me?'

'A bit.'

'Are you eating enough?'

'Yeah.'

Caris feels like crying. Everyone looks at her as she speaks. She wants to take Louise's voice away with her, to a quiet place, where she can tell her about Layla and the tree, but Louise just seems to want reassurance.

'When are you coming home?' asks Caris, in a tiny voice.

'A few more weeks. Not long.'

'How's your friend the murderer?'

'Carol? She's all right. She's waiting to hear about her appeal. The food's awful. It comes in plastic trays, like on aeroplanes. We get locked up a lot.'

Caris thought that was the point of prison.

'But there's classes you can go to,' Louise says cheerfully.

'Can I speak to her?' interrupts Stella crossly.

'Wait,' says Caris.

'I miss you, Caris. Will you write to me? It's lonely when you don't hear anything.'

'I'll try,' says Caris. 'Here's Stella.'

She passes the phone over to Stella, who speaks cheerfully into the receiver, babbling on about her school achievements and how she's going on a trip to London. Caris aches. Mac stands with his arms folded, and Nana Price picks at her teeth with a matchstick.

'Do you want Dad?' says Stella, and passes the phone back to Mac, who goes out of the room, talking in a hushed voice.

'I'm working,' he says. 'I haven't got time. I've got to go up and see the bloody teacher tomorrow. I don't know what to say to him. Shall I tell him, or what?'

Stella starts clearing up the plates and stacking them in the sink.

'You've got to wash up, Caris,' she says. 'You never do it.'

Caris runs from the small white kitchen, and up to her bedroom, pushing the door tightly shut behind her.

Then she doesn't know what to do. She looks out of the window at the house opposite, where a woman basks in the strange purple glow of a sunbed, as if she craves for light in this long dark tunnel of winter. Caris opens a drawer and shuffles through it, pulling out handfuls of paper scraps. She finds a small photograph album, made of pink plastic, with the words 'My Pictures' written in gold italics on the front. Like most of Caris's things, it's slightly torn, and it is only half filled with photographs. She studies a picture of her and Louise standing on a beach. Louise is slim, and looks like a girl, wearing a bikini and pushing her long hair back with her hand. Caris is a plump thirteen, too young to hold her stomach in, but self-conscious enough to look at the camera suspiciously. *It's hard to believe that I started my life in Mum's flat stomach*, thinks Caris. *My mother was only twenty when she got pregnant with me.* This thought triggers an unpleasant image of Louise and Mac having sex, and Caris can hardly bear to think of her petite mother beneath the overweight Mac. She stuffs the photograph back into the wallet and pulls out another. This time it's a photograph of her as the Virgin Mary in a play at primary school, sitting on a hay bale, holding a plastic doll, with a pious expression. She remembers being told she was the most beautiful Mary they had ever had and Stella being so jealous that she had cried all through the play, and how Caris had rejoiced in Stella's misery and felt even more superior with the baby Jesus looking up at her with fake eyelashes.

I'm not a nice person, thinks Caris. She throws the photograph on to the floor where it gets lost among a pile of unwashed knickers and T-shirts. She lights a cigarette and stands next to the slightly open window, blowing smoke out of the crack.

I'm going to have sex, she thinks. *I'm going to do what I like and no one's going to stop me.*

school visit

Caris, Mr Fortoba and Mac sit too close together in an overcrowded brown office with high metal windows, surrounded by piles of ragged exercise books on shelves. Mac looks like a boy who is waiting to see the headmaster, while Caris twists in her chair, staring at a threadbare patch of sky through the high window and wishing she was somewhere else.

Mr Fortoba reads out a list of Caris's absences from the class register. In the distance they can hear the sounds of other children hurling themselves around the school, crashing through doors and running in wild frustrated circles outside on the playing field.

'So,' says Mr Fortoba, putting the register down, 'what have you got to say for yourself, Caris?'

Caris doesn't answer. She looks instead at Mac. He always looks washed. His skin is smooth and pink. When she was little she liked to stroke his shaved chin. She loved the smell of him, of car interiors and leather.

Mac coughs and says, 'Caris, what about your exams?'

'I don't know,' she answers in a small voice.

'Now's the time to talk about it, Caris,' says Mr Fortoba, his neat face sharp and interested. 'Let's try and sort things out.'

Caris crosses her arms and tries to be invisible. She concentrates on the tree, and imagines Mr Fortoba's shoes hanging in it.

'Say something, Caris,' says Mac loudly. 'Show some respect.'

'I don't know what you want me to say,' sniffs Caris.

'I wish I'd passed my exams,' says Mac. 'I wouldn't be a taxi driver now if I'd listened.'

'Why didn't you?' mutters Caris.

Mac has an image of lines of schoolchildren in a large airy room, all writing diligently, while he and his friend Joey crouched at the back staring out through the window like incarcerated dogs that longed to be outside.

'I had to start work. But you've got a chance to be something,' Mac says in what he hopes is an encouraging voice.

'I don't want to be anything,' says Caris.

Mr Fortoba sniffs. He puts down the register and uncrosses his legs.

'We've had some stress,' says Mac. This sounds wrong. He tries again. 'Trouble. It might be affecting her.'

'No, it's not,' says Caris.

'You might not even know it's affecting you.'

'Perhaps you should let us know,' says Mr Fortoba.

Nosy bastard, thinks Caris.

'It's her mother, my wife,' says Mac.

Mr Fortoba leans forward, his eyes fixed on Mac.

'She's been arrested,' says Mac.

Caris sighs loudly.

'I see,' says Mr Fortoba.

'Imprisoned,' adds Mac.

This has a fairy-tale ring to it.

'Locked up,' says Caris.

'Recently?' asks Mr Fortoba.

'Very recently. Not for long. She'll be out by May. It wasn't anything serious.'

'How does Caris feel about this?' asks Mr Fortoba, swinging round to look at her. In fact he is consumed by curiosity. He remembers Louise from parent-teacher evenings as a shy, youthful parent with a slight lisp and shiny long hair parted in the middle. Caris knows Mr Fortoba wants to know what her mother's crime was. She delights in knowing something that he doesn't.

She screws up her face and says meekly, 'I'm worried.'

Mr Fortoba nods. Mac reddens. He is afraid that Caris might cry. He wonders if his daughter is irreparably damaged. He thinks of cars breaking down and having to be scrapped.

'She robbed a shop,' says Caris childishly. 'She got caught.'

'Ah,' says Mr Fortoba, unsure how to react.

'We think she was depressed, like,' Mac explains. 'It happens to women sometimes . . .' And his voice trails away. He tries again. 'She only took a shoe!' he says defensively 'It wasn't much.'

Mr Fortoba smiles in an understanding way.

'Do you want to talk to someone, Caris?' he says.

He wishes Caris liked him more. She is one of the pupils who he dwells on, when he can't sleep at night, and he feels like giving up his job and becoming a tree surgeon, or a countryside warden. He sees her laughing at him, her head thrown back, her red hair curling down her back, her mouth wide open. He knows that Caris is clever, but that school does nothing for her. She's a girl who doesn't suit an English education. She doesn't suit the buildings, or the work. She would be better off outside, like him, mending walls or climbing trees.

While Mr Fortoba thinks these things, Caris is getting into character. She feels misery welling up inside her like sick.

'I can't sleep,' she says, 'thinking about Mum, behind bars.'

'Of course not.' Mr Fortoba frowns, thinking of his own mother, who resembles a large teapot, and how he might feel if she was incarcerated. Rather pleased, he decides.

'It's not your fault, Caris,' he says.

Mac nods emphatically. 'No, love, it's not your fault.'

'Whose fault is it, then?' says Caris.

There is a silence. Mr Fortoba wonders how to move things on. He has to teach a geography class in five minutes.

'The thing is, Caris, you've got to stop running off. You have to let people know what you're doing. Do you understand? I can arrange for you to see a school counsellor.'

'I don't want to see a counsellor,' says Caris. 'I'm scared.'

'Well, think about it.'

'Yes, think about it,' says Mac, to whom counselling is the kind of thing flaky posh people do. 'You've got to behave, Caris.'

'You can talk to me any time you like,' adds Mr Fortoba.

Caris turns to Mac with tears in her eyes.

'I need space, Dad,' she says, 'To work this out.'

'This might explain the, er . . . bullying incident,' says Mr Fortoba.

'What bullying incident?' says Mac.

'Yeah, what?' says Caris.

'Caris hit another girl, and she stole her shoes, a Layla Tumility.'

'No I didn't!' says Caris, vehemently.

'Caris!' Mac is shocked. He can't imagine Caris hurting anyone.

'She says you did. Her father came into the school. He was very worried.'

'Well, she's a liar.'

Mr Tumility is one of the parents who Mr Fortoba dreads meeting. He's built like a concrete car park, and looks like the kind of man who might burn down your house if you annoyed him.

'I think you should talk things through with Layla.'

'No way!' shrieks Caris. 'I hate her.'

'That's not going to solve anything, is it?' says Mr Fortoba, although he dislikes Layla Tumility himself.

Mac shakes his head. He thinks that Caris is acting up, and would like to slap her, but he can't do this in front of the teacher so he holds his breath and stares at his brown leather shoes instead.

'Perhaps we should meet again in a few weeks to see how things are developing. Sometimes these things pass over like bad weather,' says Mr Fortoba, jumping to his feet and shaking Mac's large hand as a loud bell rings. 'The main thing is, you must come to school,' he says. 'Otherwise how can I help you?'

'Did you hear that, Caris?' says Mac in a more aggressive tone than he intended. 'Get yourself to school!'

Caris nods. She wonders if either of these men could manage in her world. *They just want me to stop causing problems*, she thinks, *so that they can get on with their stupid lives*.

She stares at Mr Fortoba's boots. His feet are very small. His whole life is small, she decides.

'Yeah, I suppose,' she says.

the tree of shoes

George is hanging more shoes in the wide branches of the oak tree.
He hangs up pairs of his father's business shoes, and his mother's
fluffy slippers. He waits for Caris to come back and see what he
has done. The oak is a perfect shape; its branches form a generous
scaffolding that supports him as he twists between boughs. George
hangs up the shoes carefully, measuring the distance between them
so that they appear symmetrical.

He tries to make himself invisible, so that people passing beneath
him are unaware of him. He listens to their conversations. There
are arguing couples, excited children, people calling their dogs.
Some people sing out loud, or talk to themselves. A black woman
comes by carrying a basket of oranges. She stops and looks up at
him as if she had always known he was there.

'What are you doing, boy?' she calls.

'Messing about,' answers George.

'You shouldn't hang shoes in a tree,' she tells him. 'It's a bad
thing.'

'Why not?' he says.

'You're hanging people's souls up there.'

George ignores her, turning away.

The woman takes an orange from her basket and throws it at
him.

'Are you listening to me?'

The orange misses him and rolls off down the hill.

George won't look at her, and after a while she stomps off, muttering to herself. He likes the idea of capturing souls in the branches of the tree. It makes him feel powerful. He climbs up as far as he can go, to where the last branches divide. The ground is miles away, and he can see beyond the city to green hills, and the blurry edge of the land and the North Sea. Sitting there, like a king, George feels almost happy. It's an odd sensation, like sucking sherbert.

writing on the wall

Layla and Margaret have got some car-paint spray cans from Layla's father's garage. They've got pink and silver. They walk through the Vale at lunchtime, each wielding an aerosol like a gun, looking around furtively before spraying 'Caris is a slag' or 'Caris is a fat pig' on every available surface. Their writing is girlish and looped, and after a while their fingers get icy, and their wrists hurt. Then eventually the cans just rattle and won't spray any more letters, and they toss them into the brown river, watching them float off into an underground tunnel.

Then, bored, they sit on a bench in the park, and Layla says to Margaret, 'I fuckin' hate her, that Caris.'

Margaret agrees. Her friendship with Layla is built upon the foundations of hating Caris. If they had a religion Caris would be the Devil, and Britney Spears would be their Goddess. Oddly, there are physical similarities between Britney Spears and Caris, which both girls choose not to notice.

Lately Caris hasn't been at school much, which means that they have little to go on with the Hate Caris campaign. Layla would like to see Caris publicly humiliate herself. She never cries, just looks back with a tight, dumb expression. She would like to make Caris wet herself. Layla's done that with another girl, and it made her feel glorious to know that she, Layla, could incite such fear that someone could lose control of their bladder.

Layla looks down at her hands, which are smeared with silver and pink.

'What shall we do next?' she says, tired of being cold.

'Go up the Shields Road and get some chips,' says Margaret.

Margaret walks ahead, her socks falling down, the hem of her school skirt uneven. Layla follows, aware of her slender, sharp body in contrast to Margaret's, her new school clothes, singing, '*Hit me baby one more time . . .*'

The girls pick their way along stony paths, past a children's playground and up a steep path to where the shops are.

Caris is lying under her bedclothes, her eyes wide open, breathing in her own body smells. She wishes she was someone else, and imagines herself as a glamorous woman who is surrounded by courtiers. She sees herself as a queen, standing in the bows of a ship, dressed in a gown stitched with jewels, or reclining in a golden room, making decisions about a world outside. She wishes that the things she said were important. She wants to matter. Sometimes her head is filled with words, but none of them are in order. She wants to be able to say something powerful. She can almost taste sentences on her tongue, but cannot articulate them.

Caris wonders what her mother is doing at this moment. She pictures her in a dull canteen, smoking a hand-rolled cigarette, surrounded by tough-faced prisoners like the ones in documentaries, with bitten-down nails, who speak to each other in harsh, clipped sentences. She wonders if her mother has been in any fights yet.

At this moment Louise is looking out of the prison window at a neat necklace of migrating birds. She's in a dream, wondering where the birds are going, and how they manage to plan their journeys. In the background there's a group discussion going on, about good parenting. Most of the other women in the group are under twenty, talking about their children in anxious, trembling voices.

'What do you think about smacking, Louise?' says Tracey, the group leader, and Louise jumps, feeling everyone's eyes on her. She feels dazed. She tries to remember smacking Stella or Caris.

'I never did it on purpose,' she says eventually, and the group nods, each one thinking of an incident when they had ended up walloping their child out of desperation.

'Sometimes you don't know what you're doing,' says a young woman with a puffy-looking face.

'I hardly ever knew what I was fucking doing!' admits a large girl, and the whole group giggles, relieved.

Caris pushes back the bedcovers and sits up, dazzled by the light in the room. She knows the house is empty. She pads downstairs and toasts some bread, eating it as she pulls on clothes and thinks about what to do next. She wants to look at the tree again, to see what has happened to it while she slept.

She waits until the day begins to darken, and then slips out into the street and down the back lane to the park. Dogs sense her passing and hurl themselves at their back gates, snarling and barking. The light shines on to the street from Abdul's corner shop and a steady stream of customers head towards the open door as if pulled by a magnetic force.

When she reaches the entrance to the park she sees her name written in pink letters on the gatepost. Caris stares at the looped letters with a lump in her throat. She tries to rub out the words with her sleeve, but they are indelible and smug. Caris starts to run, down through the trees, as fast as she can go. There on the tarmac path her name shines out again, in silver. She runs faster and faster.

When she reaches the tree it looks kind. She climbs up into its branches quickly and easily, and the rugged bark against her skin is warm and giving. She curls up in its arms and lets the evening wrap her in darkness, while her teenage heart beats against her chest and she cringes with rage.

friday night

The Millennium bridge is winking its wide white eye to let a ship pass underneath it. It looks like a toothless jaw swinging apart. A small crowd watch from the riverside, impressed by its smooth technology.

Degna stands outside the restaurant on the quayside in her white mackintosh, her shoulders damp with rain, watching too. The older bridges crossing the river are lit up with an orange light, and the water is like glass, flat and glossy, making the surface look as if it's been varnished. It's still new to her, this city with its broad river and people that speak in leaping sentences. She considers buying a flat down by the quayside in one of the new developments; a suite with redbrick walls and low lighting.

As the winking bridge resumes its elegant, arc-like shape she has a rush of homesickness for her old life, in which she seemed to have so many things surrounding her, on shelves and in her cupboards. People, too. There were friends everywhere calling her up, inviting her round. Now it feels like her life is one simple idea, a job and a bed. It has no crevices or secrets or clutter. Degna is bored.

When Mac purrs round the corner in his blue car she relaxes, lifting her hand to greet him. Mac stops the car and jumps out, as if he's her chauffeur. Degna graciously climbs into the back of the taxi, thanking him, pleased to see him. She likes men like Mac, large, comfortable men with thick coats. Family men. She can almost hear his large heart beating.

'Home, please,' she says, and Mac looks into his mirror, pulling out into the busy street.

The quayside shines with new money. Mac tells Degna how it used to be: the flat wastes of demolished industries; the oily scum floating on the Tyne. 'It was a good place to get murdered in the old days. Look at it now,' he says. 'No one would ever know how bad it once was.'

Degna listens, and Mac feels as if he is saying something interesting. He likes the way that Degna sits in his taxi, relaxed and alert. He wants to drive slowly. To savour the atmosphere and to enjoy the company of this tired, calm woman.

'Had a good night?' he says as they turn up a steep hill towards Jesmond.

'Busy,' she tells him. 'Very busy. How are you?'

And Mac finds himself telling her about the prison visit, the school, and she nods and laughs.

'I got expelled from school,' she tells him.

'They didn't even bother to expel me,' says Mac. 'I just stopped going.'

'It's different when it's your kids, though, isn't it? What's she done?'

'Truanting and that. She doesn't work.'

'How old?'

'Fifteen.'

'When I was fifteen I was all over the place. Once I set fire to our house!'

They laugh together.

'I just used to hang about with the lads, you know, writing our names on things, climbing over fences, that kind of lark, or trying to get off with girls. It was just good clean fun. Now there's drugs and AIDS and all sorts.'

'What do teachers know?' says Degna. 'Look at me – I left school with nothing. She's probably too clever for them.'

Mac thinks of Mr Fortoba, with his bobbly jersey and his thin hair combed over his bony head, compared to Caris with all her brightness.

'Perhaps,' he says. 'You should meet my other daughter,' he boasts. 'She loves the acting, like.'

'You love them, don't you?' says Degna.

'Yeah,' says Mac. 'But they don't talk to me. I don't know what they want. Louise did all the talking.'

'I want to have kids,' says Degna. 'There isn't time. At least you've got kids.'

'Are you married?'

'No, single.'

'Why's that?' says Mac.

Degna doesn't answer. They are driving through streets that are empty apart from the odd group of student drunks. Above them the moon is a broken saucer in a cloudy sky.

Mac's radio splutters and Degna closes her eyes, leaning back in the seat.

'Are you there, Mac?' rasps Jeannie. 'You need to pick up Mr Bents from Casualty. He's waiting by the ramp. It's urgent. He broke his wrist and he wants you to take him home. Did you get that, Mac?'

He speaks lazily into the microphone: 'Yes, I heard.'

Degna opens her eyes.

'What's it like, driving taxis?'

'It's all right,' says Mac. Then he thinks for a moment. 'I can't stop it,' he says. 'I can't stop working.'

'Why's that?'

'There's always another fare, another person wanting to get somewhere. And you're hoping for the big ride.'

'The big ride?' she repeats.

'To Glasgow, or London. You want someone to get in the cab and say, "Take me to the Outer Hebrides." It happens.'

'But not often?'

'No. I should have done something else. It's too late now.'

'I wouldn't say that.'

'My daughters don't respect me.'

As he says it Mac knows it's true. He never thought he would drive a taxi for eighteen years, but that's what he's done.

'What's wrong with being a taxi driver?' asks Degna.

'It's not a career, is it,' says Mac sadly.

Then they are driving up an avenue filled with trees that are sprinkled with fairy-lights, outside closing bars and restaurants. Mac has a sudden urge to not take Degna home, to just drive and drive, up the coast road until they reach the top of Scotland, and they can just sit, with the headlamps on, looking out to sea, and forget everything, but now they're turning down Degna's street, and there's her front door, and tonight she has the right money so there's no need to hesitate. She just gets out of the car and says, 'See you next Friday, then', and then she's gone, closing her door and disappearing into the darkness.

dead people's shoes

Caris desires George. She feels it most in her stomach, and can't eat any breakfast. It feels like an illness, or a deep internal wound. She tries not to think about him. She also tries to forget that her name is scrawled all over the park.

Today she's got biology, and she likes the teacher, an olive-coloured woman called Miss Moss who brings in odd things to show them, like Venus fly-traps, live frogs, and once a shrunken head. Caris sets off for school leaving the house in a warm fug, with Nana Price humming through the open door of the boxroom. She's late but she doesn't care. Outside the air clings to her skin like a wet vest, leaves lie in the gutters among old crisp packets and cigarette ends. Carrier bags flap hopelessly in the bare branches of trees.

Caris strides across the glassy puddles, fracturing the ice with her shoes. The houses, built on steep hills, appear insubstantial to Caris, as if they could get overwhelmed by weeds and wildness if left too long. She looks up at nests in the wet branches above her. The tops of the trees in the distance blur into a pink mist. Caris wonders where George is, and if he thinks of her.

The allotments, a shanty village of sheds, pigeon crees and greenhouses, straggle down to the river, enclosed by a tattered fence. A notice flaps from one of the gates, saying that 'due to Pigeon Lung Brian has been forced to sell his champion pigeons'.

The river rattles along below her, snagged with bike wheels and water-drenched branches, sometimes disappearing into underground pipes, then bubbling up again. There's the remains of a burnt-out car pushed into a lay-by, its blackened hulk dripping with black rain. She strides on towards the tree.

Then she hears voices through the trees, and Margaret's unmistakable bray, interrupted by Layla's piercing giggle. Caris is afraid. She begins to run along the slippery path, stumbling on a root that snakes across the path.

At last she reaches the clearing where the tree glints in the mist. There are more shoes dangling among the twigs: a pair of man's boots, some sodden velvet slippers, a pair of green ankle boots. George must have put them there. The tree looks as if it welcomes her, and wants to protect her. Layla and Margaret are getting closer. She can hear their footsteps, their discordant voices getting more and more abrasive. She starts to climb the tree, her feet slipping on the bark, up to the sitting place from which she first saw George, and then further. She presses her body against a branch, trying to hide. Layla and Margaret are passing on a higher path.

'My dad's going to take me to Majorca,' says Layla.

'I've never been abroad,' whines Margaret.

'He takes me every year,' boasts Layla. 'I'll ask if you can come too.'

And then the voices begin to fade, fragmenting among the trees. Caris breathes again. She opens her bag and takes out a pair of her mother's shoes. They are flat summer sandals with pink straps. She remembers Louise wearing them on her elegant feet one summer night when she and Mac were going to a hotel, leaving her and Stella with Nana Price, watching videos. Nana was more compact then. Her buttons were done up, and she liked to make the girls little meals on trays. Mac and Louise went away for a weekend to Scotland. Louise had persuaded him to stop working and have a break. They had smart suitcases and Louise wore a bright-blue scarf that made her look sophisticated. They appeared to love each other. Caris had watched Mac and Louise getting into the car, and had noted how caring he was as he settled her into the seat, doing up her seatbelt, and making sure the seat was in the right position. When they returned they had both looked softer, and unknotted. Louise had given Caris a tinful of Edinburgh toffee. She still has that tin. She keeps her eyeshadows in it. Caris looks at the shoes and wonders if they still retain the warmth of that night. Then she hangs them lovingly in the tree, and wishes that George would be hers for ever.

As if her wish is heard, she hears a rustle on the ground below her and looks down to see George, looking up, his face pleased and expectant. Caris feels a rush of blood going to her cheeks.

'I've been hanging around for ages,' he calls up. 'Come down.'

Caris wriggles downwards clumsily, wishing George wouldn't watch her, and then lands on the ground, her heart thumping, unable to look George in the eye.

'I'm sorry,' she says, 'about last time. It's my nana. I was dead embarrassed.'

George doesn't answer. He kisses Caris on each cheek, a delicate, sophisticated, nearly not-touching kiss. George smells of tobacco and mints.

'What shall we do?' Caris says.

'Get more shoes,' says George.

They start to walk, up towards the shops above the park. George keeps on looking at Caris. Caris is hot, but brave. She feels like suggesting they have sex on the damp grass. Caris wants to see George's body. She wants to explore him. George is silent. He frowns at the sky and plays with a silver ring on his finger.

'Have you ever had a girlfriend?' asks Caris, exhausted by the silence.

'A few,' says George.

'Why did you break up?'

'I got bored with them,' he says. 'They didn't interest me.'

'Do you think you'll get bored with me?'

'No.'

They arrive at the battered row of shops. Vegetable stalls spill out on to the pavements between charity shops and cheap furniture stores. Shoppers appear stooped and Siberian, wearing motley knitted hats and baggy boots.

'Where now?' says Caris, aware that there are people everywhere and that she could be seen, but not caring. Caris feels airy and proud.

'Let's get some dead people's shoes,' says George.

'What for?'

'For the tree, of course.'

They go into the Cancer Care shop. It's full of frilled curtains and shrunken jumpers on hangers and smells of wet wool. A woman with army hair is sticking price tags on a pile of jigsaws. George goes to the back of the shop. There's a pile of shoes there with worn heels and scuffed toes. There are shoes in the shapes of old ladies' bunions, and shoes that old men have cared for and polished for years. *They look dead*, thinks Caris. *They might even have been on their feet when they died*. And then Caris thinks of her Nana's contorted toes, and feels uncomfortable. George holds up a black boot with a built-up heel. Caris imagines a bent man, dead, his last pair of boots stripped from his crooked feet. George is taking a pile of footwear to the counter. Caris picks up a pair of grey baby shoes with rabbits stitched on the front.

George is paying. Caris glances up to see him pulling several notes out of his pocket. She is beginning to feel embarrassed in this shop. 'This is a place where poor people go,' she wants to say to George. 'We shouldn't be here. With all that money you should be in Fenwick's.'

George turns to her with a recycled carrier bag and grins.

'Got this lot for a quid!' he says. 'I think that's a bargain, don't you, Caris?'

She shrugs.

'Are you art students?' asks the army-haired woman. 'Is it an art thing?'

'You could call it that,' George tells her.

'We get a lot of art students in here,' says the woman. 'Does your dad drive taxis?' she asks Caris, who grimaces.

'Yeah,' she says.

'I know your nan,' says the woman. 'I see her at the bingo.'

'Oh,' says Caris.

George picks out an old man's hat with a feather stuck in the brim.

'How much is this?' he asks.

'Fifty pence?'

'Is that all?' says George.

'You might get nits,' says Caris. 'You should be careful.'

The woman won't stop looking at her.

'I want a fag,' says Caris.

'We'll go to a café,' says George. 'One of those cheap places.'

When Caris was younger Mac would sometimes walk with her and Stella to Shields Road on a Saturday morning, so that Louise could 'get on'. They would come to one of the cramped, steamy cafés and sit and have sausage sandwiches and strawberry milkshakes. Old women with carved wrinkled faces would pat Caris's head as they passed. Mac would make jokes, sitting opposite her and Stella, taking up two seats. She would sit quietly, watching, sucking through a straw. She would feel very safe, with her affable father opposite her, drinking his mug of tea. He always knew everyone. People would shake his hand and say things like, 'Has she left you with the bairns?'

Afterwards he would buy them something from one of the cheap shops: a doll whose head would immediately fall off, or a little plastic pony with a jewelled harness.

Now she follows George into Munchies and sits down at a Formica table, feeling self-conscious. She's not surprised when a middle-aged woman in a daisy-printed plastic hood says, 'That's never little Caris, is it?' and lurches towards them dragging a tartan shopping trolley that has a small dog sitting in it in a red coat.

Caris nods, wishing George would stop looking.

'How's Stella?' says Mrs Featherly, who used to work at Mac's taxi rank before Jeannie, and is also a part-time clairvoyant.

'Canny,' mumbles Caris.

'Why aren't you at school, pet?'

'Revision day,' Caris tells her.

'I see.' Then Mrs Featherly examines George with her wrinkled eyes. She takes in his dirty coat, the silver stud that pierces his nose, his greasy hair.

George does a little bow but Mrs Featherly doesn't smile. Then George yawns.

'Who's this?' she says. 'Is it your boyfriend?'

'Yes,' says George.

Mrs Featherly licks her lips.

'Are you at the same school?' she asks.

'No,' says George.

'He's changing schools,' mutters Caris.

'You've grown. Last time I saw you, you were a little girl. Now look at you.'

It feels as if everyone in the café is looking at Caris.

'I'm sorry about your mam. I read it in the paper.'

'Oh, well,' says Caris.

'How's she managing?'

'Not bad.' Caris longs for Mrs Featherly to shut up.

'It will be over in no time,' says Mrs Featherly.

There is a long pause, filled with the shrieking of the coffee-making machine, and clashing dishes in the kitchen.

'Give your father my regards,' Mrs Featherly says at last.

'I will.' Caris bleakly stirs her coffee with a tin spoon.

'Be seeing you, pet,' Mrs Featherly says. 'Get back to that revision.' And she shambles off, leaving a sense of unease behind her.

'We shouldn't have come here,' says Caris.

'You know people, don't you? It must be funny, that. Knowing people around the place you live. I don't know anyone, anywhere.'

'You must do.'

'No, I told you. I was at boarding school.'

'Why have you come here?'

'It's where my parents live. I got expelled.'

'What for?'

'Smoking dope.'

'Oh.'

'It was a shit-hole anyway.'

'Don't you have any friends?'

'I've got you.' George smiles with half his mouth.

Caris sips the last of her coffee. It tastes like poison. She never drinks coffee. She wants to go back to the Vale, and get away from all the people in the café. She feels them looking at her and George, wondering what they are doing there. George leans back in his chair confidently. He is unaware of everyone around him. He looks at Caris as if she is a gadget he doesn't yet know how to operate, but is determined to master.

Behind him, in the street, Caris sees Margaret and Layla, still deep in conversation, sharing a bag of chips. *It must be lunchtime*, Caris thinks. School seems a long way off. She imagines Mr Fortoba saying, 'Anyone seen Caris?' and no one answering.

'Come on,' she says. 'Let's go back.'

And down in the Vale, the tree waits for them, a personality now, adorned with shoes. And the people who pass by point up to its branches and say the words 'Tree of Shoes' or 'Shoe Tree' to themselves, as if it's always looked like this, or as if the shoes have grown all by themselves. And a council gardener called Maurice passes by and stops to marvel at it, but can't bring himself to tell his superior. *Shoes in trees aren't doing any harm*, he thinks.

the rank

Mac is with a gathering of taxi drivers outside the small office. Work is scarce, and the men stand outside their cars, smoking and grumbling. Conversation revolves around the same topics: office fees, traffic lights, sleeping policemen, students, bad drivers, cyclists, other taxi ranks, crazy fares, MOTs, the price of osteopaths, bad backs, and how to get out of taxi driving.

One former driver, Sammy, has managed to set himself up in a business laying patios. The other men talk about him wistfully.

'What does he know about patios?' says Mick, a tiny man with bow legs and grey teeth.

'It's not hard, is it?' says Col, who wants to get into computers. 'You just get the paving stones and plonk them down in straight lines.'

'Oh, yeah? Straight lines? Sammy can't even walk in a straight line. He'll be back.'

Mac doesn't speak. He stands slightly apart from the others, most of whom smoke heavily. Waiting is the part of his job he dreads most. It feels as if this day will never end, and yet he can't make himself go home. He idly cleans his windscreen.

'They've made a right arse out of the Jesmond roundabout,' says Mick. Everyone nods, universally hating the town council. In their perfect world there would be no other cars in the city but taxis, which would have right of way over buses. Tipping would be compulsory. MOTs wouldn't exist.

In a car behind Mac sits a man they call 'the Reader' happily engrossed in a fat thriller. Mac envies him. He seems to savour these long workless days.

'How's your back, Mac?' shouts Col.

Mac looks up. Lately his back has begun to ache, and he knows that he should get some exercise. He feels as if his body is shaped like a car seat. The first time it went he was on his back for three months, and Louise had to go out to work. He lay on the floor, looking up at the cracks in the ceiling, thinking about his life. At first he had been so bored that he had wanted to die. Stella and Caris had skipped round him as if he was a piece of delicate furniture. That had been the only time he had read books, and he'd done it out of desperation. Louise had gone to the library and got him a selection. One of them had been called *Happiness: How to Find Your True Self*. There were mental exercises that you had to do, like visualising yourself doing unlikely things – rowing up rapids, and climbing trees. You made lists of what was important in your life. At the top of Mac's list was the word 'Family'. Strangely, after a while Mac had begun to feel like a new person. He had lain on the floor and dreamt of putting his family into a camper van and driving out of the city to a clearing, where he would build his own house, and start a business growing luxury lettuces. He read that lettuces were easy to grow in controlled climates, and that there was a huge demand for different varieties. He got Louise to borrow books about gardening and self-sufficiency. He wrote lists of 'Aims' and then 'Steps to Achievement'. In the evenings, when the girls sat on the settee eating their tea, he would outline his plans, and Caris, particularly, would ask him questions about the house he would build, and her bedroom and where she would go to school. Louise would come in late, tired from a part-time cleaning job, and look at his lists, and would say, 'Anything's better than this, love.'

It was, in his memory, a happy time. He felt as if they had been together, even if he had been horizontal.

What happened? he thinks. First he got the operation, and gradually his back improved. He'd phoned Tony at the rank to ask him if he could do some part-time work, just to keep them going while he sorted out a loan. Then Louise had a row with the woman she worked for and walked out in a huff, and he'd increased his days. *But even then*, he thinks, *I was still talking about luxury lettuce.* Weekends would be spent driving around Northumberland looking for suitable sites. They still had projected dates.

'What are you thinking about, Mac?' chirrups Mick.

'Nothing,' says Mac.

'It will get better when the students are back,' he says cheerfully, lighting another cigarette.

'Bloody students,' moans Col.

I'm never going to get out of this, thinks Mac. He feels angry with Louise, as if it's her fault that he can't make things better. He imagines himself as a single man again, living a different kind of life. He would have his own flat, be thinner, more muscular, and come and go whenever he pleased. He thinks about calling Louise his 'ex-wife', and mutters the phrase to himself to try it out. He wouldn't be responsible any more. Maybe in a different relationship he would be another kind of man; a man who had interests, who travelled abroad, who had ideas. *Divorce*, he thinks. *I want a divorce.*

Jeannie's voice calls him over the tannoy. 'Are you there, Mac? Mrs Ernest again. She wants to go to a funeral parlour this time.' And he climbs back into his taxi and realises his eyes are brimming over, like a big baby's.

home

Mac comes home to find no one there. It's early evening and the house is an empty box. He walks from room to room, searching for signs of his life, but he can't find anything. In the kitchen there's a pile of plates in the sink and a crust of bread lying on the floor. The sitting room is dusty and the curtains are half drawn. Photographs on the mantelpiece look somehow faded, and there are coffee rings on the table. He looks at the settee, which he and Louise bought together after much discussion and many Sundays wandering around furniture showrooms. When it first arrived it seemed immense and powerful; a symbol of their marriage, with its clean swollen cushions and soft recesses. Now it looks like something in an auction room. He makes himself a cup of instant coffee and finds that there is no milk. He doesn't know where to sit, so he plods upstairs to his bedroom with the unmade bed, and sits on the edge of it thinking of all the times he and Louise have climbed in beside each other and how she would lay her head against his shoulder and he would stroke her hair. He opens the wardrobe and stares at her clothes: the blue dress, the suede coat. He touches them and smells them, hoping to catch a glimpse of his marriage in their folds.

He looks into the mirror and sees himself, looking smaller, defeated. He hates Louise. *She might as well have set fire to this house*, he thinks, *the damage she's done. Things are going to be different. I'm going to be a divorcee. I'm going to do what I like.*

I'll go out on dates. I'll live somewhere smart with one of those wide televisions.

'You only live once,' he mutters, a phrase which his passengers are fond of, especially those on their way to the airport.

Then he hears the door open downstairs, and slam shut. He knows that it's Caris. He can sense her impatience, hear her pulling off her coat and carelessly dropping it on to the floor.

'Caris!' he calls.

She doesn't answer. He hears her walking through the house, dropping a bag on to the floor. Mac walks to the top of the stairs and looks down.

'Caris,' he says again, softer this time.

She appears in the hallway and stares up at him. She's chewing gum, and it seems to Mac that something is different about her.

Caris sees a man in crumpled brown trousers looking down at her. She despises him. *He looks like a taxi driver,* she thinks callously. As he steps down towards her she moves away, pulling the chewing gum from her mouth.

'How was school?' asks Mac, following her into the small kitchen.

Caris shrugs. She opens the fridge and for a moment her face is lit up by its icy light.

'Answer me!' says Mac.

'What do you want to know?' she drawls.

'Have you been to school?'

'Course I have.'

She looks at his round smooth face, and the stubble on his chin. She takes a mug from the cupboard and fills it with water from the tap.

'How's Mum?' she asks.

Mac wants to say, 'I don't know, and I don't care.' He imagines telling Caris that he is divorcing Louise.

'She's fine,' he says.

'Enjoying prison?' says Caris.

Mac doesn't answer. He can't think what to say to this young woman in his kitchen. Not long ago her voice would fill rooms, like music. A few months ago he would come home and she would pester him with demands. Now she doesn't seem to want anything.

'Shall we do something?' he says. 'Go bowling?'

'Bowling!' shrieks Caris, too loud. 'You must be joking!'

'What's wrong with bowling?'

'No thanks,' says Caris.

She leans against the sink, sipping water from the cup, looking past Mac as if he's not there. Mac feels a spasm of anger. It feels like a power surge revving through his veins. He grabs Caris by the arm and forces her to listen to him. He feels his mouth open and hot air come rushing out.

'How do you think I feel, Caris? Eh?' he spits at her.

Caris pulls away. 'Get off me!' she shouts, struggling to get away from him.

Mac lets go and picks up the bag that lies on the floor in the doorway. He tips the contents on to the floor. There's a packet of cigarettes, some make-up, but no school books.

'What's this? Smoking?' He picks up the cigarettes and shakes them in Caris's face.

'So!'

'You haven't been to school, have you?' he bellows.

'Leave me alone!' she shouts.

'You're not trying!'

'Not trying at what exactly?' she repeats slowly.

'At being a family.'

'This isn't a family,' says Caris. 'This is a horrible house. I hate it here. I hate school. I don't care what I do. I don't care about anything!'

She shocks herself. Mac feels as if she's possessed, a different girl to the one he knew before. He looks at her in horror. Next door, the neighbours, a young couple with two milky-coloured children with fair hair and eyelashes, exchange a glance as the walls shake with raised voices. The mother shakes her head disapprovingly.

Mac turns and crashes out of the small house and into the street.

112

Caris knows where he's going. He'll drive around the city until he's calmed down and then he'll come back, and say he's sorry. *It's the car*, she thinks. *He loves that car more than he loves me. That's why Mum went stealing: she couldn't bear it any more. She lost her husband to a Ford Mondeo. She can't compete with its velvety seats, its dashboard, its purring engine.*

Caris wants to cry, but she won't. Instead she runs upstairs and takes a pair of Mac's heavy man's shoes from the back of the wardrobe and runs out to the shadowy Vale.

stick insects

George keeps stick insects in a glass cage in the corner of his room. Caris stares at the creatures that are so cleverly camouflaged they blend into the branches of green leaves behind the glass. *This is the only thing that is really interesting about stick insects*, she thinks, *the way they know how to disappear.*

'This is where I live,' says George. 'Forget about the rest.'

George has his own bathroom, video and television. He has a drum kit and an electric guitar, and computers and digital cameras.

Caris stands in the middle of the room feeling cheap. She shakes her head and runs her hands through her hair.

'Wow,' she says.

'What shall we do?' asks George, handing her a beer.

'I dunno,' says Caris. 'Sit about, I suppose.'

George lights a joint. The room fills with overpowering blue smoke. He lies down on the bed and beckons Caris over to him, but she doesn't go. She walks around the room, like an animal feeling the boundaries of a cage. She wonders what will happen. Now they are alone, in a room, she isn't sure that's what she wants, only that she feels hungry.

'What are you doing, Caris?' asks George.

'Is all this stuff yours?' she says.

'Yeah.'

'You got any brothers or sisters?'

'No.'

'Do they buy you anything you want?'

'No.'

'You've got a lot of things,' says Caris.

'Take your clothes off,' George whispers.

Caris ignores him and goes to the window. Outside the driveway of the house is lit up. The gravel glistens like diamonds.

'Why don't you go to school?' she asks, not looking at George.

'I told you, I got expelled.'

'What will you do?'

George considers his answer.

'They'll send me somewhere else,' he says eventually. 'That's all they talk about, what I'm going to do.'

'What do you want?' Caris asks him.

'To get away from here,' says George. 'You and me.'

Caris looks at him hopefully.

'Where?' she says.

'I don't know yet.'

'What was it like, your school?' she asks him.

'I hated it. It was miles from anywhere. It was full of weirdos.'

George doesn't tell her about Wilson. He lets her wander around the room, touching his things, and looking at his music collection. He rolls another joint, and notices how Caris sniffs out the place, looking wary. No, he doesn't tell her about Wilson with his meaty face and white flesh. How George would find him wherever he was, in the corner of a library in the twilight, or the edge of a school field. He always knew where Wilson was, and how to isolate him from the flocks of chattering boys, the vague masters in their comfortable tweeds. He doesn't tell her about the sound Wilson made, a kind of soggy squeal, whenever George touched him, how easily his flesh would bruise or burn, and how he had pleaded with George, with copious tears running down his slab cheeks. George himself is not quite sure why it was he got so much pleasure out of being cruel to Wilson. It became a sport, like a computer game, or a kind of quest. Even at the sight of Wilson he would begin to salivate, to feel a queasy pleasure that began somewhere in his stomach, and which flickered warmly across his genitals.

George doesn't tell Caris how, when Wilson finally broke, like a ball deflating, a string snapping, and leapt from the upstairs dormitory window only to fracture his arm in two places, George felt nothing but tiredness. It was the same feeling that one had at the end of a summer when the cold winds began, a kind of weary dread. So when George was summoned to explain himself and stood in front of a puzzled headmaster with eyebrows like small rodents, he found that he could hardly be bothered to excuse himself. He had said only that Wilson had bothered him, and that he hadn't realised that he was so sensitive. 'I was just messing about,' he'd said, and the headmaster had got up and walked over to the window.

He'd said, 'Farrish, you are an extremely unpleasant human being, and I don't want you in my school. I suspect that you'll end up in prison. Get out.'

George doesn't tell Caris any of it. He just lies on his unmade bed, getting stoned, examining this creature he's found. She is like a gift that has fallen into his lap, with her shining eyes that are full of anger, her angel face, her almost edible pink ears.

road rage

Mac drives round and round the clogged streets of the city. Passengers become dark shapes behind his head, their voices badgering him with questions and commands. He swears at traffic lights. He wants to kill pedestrians.

'You see,' he says to no one in particular, 'they've made a mess of this intersection. It's the planners, they're corrupt. What's the point of it? Get out of the way, you stupid fool! These people shouldn't be allowed to drive. They should never have passed their tests. Look at that! Who does he think he is? That's a bus lane, you cretin!'

He taps the steering wheel, sounds his horn, hates being still, careers down bus lanes in traffic queues. He moans about the sunlight hurting his eyes, the rain that gets in the way of his vision. He curses jeeps and Land Rovers, and drivers who don't indicate.

He loathes students with their high-pitched laughter and their drunkenness, who try to persuade him to take five passengers 'just this once'. He doesn't make any effort to help when old ladies drop their change. He wants to rant when peaceable businessmen ask him if he's had a busy day, and he refuses to discuss the weather. Round and round he goes, up and down from the quayside carrying those too lazy to walk from the station. He waits in endless queues outside the station and then gets a fare to the Swallow Hotel, five minutes' walk away. He starts to hate Jeannie at the switchboard, her whining voice splintering his silence.

He drives past Degna's restaurant and tries to see inside. He counts the days until it's time to pick her up again. He thinks about her as he waits in traffic queues, fantasising about conversations they might have, and imagining what might have happened if he hadn't married Louise. He feels sorry for himself. *I deserve better*, he thinks. *I deserve respect.*

His back gets worse, and his neck is stiff. His bones are like rusted iron. He swallows painkillers. When he goes home he opens up a newspaper and reads about celebrities having adulterous affairs. He lies upstairs on his bed, with the curtains half closed, the radio muttering next to him on the bedside table, dozing deliriously, dreaming of road blocks and motorway pile-ups and plates of buttery spaghetti.

light and shade

The art room of the prison is a wide, airy space. There are no obvious bars, and sometimes, when you get absorbed, it's possible to forget where you are. Today Louise is painting vegetables. The tutor is a sweating, menopausal woman with enthusiasm, who is doing an artist's residency. She is creating a series of paintings based on the theme of imprisonment. Sometimes she shows the women her work. It looks like black smudges on white canvas. She runs a workshop three times a week for anyone who wants to go, and Louise finds herself looking forward to these quiet dabbing hours. The tutor, Vanessa, wanders the room exclaiming and murmuring. She sounds like a child with her 'ooh's and giggles, but Louise likes her. She likes the way she points out the finer details of light and shade within the still life of tomatoes, onions and lettuce, as if it really matters, as if they really matter.

The small group of women hold their brushes tentatively, making bewildered expressions with their mouths as if their arms are not really connected to their brains, laughing at their attempts to paint, but glad to be out of their brick cells, and not to be talking about parole or families. Louise feels that she is beginning to emerge from a long winter in which tomatoes were not so different to onions.

She mixes up green paint and starts to dab the outline of a lettuce. She tries to remember when it started, the feeling of fogginess, the sensation that her hands were not her own, that her feet were not connected to her brain, that her daughters were not her daughters but are substitutes, that Mac was just a shape, filling up the spaces in rooms.

Louise drifts back years, to a time when Mac had a bad back, and was lying on the floor, talking about setting up his luxury-lettuce business. She'd gone out to work, out of desperation. The girls were just little things, darting from room to room, jumping up and down on their beds, pushing stiff-armed dolls around the back yard in plastic prams. Caris had an apple-cheeked shining face and a brace on her teeth, and Stella was pale and dark-eyed with a heavy fringe. It was the first job Louise had since having children. It was just a part-time thing, advertised in the local newspaper, cleaning a grand house just a few streets away on the other side of the Vale. Louise remembers polishing a long brown hallway, down on her knees, and the huge quietness of the place. In a distant room she could often hear the fragmented sound of a child playing alone. Louise would feel almost invisible as she wandered through rooms with her duster and tin of beeswax polish. The woman who paid her was young and perfumed, in tailored clothes. She was called Marina Farrish and she was sharp all over, with tight eyes and pampered skin. She stalked out of the house early in high heels and tight jackets, leaving a list of instructions for Louise on the kitchen table.

Tidy linen cupboard
Change beds
Clean study windows inside and out
Polish silver

There was a Spanish nanny, too, looking after the child. When they appeared at mealtimes the girl would follow the child about as if she was powerless to make decisions, watching him with dull eyes as he sat at the dining table eating his lunch. Louise remembers his fair curls, falling over his face. She had tried to charm him, winking at him, and asking him questions, but he didn't answer, just looked at her with sorrowful eyes. Once she brought him a ten-pence mix from Abdul's shop, but the Spanish girl had shaken her head morosely and said, 'No sweets for Georgie', in a low secretive voice, as if something terrible might happen if he ate a Smartie.

Louise starts to paint the under-part of the lettuce in dark greens and yellows. It looks like the roots of a tree, veined and earthy. She thinks about all the things she cleaned in that house: the silver teapot collection on the shelves, the china sugar bowls, the bidet in the pink bathroom, the photograph of the mother and father and baby sitting on a high-backed sofa, the complicated compartments of the immense fridge, the ornate candlesticks, the corners of staircases. And she thinks of Mrs Farrish's long fingernails, the insides of her drawers that were filled with ironed lace underwear, her powder puffs, her French soaps, her austere, organised life and the racks of shoes in a cupboard in her bedroom: hundreds and hundreds of shoes. Sometimes Louise would sit cleaning these shoes, even though Mrs Farrish hadn't asked her to. She would sit on the floor, surrounded by pots and jars of different-coloured polishes and suede cleaner and brushes. She'd polished them lovingly, got to know them, rubbed her spit into them, even spoken to them.

Louise had tried to lighten the atmosphere. In spring she took in daffodils, she opened windows, she sprayed room-freshener. She would tell the monosyllabic nanny about Caris and Stella, the things they said, and about holidays she was planning with Mac. She even told her about their plans to grow luxury lettuce, listing the types that Mac said he was going to grow, when he left taxi driving. Lollo Rosso, Perella Red, Paris Whites, Butterheads and Besson Rouge. They sounded glamorous and silky, more like underwear designs than varieties of lettuce.

She had sat on a high chair in the kitchen, filling the silence with her young voice, moaning about being a taxi driver's wife. The nanny would say things like 'I see' and 'Yes' and Louise would feel like a ridiculous chattering monkey.

Back home, with Caris and Stella, she would describe the house as if it was a palace. She would tell them about Marina's lace tablecloths, her elegant oak bed, the unopened soaps in her bathroom chest of drawers, the chandelier in the opulent drawing room, and of course, her shoe collection. Caris was fascinated by these stories. She wanted to come to work with Louise. She would ask Louise questions like, 'Do they go to the toilet?'

Mac would be lying on the floor, calling through to the kitchen, 'Tell that Mrs Farrish you want a rise. It's ridiculous what she pays you, Louise, bloody ridiculous!'

Vanessa stands behind Louise now, and Louise feels self-conscious. The lettuce looks huge, dwarfing the onion and tomato.

'That is fantastic!' shouts the tutor. 'Look at this, everyone.'

A couple of the women put down their brushes and peer curiously at Louise's painting.

'What a lettuce!' sniggers Carol.

'It's sort of abstract, isn't it?' says someone else.

'It looks psychological,' Carol giggles.

'I love it,' says Vanessa. 'Carry on!'

Louise is bemused. Courageously, she decides to paint in a Mediterranean background, and mixes up a bright blue.

Louise hardly ever saw Mr Farrish. He was a little, sinewy man with small feet. He ran a factory somewhere; something to do with electrical systems. *All their money came from something ordinary,* she thinks. Mrs Farrish worked too. She was in make-up or scent, or something like that. She had lots of samples in her bedroom, but she never gave Louise any. They were mean people.

It was a time when Mac was talking about giving up driving, and there had been this window of hope, when he was lying on the floor, unable to move, when she'd believed that they could move on.

Also, thinking about that time, she realised she'd enjoyed Mac's immobility. She knew where he was, and there was something comforting about the way he'd needed her, lying there, straining to hear her coming through the door. Even though they had no money, she'd felt oddly rich.

Back in the loneliness of Mrs Farrish's house she carried on with her underpaid work, hoovering balls of fluff from under beds, ironing immense duvet covers, singing as she worked. And it's true that she'd sometimes been nosy, and spent too long tidying up Mrs Farrish's drawers, and when the house was especially quiet she had liked to play with her make-up in the bathroom with the golden taps and the sunken bath. Once she had tried on a pair of leather trousers and some Gucci sandals, but she had never taken anything.

The day she left she was cleaning shoes in Marina Farrish's dressing room. It was a small, oak-panelled room with fitted, mirrored cupboards, so if you sat in the middle you could see yourself from every angle. You could look at your back and see yourself as others saw you. Louise found the room intoxicating, but horrible. She often felt a little sick after a morning in there, as if she had gorged herself on her own image. That day, she heard a door slam and the high register of Mrs Farrish's voice calling out in the hallway. Louise was cleaning a pair of Italian boots. They were rather like riding boots, with straps at the top. The nanny had left earlier with the child in a harness. They were going to the park, she'd said, to feed the ducks. She had held the boy's reins plaintively in her hands and looked pathetic, as if she was going out into the ice wastes and was hoping the child knew the way.

Louise could hear Mrs Farrish coming up the stairs and into the bedroom. She'd straightened her face into a meek servile expression and was neatly brushing the black boot, holding it like a baby in the crook of her arm. It was clear when Mrs Farrish came in that she was drunk. Louise could smell her breath even before she opened the door. When she came into the mirrored dressing room she stood swaying, staring at Louise. Her cheeks were flushed red, and her mouth kept slipping open.

Louise was surprised, but she kept on brushing. She was used to drunks. Her own mother was often harmlessly tiddly, and Louise frequently tucked her up in bed after one of her sessions. But there was something frightening about Mrs Farrish's drunkenness, as if all her tight laces and knots had come undone and something unpleasant was about to leak out.

'What are you doing?' she slurred.

'Cleaning shoes,' answered Louise.

'I never told you to clean my shoes.'

Louise replaced the boots and began to gather up the pots of polish.

'You can go home,' said Mrs Farrish rudely. 'I don't want you here.'

Louise stood up. The room was too small for the two women. A thousand reflections looked back at them.

'Of course,' said Louise politely, but she was due her money that day, and she didn't want to go without it.

'Go on, then.' Mrs Farrish suddenly slumped into an armchair, her hair hanging down, her mouth ugly.

'Can I have my wages, please?' Louise had said bravely.

'No,' answered Mrs Farrish. She'd lolled towards Louise, looking like one of the winos who sat in the square in the town.

'I need my wages,' said Louise.

There was a long pause while Mrs Farrish tried to focus on Louise.

'What?' she'd slurred eventually.

Louise felt embarrassed, as if she was begging. She'd pushed past the drunken woman into the bedroom. Mrs Farrish followed her, falling on to the wide bed.

'I hate this house,' mumbled Mrs Farrish.

'You can leave,' said Louise practically.

'I'm not a good mother,' she went on in a maudlin voice. 'I don't like children.'

'George is a lovely boy.'

'I find him boring,' she said. 'I don't love him.'

'I'm sure that's not true,' said Louise. 'Look, a cheque would do. It's just that my husband isn't working. He's got a bad back.'

'Oh, Christ,' said Mrs Farrish, and began to cry, deep, self-pitying sobs.

'Can I get you a coffee?' asked Louise.

'Get me a drink.'

'I think you've had enough.'

'I got drunk,' she said. 'I went to a bar.'

'Yes.'

'Do you want to know why?'

Louise shook her head. The sight of Mrs Farrish, drunk, in her grand bedroom disgusted her.

'Not really,' she said.

'I hate my life!' Mrs Farrish wailed.

'Oh dear,' said Louise, glancing back at the glorious room of listening shoes.

'I want a fag,' Mrs Farrish snapped.

Louise had given her a cigarette and lit it. She'd watched the ash fall on to the recently ironed white bedcover.

'You'll be all right,' said Louise wearily, 'when you've had a rest.'

'I'll never be all right,' she moaned.

'Can I have my wages?' Louise asked again.

Mrs Farrish had frowned at her then, as if she was seeing her for the first time. 'Is that all you can think about?' she'd slurred. 'Can't you see I'm upset?'

Louise was angry, but didn't show it. She'd turned and gone downstairs. Mrs Farrish's handbag lay on the floor in the hall. She'd picked it up and found her soft leather purse. Inside it there was a sheath of crisp notes. Louise had taken her wages and an extra twenty-pound note. She hadn't cared. She'd felt as if she was owed it. Then she had left the house, slamming the door behind her, never to return. She'd walked home along a winding path through the trees, lit with sunlight after rain. Everything had been silver and gold, with birds singing loudly. Louise hadn't cried, or felt anything. Later on that day Mr Farrish had phoned to say she wouldn't be needed any more. She'd told Mac she'd had a row with her employer, and that was that. Then Mac had gone back to the taxis, like an addict returning to the needle, and after a while she had got another job as an usherette in the new cinema up on the coast road, working in the dark in the carpeted afternoon, watching Hollywood films full of women with shining skin and perfect eyebrows, over and over again.

*

In the art room, Louise shudders. She's nearly finished her painting. The lettuce is a vast, veined miracle against a blue background. Louise puts her brush into a pot of water and watches the water cloud from clear to blue.

lovebites

Weeks pass. There are cloudy bluebells in the Vale, and tight buds on the Tree of Shoes.

Today Nana Price can't get out of bed. She lies flat on her back, looking at box files on the top of the wardrobe in her windowless room that have the words 'LETTUCE VARIETIES' and 'COMPUTER TRAINING' written on them.

Nana wants someone to look after her. She calls out in her crackling voice. Her hair is all undone and it rises up from her head like straw, and she hasn't put her teeth in. Stella sits in her bedroom, the door locked, at a desk that is arranged with books. Every few minutes she stops writing to sharpen a pencil, or to straighten a piece of paper. She can hear Nana's voice, like an ancient beached seal, croaking through the house, but she waits for the sound of Caris's feet on the stairs. She is writing an essay about portraiture. She has written the words '*Since the beginning of mankind, man has always wanted to find ways to reflect the human face*' but this sentence sounds wrong, and it's got too many men in it. She crosses out '*man has*' and writes '*people have*' instead.

Caris lumbers to the door of the darkened room and sees the old woman lying there and blinks. Nana pats the bed and makes Caris come and sit next to her. *She stinks*, thinks Caris, *of something mouldering*. Nana Price smells sex on Caris. Her old nose twitches and wrinkles.

'What's that up there?' says Nana, waving her arm vaguely.

127

'What?'

'That file on the wardrobe, about lettuce.'

'I don't know,' says Caris. 'One of Dad's stupid ideas.'

'He was going to start a worm farm once,' says Nana, her gums making a sucking sound as she speaks. 'When Louise first met him she came home and said she'd met a worm farmer.'

'He'll never do anything except drive pissy taxis,' says Caris carelessly. 'What do you want, anyway?'

'Lucozade, and a KitKat.' Nana puts on her pleading face. Caris grimaces.

'Oh, Nana.' The room stinks of her grandmother's bad dreams, of a long, restless night, of unwashed underwear.

'Well, well,' says Nana, reaching up and lifting Caris's hair from her neck. 'Look at that.'

'What?'

Nana prods the red mark on Caris's skin.

'Did you suck it yourself?'

Caris moves away, annoyed, and picks up a hand mirror on a table to examine her neck. There is an ugly hicky just below her ear. It looks raw and blue red. She rubs it, as if she wishes she could remove it, like a stain. She thinks of George's blond head, nuzzled beneath her hair, his bony body pushed up tightly against her.

'It won't come off,' says the old lady, cranking herself up in bed. 'You're going to get yourself into trouble, the way you're carrying on.'

'It's only kissing,' says Caris.

'It's your cherry he wants,' says Nana lewdly. 'Is it that Georgie who gave me the shoes?'

Caris doesn't answer.

Nana starts to cough, loud syrupy coughs that squelch and rattle in her chest.

'Get us some water, pet,' she gasps, and Caris fetches her a glass. Nana gulps it down and looks at Caris with rheumy eyes.

'What would your mother say?' she says.

'She's not here, is she?' says Caris. *She's lounging about with murderers*, she would like to add.

'You don't want to get into trouble, that's all.'

'I won't,' says Caris.

The old lady shudders. On mornings like these she feels every cell in her body. Inside her a ghost of her former self flutters; the woman who strode out on a Saturday night in new stockings, arm in arm with Mona and Sally. There is nothing she doesn't know about sex. She remembers its rough texture; the taste on her tongue, wartime songs playing, a humming in her whole body. She loved those men with thick arms who worked on ships, or in factories and who smelt like tar, or paint, or salt. Nana Price had enjoyed sex, found it hilarious and delicious. When she married she found it almost impossible to be faithful to Louise's father, sweet Walter, who spent his spare time on his model railway in the back room. She liked nothing more than to pursue a handsome man, running him to ground like a hound chasing a fox.

No, Nana Price had nothing against sex, but something isn't right with Caris. She doesn't look as if she is enjoying herself. Nana doesn't like noticing other people's unhappiness. She prefers to shove things under the carpet, and to believe that everything will turn out right in the end. When she looks at that hicky on Caris's neck it makes her feel giddy and unsure.

Things get lost, she wants to say to Caris, *without you realising that they are beginning to disappear.* Like the real white teeth that she once had in her mouth, like the forest of pubic hair she once had down below, like her husband, Walter, who had walked out one day, leaving his model train aimlessly circling the railway track in the back room.

But even if she did tell Caris to behave herself, that men are only after one thing, that there is plenty of time to have babies, Caris wouldn't listen.

'Why don't young women listen to old women?' she says out loud to Caris, who is brushing her hair, trying to arrange it over the mark on her neck.

'What are you talking about, Nana?'

'Why doesn't anyone ever learn?'

'Learn what?'

'Not to make mistakes. Things go round and round and never get better.'

'I don't know what you're talking about,' says Caris.

But even though Nana Price doesn't spell it out Caris knows exactly what she's saying. But she's thinking about something else. She's thinking about space. About how high you need to climb to have room, how many rooms you need to be able to stretch out. She thinks about George and her climbing up to the top of the oak tree and owning all the land that is around them.

'I don't want to go to school, Nana,' she says, her voice like a child's.

'I know you don't, pet,' says Nana, who needs to pee. She grasps Caris's young arm in her haggard fingers. 'Don't give it all away,' she says urgently. 'Hold out for quality. Think it through, Caris.' Then she falls back on the pillow. 'I wouldn't mind a Ginger Nut,' she says weakly.

Caris hears her, although she would rather not. She feels as if she's floating down a river and her old nana is trying to throw her a life-jacket, but she can't reach it.

driving to school

Caris and Stella get into Mac's taxi. He's trying to take control of his daughters, and the only way he knows how to do this is to drive them somewhere. The two girls sit as far away as possible from each other in the back, each staring out of opposite win dows. Caris looks at the sky that is full of clouds like threads. Stella sees a boy she fancies who did the lights for *Macbeth*. The bag he carries is full of books. *Caris would call him a swot*, she thinks.

'Where to, ladies?' Mac asks, trying to be lighthearted.

Neither of them answer. Mac turns on the radio, and there's a burst of loud music and chatter.

Caris feels afraid. She rarely makes it to school these days, spending most of her time with George, either in his attic, or down in the Vale. When she does get there she has to spend all her time avoiding Layla and Margaret, making sure she is never alone, attaching herself to other teenagers who she hardly knows. Days are obstacle courses full of dangerous journeys from one room to another. She can't even go to the toilet alone.

She looks at the back of her father's head, at his thick neck that bulges over his collar. He keeps looking at her in his mirror, as if he's checking that she is still there. As they drive along the familiar streets, filled with blue-coated teenagers loping to school, she feels sick. Mac pulls up, and Stella jumps out of the car and runs to join a group of girls with identical ponytails and sixth formers' shaved legs.

'Off you go, Caris,' says Mac.

'I can't,' she says.

'What do you mean, you can't?'

'I don't want to go.'

Mac is irritated.

'You've got to,' he says roughly.

Caris leans forward. 'I hate it,' she says. 'Don't make me.'

Mac shakes his head. 'Come on, Caris,' he says.

'Why do I have to go?'

Mac has a horrible image of himself as a big red boy in ill-fitting trousers, standing outside the school gates thinking the same thing, wishing that a spaceship would appear and take him away from it all, knowing that there was nothing there for him.

'Please, Dad,' pleads Caris.

'It'll be all right when you get there,' he says in a diluted voice.

'It won't.'

Just then Layla and Margaret pass; they peer inside the car and wave at Caris.

'There's your friends,' says Mac.

'They hate me. Everyone hates me.'

Mac is startled. He doesn't know what to do.

'Please try, Caris,' he says. 'If you don't go to school then what will you do?'

Caris doesn't answer. The gate is empty now, and in the distance they can hear a bell.

'Off you go,' says Mac.

She gets out, feeling the cold air on her face. She doesn't say goodbye. She slams the car door and the ornamental dog shakes its head. Mac wants to call her back, but what then? He watches her walking, alone, towards the open mouth of the school. She looks tiny, like a little girl. *I should have let her come with me*, he thinks, but squashes the thought. He waits until she has disappeared then drives away, uncertain, guilty.

potential

Everyone at school is shrinking. *They look like midgets*, thinks
Caris, as she stands in a concrete quadrangle eating crisps. She
watches feet moving about on the ground, kicking the tarmac.
Girls, she notices, often stand with their toes turned inwards, in
black-heeled shoes, like unsteady calves, while boys bounce
confidently from foot to foot in practical boots, soles firmly on
the earth.

Caris breathes, in and out, thinking of George, and the feeling
of his mouth against hers and his hand creeping up the inside of
her shirt. She has hardly thought of Louise, who has also shrunk,
into a small plaintive shape behind bars, dressed in an overall,
waiting dumbly for whatever happens.

'*Why am I here?*' thinks Caris, aware of the fences and walls
around her.

Layla and Margaret appear in the corner of her eye. They stand
looking at Caris like figures in a dream, chewing sandwiches,
glowering, sheep-like. Caris scrumples up her crisp packet and
throws it on to the ground. Margaret comes closer and Caris
closes her eyes. She thinks of George's stick insects, disappearing
into the foliage.

'What are you doing, Caris?' says Margaret, close now, with her
mule face.

'Nothing,' answers Caris.

'Why do you keep on hanging shoes in that tree?' says Margaret.

'Why not?' says Caris.

'It's weird, and who's that boy?' questions Layla.

A ball bounces against a wall next to them, making a thwacking sound. Caris jumps, then shrugs. Even speaking to these two somehow lessens her.

'Yeah, who is he?' says Margaret.

'What's that hicky on your neck?' says Layla, craning to see.

'Slag,' says Margaret primly.

A buzzer tears through the conversation. Caris picks up her bag and walks off.

'How's your mother?' sneers Layla after her.

Back at the classroom Mr Fortoba is wiping the board. Today he's wearing a green polo-neck jersey. The bald patch on the top of his head seems whiter and is as polished as his brown shoes. He turns and beckons to Caris.

'How's it going?' he says.

'Not bad.'

'When are you going to start working?' he asks her. 'When are you going to make something of yourself?'

'I'm here, aren't I?' says Caris, knowing that he, like her nana, is searching for words to say that might mean something.

He wants to say, 'Caris, you've got potential. You can do something with your life, like maybe become a dental receptionist, or a beauty therapist. You can do better than your father and mother. Do you know what happens to girls like you when they let go? They end up just like their parents, living in a Tyneside terrace with an Alsatian barking in the hallway, standing at the doorway with a baby on their hip, telling the milkman to come back for his money next week.' But even Mr Fortoba knows that these words are empty when he himself is sitting in a badly decorated classroom wearing a jumper knitted for him by his mother, who he still lives with. Mr Fortoba lies in bed at night wondering how he can get out of teaching and do something brave, like white-water rafting, or scuba diving. Looking at Caris makes him angry, and

134

he has to look down at his hands, which are pale and delicate, like a girl's.

'You can sit down,' he says.

Caris drags herself back to her tinny chair and plastic desk. She wonders what George is doing now, and envies him his long, unstructured days. She knows he waits for her. Mr Fortoba is talking about different kinds of terrain. He hands out textbooks and tells them to turn to page 103. He wants them to copy a map of South America from the book into their exercise books.

I could be anywhere, thinks Caris. *Why am I here?* And she shuts her eyes, listening to the squeaky marker pen against the whiteboard, a thunderous rumble of chairs being moved in another classroom, the rattling of the ancient heating system, the echo of braying voices from other classrooms. Mr Fortoba looks over and sees her sitting there with her eyes closed. He can't bring himself to shout at her, so he ignores her.

In prison Louise is having a tea break. A group of women sit eating digestive biscuits in the common room, talking about their children. Sometimes it feels as if that's all they talk about, as if they are still attached by thin wires that cannot be severed by locks and keys. Louise doesn't join in the conversation. She notices the catch in their voices, and all the lines of worry etched upon their foreheads, and around their anxious mouths, and the agitated movements of their fingers around the handles of the mugs of tea, and the endless descriptions of happy days with children, when things were as they are in photographs.

Louise thinks of returning to her life, of Caris and Stella, and Mac, and the terraced street, of birthdays and Christmases, and suppers, night after night, and Mac in his driver's seat, and her shining her torch along the aisles in the cinema, and the couples sitting together crunching popcorn in the dark.

I don't want to go home, she thinks.

driving degna

It's Friday night and the quayside is a mess of incoherent people, swilling around the streets, falling against each other, limping between bars. Mac waits outside the restaurant for Degna, listening to the shipping forecast on the radio. He closes his eyes, picturing the wild islands of Scotland, and noble lighthouses beating out a light to lost ships. *It's all there*, he thinks, *outside this bubble I'm in. It's all happening now.*

The forecast finishes with a fizzing symbolic silence and Mac starts awake to see a man in a denim jacket vomiting into the gutter, while his girlfriend stands watching, wearily smoking a cigarette, unmoved, in a pink party top and a hairband with lights that flash on and off. Mac sighs and looks into the mirror, wondering if he's attractive. He wishes he was thinner. Inside the restaurant Degna is sorting through the money, checking the tills. She's tired. She's been working in the moist kitchens all night and the smells of food have permeated her skin. The younger chef has been getting on her nerves, bumping into her whenever she turns. Some of the customers have sent meals back, complaining of things being under- or overcooked, and one had found a long blonde hair wrapped around an aubergine.

She thinks of the calm of Mac's taxi and smiles, knowing he's out there. She can feel him waiting for her.

Mac watches the Tyne. All day a river of passengers have climbed in and out of his taxi; they merge into a memory of slamming doors, exchanged coins, each one with their own smell, their own destination. It seems as if it will never end, this continual line of people who want to go somewhere. *But where do I want to go?* thinks Mac. *When will I ever be a passenger?*

He thinks about Louise driving. She had lessons just after they were married. She would tremble in the driver's seat, afraid to touch the steering wheel or push her feet down on the pedals. Mac took her out before her test. They would drive around the quiet roads of housing estates and Mac would hardly be able to breathe as he pressed his redundant feet down on to the floor of the passenger's side and tried to keep his voice even. Often such outings would end in tears, and Mac would have to drive Louise home, her long hair draped over her blotchy face. He would recite his actions as he drove, but she didn't seem to hear. 'See, Lou, how I *slowly* push my foot down on the clutch. See!' He preferred doing it this way to letting her drive. Frankly he was horrified when she passed her test third time. He hadn't expected her to be so persevering. She'd wanted a banger to drive the kids round in, but that made Mac nervous. He couldn't bear the thought of his little girls being driven by his trembling wife, so he'd put it off. Sometimes he let Louise drive, but the experience was so stressful that it was easier for him to take over. He can't remember the last time he saw her behind a steering wheel.

Degna opens the car door. 'I'm here.' She climbs into the cab. Mac turns on the car engine.

'How are you?' she asks, as if his melancholy is tangible, something that he displays on the dashboard.

'Good,' he says. 'Canny.' But she knows this isn't true.

She smells of rosemary and vanilla, thinks Mac. *She smells like Spain, or Italy, not northern England.* He notices her hands in the mirror, white and ringless, and then starts up the engine.

'How's your wife doing?' she asks.

'I don't know,' he says, and he doesn't.

Degna leans back in the seat and closes her eyes. A part of her doesn't want to go home. When she finishes work she often feels the adrenalin rushing through her for hours afterwards. It stops her sleeping, and when she does sleep she dreams of pans of bubbling soup, squashing cloves of garlic, chopping parsley, and responding to endless orders lined up on the counter.

'Do you fancy a drink?' she asks.

Mac is due to work until four in the morning. He could stop earlier; there is always more money to be made out there. But when Degna asks him to stop driving he feels a huge sense of relief, as if all his life he has waited for her to step into his taxi and ask him this one question.

'Yeah,' he says, casually, as if this is something he does all the time, 'why not? Just the one.'

The quayside bars are all closed, but Mac draws up outside a hotel on Dean Street, where he knows there's a small snug, for residents only, but they know him, so they'll let him in. He parks his car and walks round to open the door for Degna. She steps out, taking his arm, and they walk through a stained-glass door, past a receptionist who Mac salutes, before stepping up to the red velvet bar upstairs, which is deserted apart from one Swedish businessman who leans against the bar with a half-pint of beer in one hand, talking to the barman about his heart-bypass operation.

Mac feels large and self-conscious. He orders a pint of shandy for himself and a white wine for Degna and they sit in an upholstered corner and place their drinks carefully in front of them on a polished round table. Mac wonders if Degna smokes; but, unlike Louise, she doesn't nervously reach into her bag and pull out a packet of fags. She sits there calmly, as if she doesn't need anything.

'Why did she steal, then, your wife?' asks Degna, ready to earn Mac's company with probing questions.

Mac looks into his drink. 'She said she was bored,' he says mournfully.

'You mean she was depressed?'

'She said she didn't understand it herself. I mean, it was selfish.

She didn't think about the kids or anything. She's always had trouble with her nerves.'

Mac sips his drink, which tastes like moral indignation.

'What does she do, your wife?' asks Degna.

'She works as an usherette, in a cinema. She sees a hell of a lot of films. Sometimes she watches the same film seven times in a week. She knows the stories inside out. Christ, sometimes she talks in an American accent.'

'And you drive taxis.'

'For eighteen years. Too long. Louise said she was tired of me working all the time.'

'Do you?' says Degna.

'Yes.' Mac laughs, but he doesn't feel like laughing. For a long time Louise has been a heap of duvet in the bed when he comes in, the birds singing outside at dawn. He can't remember the last time they had sex. Perhaps it was on holiday. That was what it was all for, the holidays. That was how he saw it. And when they were away that was when he loved Louise, when she put on her dark glasses and linked her arm up to his. When the kids were splashing about in a swimming pool like little otters playing, their hair plastered to their heads, bursting out of the blue with snotty shrieks.

But he doesn't want to talk about Louise, he wants to get to know Degna.

'Been in the restaurant business long?' he says, as if she's still in his taxi.

'Don't change the subject. What else does she do?'

'Louise looks after the house, the girls. And she's got her own life.'

'Friends?' asks Degna.

'Yeah, she goes out with her friends sometimes.' Mac frowns. Louise always used to be with a flock of women, all done up, going out together, but he can't remember when he last saw Maria, or Julie, or Debs. He recalls the smell of them, of wine and perfume and skin cream, and the way they glittered and filled rooms.

139

'Do you miss her?' asks Degna.

Mac struggles. He doesn't miss his wife as much as he misses not having to think about her.

'No. I think I want a divorce,' he says, and when he says this he sees a door opening and Degna standing there to meet him. 'It's finished,' he says dramatically. 'My marriage is over.'

'Have you told her that?'

'Not yet,' says Mac. 'But I will.'

'I'm divorced,' says Degna.

'When?' asks Mac.

'Last year. He went off with someone else.'

'Oh.'

'He said I worked all the time.'

'Do you miss him?'

'A bit.' Degna gulps her drink. 'What about your daughters?'

'Yeah, well, they're nearly grown up. She should have thought about them before she went out stealing.'

Mac considers hotel rooms. He hasn't stayed in very many. He has never been unfaithful to Louise, but he presumes that adultery often happens in a hotel room with drawn curtains, anonymously. He would lie with Degna on a king-size double bed, in a dimly lit room with closed blinds and an en suite bathroom. There would be tea- and coffee-making facilities, and complimentary soaps, and room service. They would order wine in a bucket. *No one would know*, he thinks. *No one would even notice*. People would assume he was working. And even if someone found out, who could blame him, with his wife being a thief?

In one of the braver movements of his middle age, Mac reaches out, across the abyss of table and glasses and beer mats, and puts his large hand over Degna's, but she pulls back and shakes her head. Mac blushes.

'I'd better get home,' says Degna, wrapping a white scarf round her neck. 'I think you should go home, too. Who's looking after them?'

'They look after themselves,' says Mac.

'Are you sure about that?' says Degna.

As Mac ushers Degna into his taxi, Caris is walking in the Vale with George. They are smoking in the dark, the red ends of their cigarettes dancing in the night, listening to the owls and bats that fly above them. Caris leans against the rough bark of the Tree of Shoes, a host of shoes above her, hanging on the branches; shoes that have walked, danced, kicked balls, stamped, tapped, walked for miles or relaxed under armchairs, and George is setting a match to a pile of sticks, looking up at Caris as the flame catches and sparks whirl into the air, lighting a hole in the darkness. Then he's licking Caris's palm with his pink tongue, and pulling her down next to him on the damp earth, and Caris is looking up at all the slippers and trainers and stilettos and brogues and boots and sandals and moccasins and Kickers and flip-flops above her while George feasts on her young body, and she's thinking about all the things George promises her, and how he will take her away from the Vale, and the mesh of streets she's grown up in, and that it doesn't matter that the ground is hard and that George's bones bruise her, and that the smell of him is slightly disgusting. *I love him*, she thinks.

And back at home Nana Price can't sleep and is waiting for Caris to come home; she is sitting alone on the settee, swilling down a bottle of sherry, remembering Caris as the small, red-haired girl who sat on her lap and who wore her jewels and high-heeled shoes, and who Walter used to call Princess. Nana Price cries into her glass. She cries rough salt tears for all her mistakes, which are hardened within her now, like fossils in an old quarry. Upstairs Stella curls up under her blankets dreaming of stains that can't be removed, and somewhere in Scotswood Mac is back in his taxi driving drunken students home, listening to them telling each other how they will love one another for ever and ever, and Louise cries out in her sleep as she dreams that her daughters are trapped in a castle and she cannot reach them, and an immense wall of water breaks over the rocks at Finistere.

stella's black boots

'Have you seen that tree?' people ask each other. 'The one that's filled with shoes?'

'Who's doing it?' they say.

Parents take their children to see it. It's like something from a story. Sometimes people make a wish, as if it has magic properties.

Some art students paint some boots bright colours and throw them up into the branches, so that they look like fruit. Each day when Caris goes there something's changed, and even the trees around have the odd shoe dangling from their branches. Increasingly she and George go there at night when the paths are eerie tunnels, and there is no one about.

And even Stella knows about it, and says to Caris one morning as she scrapes a knife of jam over a bit of toast, 'Have you seen that tree?'

It's the first civil thing that Stella has said to Caris for weeks.

'What tree?' she says.

'The one that's filled with shoes,' says Stella. 'It's weird.'

'I don't know what you're talking about,' says Caris, but inside she feels proud, as if she has made something important.

Stella writes to Louise every day. She sits in her room, at the desk that Mac bought her from Ikea, and writes to her mother about her life. She tells her about her success in *Macbeth*, the play that no one came to see. She tells her that Caris is bunking off school, and has a lovebite on her neck, and that Mac works all night long. She sends Louise her school photograph, with her hair glossy and clean and her smile symmetrical. She tells her what she's been watching on the television, and about the clothes she's bought from town. The bottom margins of these letters are filled with kisses and hugs, and Louise reads them out loud to Carol and pins them to the noticeboard in her tiny cell.

But Caris never writes, and the only image that Louise has of her is an old one, of a grinning twelve-year-old.

Stella folds her clothes into squares and places them in her drawers. She irons her knickers and keeps her jewellery in a locked box on her dressing-table. In her room, everything is straight. Sometimes she wakes up in the night and has to get out of bed to adjust a fold in the curtains, or rub at a mark on the wallpaper. She has a calendar on her wall where she marks off days until Louise's return. She feels the absence of her mother like a pain in her stomach, and she has taken to rubbing this place, while she sits listening to her teachers, or watching television.

The dirt in the house upsets her. She tires of trying to wipe it up. She locks her bedroom every day, to keep anyone else from going in there, especially Caris, with her germs and grubby fingers.

She sits in her room covering her exercise books with clear plastic, so that they can be wiped clean. The smell of her grandmother's cigarettes winds up the stairs, so that she must stuff a towel along the bottom of the door to keep it out. Her father stinks of car fumes, of garages, and petrol and other people's money.

Caris smells peaty, of fires and tree bark. Stella imagines that her sister's hair is full of small insects, her underarms unwashed and unshaven, her underwear stained, the skin on the soles of her feet cracked and grimy. Caris makes Stella feel sick; she finds it hard to be in the same room.

One day, Stella opens the door of her wardrobe and looks inside, right at the back where the old things are that she plans to throw out. Stella likes to keep things that are important to her. She keeps her old Brownie uniform and every certificate she's ever won. She

143

has a basket filled with shoes she wore as a girl: her first high-heeled shoes, the sandals she bought with her pocket money in Greece. Now she picks out a pair of high-heeled black boots that she had begged Louise and Mac to buy her when she was twelve. She wanted to wear them on a school trip to Edinburgh, and she had thought about nothing else for weeks. They were in the window of Dulcies in Northumberland Street, and she was terrified that someone else would buy them. Then, as she feared, one day the boots were gone, and Stella felt as if a part of her had been amputated. She cried, in public, on the bus on the way home.

Then, as she sat on the settee, thinking that she couldn't go on the school trip, and she would never go anywhere again, Mac had walked in, carrying a green plastic carrier bag containing the boots, chuckling like a man with the key to happiness. And the boots had made her happy. She had strutted round Edinburgh like a thoroughbred mare.

Now she takes the boots and joins the zips together with a piece of strong string. She walks to school through the Vale, carefully picking her way along the muddy paths, until she reaches the clearing where the Shoe Tree stands. There's a chainsaw screaming in the distance, and a woman under a heavy umbrella walking an old mongrel very slowly. Stella waits until she has shuffled out of sight, then she takes the boots from the bag and hurls them into the branches of the tree. They look as if they might slip down to the ground, but then a twig holds them steady and they kick the air for a few seconds before settling, next to a pair of child's sneakers.

'I wish,' whispers Stella fiercely, 'that my sister would piss off and leave me alone, and that I could get my mother back.'

hanging around town

Caris holds a cup of hot chocolate close to her lips, sucking hot brown foam through a hole in the plastic lid. She listens to a train wailing as it pulls out of Newcastle Central station, as if it plans to go away for good this time. A group of women with red plastic noses stand around a collection tin singing an out-of-tune folk song and shaking tins. A cheerful amplified voice apologises for late trains.

George leans against a wrought-iron staircase outside a photograph booth in the station. Trapped birds fly above their heads, confused by the high glass ceiling. A cleaner gracefully polishes the wide marble floor, as if in a trance. George fidgets with his change, pulling out palmfuls of silver and bouncing the coins about, then putting them back into his pocket. Caris notices the way that he holds his shoulders tensely, as if something or someone is behind him. He's much better-looking than most of the boys at school, whom puberty has made monstrous, with acres of angry spots, sprouting hair, huge shoulders and high, squeaky or low, growling voices, overgrown legs and moist, sweating hands. George could easily be a sulky model in a magazine. Clothes hang easily on him, and wherever he goes he stands out. But the city is a garment that won't fit him. It's something to do with the way he holds his head, as if he is superior. Caris knows that George needs her, could not survive without her. She feels like a guide, an interpreter. She tells him to keep his posh voice down. She sees other young men watching him, sizing him up, hating him. She shows him routes down backstreets and alleys that thread away from the main streets. She takes him to cafés and bars where they'll be left alone. They spend whole days like this, drifting around the shops and precincts and nooks of Newcastle. Caris has never drunk so much tea and coffee. She's forgotten all about school. It's a dreary memory, like remembering a period of illness.

Mr Fortoba talks to Miss Moss, the biology teacher, in the staff room. Something has to be done. He tries to phone the father, but he's never there. Miss Moss tells him to hand it over to the truancy officer. They haven't got time to chase up kids who won't come to school. They haven't got time to eat their lunch, or to go to the toilet. Mr Fortoba asks Miss Moss what she thinks of Caris, and Miss Moss sighs and stirs dried-milk powder into her coffee, and tells him how much she likes Caris, and how she was the only girl who wasn't squeamish about dissecting a rat, even though she left the job half done.

'I can't keep a half-dissected rat for ever,' she says sadly.

Now George is bored and wants a photograph of him and Caris. He pulls her into the nearby plastic booth and they squash together on the swivelling seat. Caris giggles, but George is serious, vain. He pulls his collar up, and looks at the image of him and Caris together, her face next to his, her hair brushing against his chin. She's still holding the hot chocolate, and some of it spills on to his hand, burning him. He curses, and Caris dabs at the burn with her sleeve. George is impatient, breathing quickly. He puts some coins into the slot and a light flashes, holding them there, her leaning forward with her mouth open, him sucking in his cheeks. The machine asks if they want to proceed.

'That's terrible,' says Caris crossly. She presses a button and this time she stops smiling, and looks at the camera with a pout, but now George is caught out of focus, his eyes half closed, his expression slightly alarmed.

'We'll have to do it again now,' he snaps angrily.

'All right, all right,' she says. This time George turns away from her, showing his profile, his straight nose, leaving his hand around Caris's neck. She pulls back and the photograph catches her grimacing, her mouth crooked and open, her eyes distracted. 'That's bloody awful!' she complains, but George has pressed the 'PROCEED' button and the machine is burping away like a stomach, digesting their young faces.

They go outside and wait, leaping forward when the booth finally spits out four identical wet portraits of the two of them. George grabs them and blows on them. Caris is irritated.

'Can I see?' she says, and George tears the photo into four, giving her one copy. 'I look terrible,' she says, but George isn't listening. He stuffs the photographs into his pocket as a train screeches into the station, and suddenly the quiet expanse is filled with people bundling past them with flapping coats like wings.

'What now?' she says, and George shrugs and walks away from her. She throws the cup into a nearby bin and runs after him.

George walks out of the station and up a busy street into a tiled arcade, followed by Caris. Above them surveillance cameras swivel and record them as they move aimlessly and without purpose. George sneers at them. In the arcade light glitters through stained glass and a busker plays a violin. *Mum liked this arcade*, thinks Caris. They used to walk this way for a bit of peace, to get away from the crowds. George doesn't respond to the world around him. He roams about, hungry for something new, uncomfortable in daylight.

'We'll go and break in somewhere,' he announces, leaning against a shop window. Behind him a shop dummy in a tailored suit looks affronted.

'Have you ever robbed anyone, Caris?' he asks her.

'No.' Caris lights a cigarette and frowns. 'I'm hungry.' She catches a glimpse of herself in a mirror in the shop. *I look like my mother*, she thinks with a start. *I'm holding my head the way she does, like a little girl*. She blinks and sucks in her cheeks.

'It makes your heart beat fast, and you sweat all over,' George continues airily.

'What would we steal?'

'Shoes,' he says, grinning. 'We'll steal shoes!'

Caris considers the tree. It stands there in her imagination like a kind of promise. *It's a work of art*, she thinks. *We've made a mystery*.

'What if we get caught?' she asks, thinking of her mother, red-handed, standing in Northumberland Street.

'We won't get caught,' says George. 'We'll break into a house. We'll watch until the people go out.'

Caris drops her fag on to the shining tiles below her feet and stamps on it. She hears the distant chatter of city starlings. The violinist is playing a ballad that makes her feel like crying.

'No,' she says. 'I don't want to.'

George scowls. Caris has never disagreed with him before.

'Why not?'

'I just don't want to,' Caris says.

George turns away, his hands in the pockets of his long overcoat, and walks out of the building into the hard sunlight. A man holding a Bible shouts, 'The Lord will save you!' and George snorts and continues down the wide street. Caris runs after him, calling him, but George doesn't turn round.

'Wait!' she shouts and people turn to stare at her.

But George doesn't wait, and Caris stops running. She stands there watching him disappearing among a crowd of schoolchildren with eager faces turned towards the sky holding pencils and notebooks. Without George, Caris feels cold. The square is filled with people wanting something; *Big Issue* sellers bleakly offer magazines, women holding questionnaires plead with passers-by, a gypsy with too much lipstick tries to sell her a bunch of heather, a group of early drunks with swimming eyes lean towards her, wondering if she might give them their bus fare home.

Caris is afraid to walk any further. She knows how Mac drives round and round these streets. Like a child in a game, she is safe in pedestrian precincts, but beyond them she could be seen; and, more than anything these days, Caris would like to be invisible.

She's angry with George for walking off like that. Without him she doesn't belong anywhere. She doesn't want to go home, where Nana Price will envelop her in her smoky questions, but she hasn't got any money. It's George who has money, endless supplies of it, as if his pockets are limitless. Caris sulks. She has no choice but to walk back over the bony motorway bridge, and through the concrete estate where there is always a dog barking like a wolf howling at the moon.

Everything is crap, thinks Caris as she hunches her shoulders against the hard wind on her way home.

the visitor

Some days Mr Fortoba finds himself looking for Caris as he drives home along the narrow roads through the Vale. She seems to represent his failure as a teacher, his inability to inspire his pupils. Her empty desk appears in his dreams sometimes, placed in other settings, like in his own back garden, or in the middle of a football pitch.

Today it's Friday, and there is a cold pink sunset, and the day feels unfinished and undone. After he has sat in a staff meeting for an hour, talking about the condition of the boys' toilets, Mr Fortoba asks Mrs Petty, the school secretary, for Caris's home address and climbs into his car and runs his finger over a grid of streets in his *A to Z*. He thinks his motive is to save Caris, but he is embarrassed to admit that it's also to save himself.

When he reaches Caris's front door it's exactly how he would have imagined it: a redbrick house set in a terrace in a quiet street, with nine-year-old boys kicking footballs across the tarmac, and a cat lying in a pool of unusually golden light on the pavement. Green wheeled bins stand to order in the back lanes. *Respectable working class*, he thinks.

The house looks unloved. The curtains are half closed and in the front garden dandelions and nettles are emerging among dirty rosebushes.

He stands there, in his navy-blue zip-up anorak, ringing the doorbell, thinking about what he might say. No one answers, and

Mr Fortoba turns to leave, but then hears a scraping behind the door and the shift of a key in a lock.

Nana Price peers out at him with small frowning eyes. She sees a thin, balding man with nervous fluttering hands making signs at her. She pulls the door wide open and Mr Fortoba is overwhelmed by a cloud of cigarette smoke.

'Is Caris here?' he asks.

'No one here but me, petal,' croaks the old woman, patting her hair straight. 'What do you want her for?'

'Are you a relative?' he asks.

'I'm her nana,' she says. 'Who are you?'

'Her teacher, Mr Fortoba.'

'Oh, yes, I know who you are. You're the one that phones up.'

'That's me.'

'You'd better come in.'

He follows her into the house. There's a pile of junk mail pushed into a corner of the porch. Ahead he sees the predictable flight of stairs. It's the geography of his youth; the stairs leading up to three bedrooms and a bathroom, the door to the left leading into a sitting room, and behind that a dining room, and, built on the back, a small kitchen. Nana Price leads him into the sitting room and points to an armchair.

'Go on,' she says, 'sit yourself down. I'll put the kettle on.'

Mr Fortoba would rather not sit down.

'I'll come back later,' he says, 'when Caris is here.'

'There's no knowing when that will be,' she mutters. 'You might as well sit and wait.'

Unwillingly, he sits on the arm of the chair, listening to the sounds of the old woman shifting about in the kitchen, turning on taps, opening the fridge, getting cups from an overhead cupboard. He looks around him at the room, with its obligatory happy photographs on the mantelpiece, the three-piece suite, the bay window with yellow, buttercup-patterned curtains.

'Here we are!' says Nana Price, wobbling in with a tray, which she sets down on the coffee-table. She plumps herself down on the settee, and smiles her grey-toothed smile at Mr Fortoba, delighted to have company after a dazed afternoon with the television. 'So, what can we do for you?' she goes on, making a palaver of lifting the tea cosy from the teapot and ceremoniously pouring the tea from an extravagant height.

'Thank you,' he says. 'I was wondering if Caris had been ill?'

'Ill? No, I don't think so.'

'She hasn't been at school.'

'Oh, I see. Well, she's going through a sticky patch. Like they do.'

'Where is she, then?'

An expression of well-practised innocence flickers over Nana's face. 'I couldn't tell you that,' she says.

'I'm worried about her, Mrs –'

'Price.'

'I think she's in trouble.'

'What kind of trouble?' asks Nana, nibbling a biscuit and scratching her nylon stocking.

'With her mother gone.' Mr Fortoba's voice drains away.

'That's my Louise,' Nana points a trembling finger towards the photograph on the mantelpiece.

'Yes,' says Mr Fortoba, trying to drink his tea quickly.

'Shall I tell Caris off?' says Nana, pragmatically.

'No, that's not why I came round. I thought we could talk.'

'Talk?' echoes Nana.

'Try and find out what's she's up to.'

'You like Caris, do you?' asks Nana suspiciously. She tries to remember the word 'paedophile' but it slips away down a river of forgotten words, leaving only an unpleasant aftertaste.

'It's my job, that's all,' says Mr Fortoba.

'Are you sure?' sniffs Nana.

'I'm her form teacher,' explains Mr Fortoba, trying to sound respectable.

'I think she's got a lad,' whispers Nana. 'She comes in late. Like a bitch on heat.'

'Well, exactly,' says Mr Fortoba.

'She goes down that Vale,' says Nana, and Mr Fortoba sees the

dark canopies of trees, stretching out like a scab on a limb of
the city.

'Who's the lad?' asks Mr Fortoba.

'I dunno. She must have met him down there. Young people go
there. They turn into wild animals, attacking people,' says Nana,
warming to the story.

'Where's her father?'

'Out.' Nana smacks her lips together, crossly. 'He's always out.
Taxi driving.'

'Who looks after Caris?' asks Mr Fortoba.

'I do!' exclaims Nana. 'Would you like a tipple, Mr
Cortina?'

'No thanks. I've got to go,' he says, standing up.

'Already? What shall I say to Caris?'

'Tell her to come to school,' says Mr Fortoba lamely. 'Tell her
that I'm not angry.'

At this moment they both hear the door. Nana swivels in her chair.
Mr Fortoba sits down again, feeling trapped in the oppressively
hot room.

Stella appears in the doorway. Her skin looks very white, and
her lips are stained red.

'What's going on?' she says.

'Ah, Stella,' says Mr Fortoba. 'How are you?'

'Very well, thank you,' answers Stella mechanically. She sits
down, looking at Mr Fortoba with a questioning face.

'I came to see Caris.'

'What's she done now?'

'She's wagging off with some lad,' interrupts Nana.

'Oh,' says Stella.

'Stella's all right,' confides Nana. 'She works all the time. Don't
you, Stel, in your bedroom?'

'Sssh, Nana,' says Stella.

'I'm just saying,' Nana says.

'We don't know where she is,' says Stella in a loud voice. She
doesn't like Mr Fortoba being here with her grandmother.

153

She notices how uncomfortable he looks, and how he keeps glancing around, as if he's checking the place out.

'When do you think she might come back?'

'I don't know,' says Stella. 'Has she been missing school again?'

'She hasn't been to school for weeks.'

'Weeks?' echoes Stella, feeling tired.

'I'll have to give her name to the truancy officer.'

'What does that mean?'

'He'll come round.'

Stella nods. 'So this is like a last chance?'

'I suppose so.'

Mr Fortoba hadn't meant it to be like this. The atmosphere in the room is grave and dark.

Nana clears her throat. 'We'll tell her, won't we, Stella?'

'Yes.'

Stella longs to go and wash. Her fingers itch with dirt.

'Well, I'm sorry to disturb you,' says Mr Fortoba, in what he hopes is a relaxed voice. 'I'm going now.'

'Yes,' says Stella.

Then they all hear the front door opening. Stella looks afraid, and angry too. Nana puts her hand to her mouth, as if she is hiding and doesn't want to make a noise. Caris walks into the room, dropping her coat on to the floor. *She's like a young bull*, thinks Mr Fortoba, *like a bull that might start stamping on the carpet. She looks as if she's going to lose it, to have the screaming abjabs with her tangled red hair and shining eyes.*

Caris sees them like a photograph. Her grandmother blurred and out of focus, Mr Fortoba on the edge of his seat, his mouth half open, Stella with her face stuffed with moral rage. She hates the way they all look as if they expect something.

'What the hell are you doing here?' she says rudely.

'I came to see how you were,' answers Mr Fortoba.

'Oh, Christ,' says Caris, and turns and stamps upstairs.

'Come back here, Caris!' shouts Nana, but then there's silence.

'It's just it's a shock, you being here,' Stella tells him.

154

'She doesn't like school,' says Nana. 'I didn't either. Waste of time, if you ask me.'

'Can you go up and ask her to come down and speak to me?' says Mr Fortoba. He feels upset, as if Caris has personally shunned him.

'I'll try,' says Stella and drifts out of the room, leaving Mr Fortoba staring at the closed door. He hears voices from upstairs, some more slamming and crashing. Then Stella appears again.

'She's got a headache,' she tells him. 'You'd better come back another time.'

'She's throwing her life away,' stammers Mr Fortoba. 'She needs support.'

'I told you, she's got me,' chips in Nana complacently. 'I haven't got any qualifications, and there's nothing the matter with me.' She raises her mangy eyebrows and winks at Mr Fortoba.

'Tell her father to phone me.'

'If I see him, I will,' she says, not getting up to show him out. Stella jumps to her feet and ushers him into the hallway. Mr Fortoba hesitates at the foot of the stairs. He looks up and sees Caris standing there, looking down at him. It's an image he will always have, of a red-haired girl staring down at him with an expression of contempt and compassion. Long after this, when he's a happier man, in a different place, wearing a pair of shorts and a T-shirt with the words 'WATER WARRIOR' written on it, he will think of this as a transforming moment in his life.

'Caris,' he calls softly.

'I'm not coming back,' she tells him. 'I've got other things to do.'

'But . . .' he stammers.

'I'm sorry, Mr Fortoba.'

And then she's gone, closing the door firmly behind her.

flatpacks

Mac sits outside Ikea in his taxi, waiting for a woman called Felicity. He chews gum and watches families emerging with large boxes, arguing with each other as they pack up their cars. Mac and Louise once went to Ikea to buy Stella a desk. They had walked round the shop slowly, drifting helplessly among the crowds. He had felt suspicious, as if the shop was trying to trick him into becoming something he wasn't, a man with cupboards and hooks. Everything had looked so neat and organised. Louise kept on stroking the sofas and chairs as if they were animals in a zoo.

When his fare appears she's carrying a paper lampshade. She wears a sheepskin coat over a pregnant belly and she has straight, fair Swedish hair and a bored mouth. Mac gets out of the taxi and puts her stuff in the boot.

'I nearly bought a bed,' she says when she gets in the taxi. 'It was only two hundred pounds. My name's Felicity, by the way.'

'I know,' says Mac. 'From the radio.'

'Oh,' she says.

Mac chews his gum and joins a queue of cars.

'Where to?' he says.

Felicity tells him an address, then starts to hum in a tuneless way. Mac's phone rings. It's Stella.

'Caris's teacher came round,' she says.

'Oh,' says Mac.

'He says Caris hasn't been at school.'

'Oh, Christ,' says Mac.

'She's in her room. She won't speak to us.'

'Oh.'

'What shall we have for tea?'

'I'll get something in,' says Mac. He throws the phone down, swearing.

'It's illegal to talk on a mobile while driving,' carps Felicity.

The queue of cars begins to move.

Mac wishes that children were like Ikea furniture. He wishes that he could pack them into a box and keep them under the bed. He laughs at this thought.

'What's funny?' says Felicity.

'Nothing,' he says, hoping that she won't start talking again.

'All I got was a lampshade,' she says in a doleful voice.

'What did you want?' Mac asks her.

'Everything,' she moans. 'I just moved into a flat with no furniture. Now I've got a lampshade, but no bed, no wardrobe or anything.'

'Mmm,' says Mac.

'I'm having a baby.'

'I see.'

'I need furniture.'

Mac turns on to a motorway and accelerates into the fast lane, feeling a momentary sense of relief as he glides past lorries.

'I don't know what to do,' says Felicity.

'Can't your family help?'

'I haven't got a family,' she says.

'Oh.'

'Baby's due in a month.'

Mac is irritated. Why is she telling him this? He wishes his passengers wouldn't leave their problems in his taxis. Sometimes he can recall them days after they've left the car.

'What are you sleeping on now?' he snaps.

'The floor.'

'Where's the father?'

'Iraq.'

157

Mac can't face it. He shakes his fist at a woman driver and then turns the radio on loudly. He doesn't want to know about Iraq, or the pregnant girl with no furniture. All he wants is to buy some processed food, go home, eat it and shout at Caris. He is filled with a dictatorial rage. He would like to make Caris wear a veil and attend a strict boarding school. *Don't they have places in America for troublesome teenagers?* he thinks. *Where they reprogramme them. That's what she needs*, he thinks, *bloody discipline. This whole thing has gone on too long.*

'Third on the left,' says Felicity. They turn into a street of bungalows with dripping gardens. The fare is four pounds.

'I've only got three pounds fifty,' says Felicity. 'Will that do?'

Mac snatches the money from her and watches her struggle out of the cab.

'Sorry about that. Thanks,' she drones. She slumps towards her front door.

'*Stupid cow,*' thinks Mac as he speeds away.

mac makes tea

Mac stands in the over-bright supermarket watching a packet of
fish fillets in batter, frozen peas, oven chips, four individual trifles,
a sliced loaf, aspirin, coffee, margarine, cornflakes, tinned peaches,
marmalade and a large bottle of orange squash glide through the
checkout. The girl who serves him never looks up once. Behind
him, a man with an eye-patch stands too close to Mac and forgets
to put the partition between his wares (a tin of corned beef, a bottle
of red wine, Dairy Lea cheese and a packet of plain crisps) and
Mac's, so that there is a small confusion over the bill and the corned
beef.

Mac grabs the shopping and drives home, through the crush of
teatime traffic. When he opens the door the house is steaming
with bad-tempered women. Nana Price lies on the settee surrounded
by empty cups and bottles, watching a snake charmer on television.
Mac hardly speaks to her. He picks up the tray and carries it into
the kitchen, and shoves the oven chips on to a metal tray and
into the oven with the fish fillets, without reading the instructions
on either of the packets. He rips a hole in the corner of the frozen
peas and tips them into a saucepan, and switches on the electric
kettle. Then he stamps back through the sitting room, ignoring
his mother-in-law, who is sitting up now, with her eyes unfocused.
He strides up the narrow stairs, knocking first on Stella's locked
door.

Her tidy voice answers: 'Who is it?'

'Dad,' he says. The door opens, and Stella sees her father standing there breathing heavily.

'Can I come in?' he says. But Stella doesn't like other people's smells in her room, so she tells him she'll be down in a minute.

Mac knocks on the door of Caris's room. There is no answer at all so he opens the door. Caris lies on the mattress. Loud music fills the room and it stinks of smoke. Mac turns off the music and she sits up.

'Well?' he asks.

'Well what?'

'What's this about you not being at school?'

'Oh, leave it,' sighs Caris, lying down again.

'No, we're not leaving it,' snarls Mac. 'Get downstairs!'

'What for?'

'We're going to sort this out.'

'How?'

Mac walks out of the room, leaving the door wide open. The house is beginning to smell of cooking chips. Stella is waiting downstairs, her hair pulled back, her nails spotlessly clean. Nana smiles at him vaguely, but Mac takes the television remote from her and turns off the television.

'I was watching that,' she squeaks. 'I like snakes.'

'Would you like a bath, Nana?' says Mac.

'Not particularly.'

'You need a bath,' chimes in Stella.

Nana looks at them both suspiciously. This is patronising talk. *It's the start of the downhill slope*, she thinks, *when people start suggesting it's time for a bath.*

'Then you can have your supper on a tray. It's fish,' says Mac.

'What's going on?' says Nana.

'I want to be alone with Stella and Caris.'

'Why didn't you say?' says Nana crossly.

'I am saying.'

Nana wobbles to her feet, her hair sticking up, her cardigan mis-buttoned, and makes it to the door.

'Mr Cortina was here,' she says.

'I know,' says Mac.

'I made him a nice cup of tea. It's a good job I was in.'

'Yes, I saw.'

Stella likes the way Mac is taking control at last. She can smell the fish now, swelling from uncooked grey to white in its batter coat. Caris comes into the room, her eyes swollen, her hair tangled. She falls into the settee and stares at them both.

'What?' she says.

'I want to know where you go all day,' says Mac.

Caris shrugs.

'She's got a lad,' says Stella. 'She hangs about with him. He's not at the school.'

'Who is he?' says Mac.

'No one.'

'I want to know who he is, Caris.'

'He's called George,' she says.

'How old is he, this George?'

'Seventeen.'

'What does he do?'

'Nothing. He's changing schools.'

'Where does he live?' asks Stella.

'Over the Vale.'

'Where?'

'Oh, shut up.'

'I'm only asking.'

'She's just jealous,' snaps Caris. 'No one fancies her.'

'Piss off,' says Stella.

'Quiet!' shouts Mac. 'So you miss school with this George.'

'I told you, I hate school. Can we have supper now?'

'I want to meet him.'

'You can't.'

'Why not?'

'I don't want you to.'

'What's his surname?'

'I'm not telling you.'

'Shall I turn the oven off, Dad?' says Stella.

161

'Yes.'

Mac feels his heart beating in slapping waves against his chest. He wants to shake Caris. He hates the way she lounges in the settee that he bought with money earned from driving people all over the city, and the way she just sits there with her dull pouting expression, spots on her chin, despising him, not answering him. Stella goes into the kitchen and clanks about. Mac hears her pouring water over the peas, and getting plates from cupboards.

'I've had enough, Caris,' says Mac.

'What do you mean?'

'I'm not putting up with it any more.'

'What are you going to do, then?'

'Either we meet this George, and you start explaining yourself, or else.'

'Or else what?'

'You can get out of here.'

'What do you mean?'

'You heard me.'

Stella stands in the kitchen holding a plate of chips, pale and scared.

'Where would I go?'

'I don't care,' says Mac. 'I've had enough.'

Caris turns and runs out of the room. Mac turns the television on. He tries to feel victorious, but he just feels depressed. Stella comes in with two plates on a tray and sits down.

'Where would she go, Dad?' she asks.

Mac doesn't answer. He has a horrible image of Caris standing in a shop doorway wrapped in a blanket.

'Shall I try and find out who he is, this George?' says Stella.

'Yeah,' says Mac quietly, 'and I'll go and kill him.'

Stella laughs but she doesn't like Mac's face. He looks mean.

'It will be all right, Dad,' she says. 'It's just a phase.'

Mac smiles, like someone has winched up the ends of his mouth. He doesn't feel good. Sometimes he thinks he might have a heart attack. It happens to men like him. One day you just turn bright red and keel over, and wake up in a hospital ward with your chest covered in those plugs and an oxygen mask like an elephant's trunk over your nose. It happened to Mac's father. *I should go to the gym*, thinks Mac, remembering a period when Louise went to aerobics and he joined a gym. He had walked for miles on that machine. It felt as if he had walked the length of England. Louise's arms and legs had felt hard and energetic, too. It was summer. The doors and windows were all wide open, not like now when they crouch in box-like rooms, keeping the heat in. He had lost weight. The feeling was liberating, like letting go of heavy suitcases at the beginning of a flight and feeling that you were going somewhere. They had even started eating broccoli and wearing tracksuits.

What happened? Mac chews his battered fish and tries to think. Was it just the season changing that had made them lose enthusiasm and slump back into their old lives? He'd even tried to do a course, an evening course, in computers. But when he'd got to the classroom he'd felt out of place. Everyone else was younger. They had sharper pencils and they made notes in a way that made Mac feel stupid. He hadn't understood what he was supposed to be doing, and the classroom had that school smell. He kept on thinking that someone was going to shout at him, and his fingers were too big for the keyboard, and you had to tell the group what you hoped to gain from the course and he had stumbled on his words.

Mac never reads or writes anything now except newspapers and taxi receipts.

'What are you thinking, Dad?' asks Stella.

'Nothing,' says Mac, and so the two of them sit chewing chips and then spooning red and yellow heaps of individual trifle into their mouths for half an hour before Stella goes back upstairs to her locked room to write notes on *Pride and Prejudice* in neat black Biro.

the pet graveyard

Louise can't sleep. She lies in her bunk and watches highlights from her life, like watching a film. She sees Caris dancing in a school pantomime in a fairy costume she'd made out of net curtains, coat hangers and sequins. She remembers Mac standing on a hill in Northumberland with his hands outstretched singing a hymn. Then there's the four of them in Spain having a swimming race across a pool, shrieking with laughter. She can make herself cry with these kind of images, like eating too many sweets. She has to force herself to look into the grimmer corners of their lives, the drab days when nothing much happened at all. Days filled with supermarkets, with waiting in bus queues, or looking into a plastic washing-up bowl, pulling wet clothes from a washing machine. Loveless winter days, with drops of rain running down the window-panes, rubbish blowing along the street. Louise considers her husband and wonders if she loves him. She doesn't know what love is really. She knows that, whatever it is, neither of them have attended to it very much lately. *It's like a garden*, she thinks, *that no one cares for. In the end it's just thistles and dandelions.*

Caris can't sleep either. She lies in her bed listening to the empty sounds of the night, thinking about George walking away, and what she should have said.

She wishes Mac would leave her alone, and she doesn't like the fact that Mr Fortoba came to her house and sat with his mouth round the rim of a mug, and placed his bony arse in one of their chairs, and saw the inside of her life. She feels exposed.

And she feels that the Tree of Shoes is beginning to belong to everyone, as every day more shoes appear in its branches. *Nothing*, she thinks, *belongs only to me*.

She is so angry that she even hates Nana Price, and the smell she leaves in the bathroom. She hates the sight of her pink and brown underwear hanging over the chair in her bedroom. *I have to get out*, she thinks. *I can't stand it any more*. Eventually she falls into a half sleep, as grey light seeps under the curtain of her room, and a sleepy choir of birds begin to sing.

By the time Caris opens her eyes, Louise has already eaten a bowl of cereal, cleaned out the shower cubicles, and is sitting looking at a spreadsheet on a computer screen in the education room. Stella is showered and ironed, her spots are concealed, her satchel is tightly fastened. Nana Price sleeps like an old cat, curled up in a pile of eiderdowns, and Mac is waiting on a double yellow line outside a tall office block.

Caris drags herself out of bed and pulls on her uniform. Stella waits for her in the hallway, standing with her hands on her hips, like a caricature of a nagging wife. Caris ignores her, picking up a pound coin that Mac has left on the table, and pushes open the door. She sprints down the hill, throwing her school tie into a rubbish bin.

She keeps on running, away from the house and the school, further down into the Vale, past the brick and iron bridge that lurches across the river, and down the steep narrow paths to the café that is always closed, and the row of stones in the corner of a flat green commemorating the deaths of rich people's pets. She hates these, too, with their smug epitaphs. 'To Suzie, much-loved Labrador and friend. We shall never forget you.' She sees the earthy skeletons of dogs, lying there, and the families who buried them, with their loose sweaters and their hair falling over their noses. She thinks, too, of all the dogs she's never had, because Mac said that he didn't have time to walk them. She walks along by the frothy river, hating Mac. When she gets to a small children's zoo she presses her face against the wire enclosures and watches peacocks swaying about, hens with bright combs squabbling among each other, and brainless rabbits staring back at her with marble eyes. She wonders if anyone sees her as she carries on between heavy, rain-drenched trees, under dripping stone tunnels and into the heart of the long Vale. What was it they said on that school trip, years ago? That the park had been created by some lord for the use of the working classes. And didn't he also invent light-bulbs or something?

What was he trying to do? Illuminate their lives? Whatever he thought, the Vale is now a dank, half-lit place where you can easily get lost for hours.

She strides on, with nowhere to go, keeping close to the brown river with its cloudy waterfalls and stepping stones. She balances on tree stumps and walls, jumping from one to the other. She passes joggers, and park keepers, and sometimes she thinks that she passes ghosts, people who are so soundless and insubstantial that they seem like spirits.

She wishes that she was lost but she also wishes that someone would find her. By the time she reaches the end of the long Vale, where the park peters out and the river disappears underground, her clothes are wet through and she's boiling hot. She climbs up some curving stone steps and starts to trudge back along an uneven road, filled with unusual and desirable houses, surrounded by trees, built into the side of the valley. She stops outside one that looks like a house in a film with wide bow windows and red ivy growing around the door. She watches it for a while, and knows that it's empty. She sees into its tidy rooms and swept hallways. She imagines its wide beds and the linen that lies ironed in its cupboards. *Why not?* she thinks. *What else am I going to do?* She walks to a phone box and dials George's number. His father answers with a voice like porridge.

He doesn't answer Caris when she asks for George, she just hears him place the receiver on the glossy surface of the table and call solemnly up the stairs, and then the soft pad of George's bare feet on the stairs.

'What?' he says.

'I've found a house,' and she tells him where it is, how lonely it looks, as if it longs for company.

'Good,' says George. But he wants to keep her waiting. 'Not today,' he says. 'Tomorrow. I'll meet you there.' And he replaces the receiver.

divorce

Louise's lettuce is going to be part of an exhibition, organised by the artist in residence, called 'Inside Art'. Carol teases her. 'What do you think this is,' she says, 'the friggin' Slade?'

In the prison, Louise is known as 'the arty one'. The other prisoners ask her to do their portraits to send to their children. Louise sits in the art room, with an easel and a large pad of paper supplied by the artist in residence, surrounded by hushed groups of admiring women, waiting for their turn to be the sitter. She manages to make them look calm, combed and relaxed, rubbing out the harshness of their experience with the soft lead of her pencil.

But today she feels restless. It's visitors' day. There's a storm outside and the sky trembles with sheets of lightning followed by low belly growls of thunder. She can't stop thinking about Caris, who is never there when she phones and never writes. She hopes that Mac will bring Caris to visit her, but when she is ushered down to the visitors' room there is only her husband sitting there, holding a bar of chocolate halfway to his mouth, his leather coat wet with rain.

He looks like he's the one in prison, she thinks, as she walks towards him.

'Hallo, love,' he says, putting the bar of chocolate down guiltily. 'Can I get you anything?'

She feels frustrated. All this tea and coffee and getting up and sitting down.

'No,' she says sourly.

'I brought you in some pyjamas, like you said.'

Mac looks guilty, like a dog that's just eaten a pie. He's trying to imagine Louise as his ex-wife. His tongue circles the word 'divorce' in his mouth. *I'm going to say it*, he thinks.

'I've got a painting in an art exhibition,' says Louise, to break the long silence.

'What's that for?'

'Why not?'

'I didn't think you liked art,' says Mac.

'Neither did I.'

Mac looks bored on purpose. He's thinking about Degna's hands, kneading dough, and frying onions in a pan. *Louise looks terrible without any make-up on*, he thinks. She's got dry skin, and her long hair is greasy.

'What's going on at home?' snaps Louise.

'What do you mean?'

'What's Caris up to?'

'Don't ask me,' he grumbles. 'She doesn't listen to anything I say.'

Louise mentally shades in the bags under his eyes, the lines around his mouth. Mac is disturbed by her silence. He picks up the bar of chocolate again and peels back the wrapper.

'D'you want some?' he says.

'No.'

'You sure?'

Louise doesn't answer. Around them there's a babble of voices, but it feels as if they are sitting in a quiet, lonely room.

'Does Caris talk about me?' asks Louise eventually.

'She doesn't talk, Louise. She goes upstairs and sits in her room smoking. She stays out late and doesn't come in. She's got some lad that nobody knows.'

'Where are you, then?'

Mac feels his voice getting louder, rising above the murmuring sea of visitors. 'Where do you think?' he says. 'I'm working.'

'She's your daughter!' she says.

'And she's your daughter too. You should have thought of that before you went out nicking shoes, shouldn't you?'

'Don't shout,' says Louise, as heads turn towards them. She looks up at the ceiling, at square grey tiles notched with black specks, at smoke alarms and water sprinklers. She feels something in her centre, in her womb, fluttering. It's like a memory of childbirth, the shifting of scars.

'I'm sorry,' she says, turning back to look at him, sitting squarely on his chair, his bald head shining under the neon.

Mac looks at his driver's hands. He gulps nervously. He forces himself to sit up straight and to look at Louise.

'I want a divorce,' states Mac. The people on the next table look shocked. He sits back, horrified by what he's just said.

'Oh,' says Louise.

'I've been thinking.'

'Have you?'

'I want . . .' But he can't find the words for what he wants. He has an image of driving up a broad, star-lit road with Degna sitting, smiling, in the passenger seat.

'Well,' says Louise, 'that's very fucking helpful.'

Mac has never heard Louise swear. He shakes his head at her, as if she's a broken, ruined thing. Louise sees the expression on his face and is filled with rage. Mac looks superior, even smug. She wants to slap his smooth cheek.

'Why now?'

'I've had enough,' he says. 'I've had enough of your mother, too.'

'And you think getting divorced is a solution, do you?'

'I'm sick of everything.'

'How do you think I feel?'

'I don't know how you feel, do I?'

Mac leans towards Louise, his face ugly. One of the prison warders glances over at the table and nudges her companion, sensing trouble.

'You're free, Mac. I'm not,' whispers Louise.

'That's not my fault, is it?' Mac feels indignant, ignored. He wants justice.

'What about our daughters?' Louise asks. 'What are you going to do? I can't do anything, can I? I write to Caris and she doesn't write back. I wait in a queue for hours to speak to her on the phone and she's not in. I get my mum talking about Mr Cortina and her bunions. Caris is in trouble, Mac. Getting divorced isn't going to help that.'

Now Mac is dismayed. He wanted his words to have more power. He wishes that Louise would cry and beg him not to leave her. He wanted to show Louise how bad his life was, but she's not listening. He wants her to tell him that she's sorry, and how much she loves him, but instead she's talking in this urgent, non-Louise-like way. Louise just studies him coldly, as if she's seeing him clearly for the first time. He catches her glancing over at Carol on the other side of the room, with an expression of understood despair.

'You've wrecked everything,' he says. 'You're a disgrace.'

'Look after Caris and Stella,' says Louise, 'until I get out of here. Then we can get divorced, if that's what you want.'

Mac stares at his shoes. They don't fit properly. Before he set off for the prison he had looked everywhere for his brown brogues, but, like a lot of things in his life, they seemed to have gone missing.

'Please, Mac, talk to Caris.'

Louise sighs. *These prisons*, she thinks, *they're full of women with creased letters in their pockets, and torn photographs stuck to the walls of their cells, but the worst thing is being powerless.*

As they sit there hard hailstones start tapping the window, like insistent fingernails.

'I've got to go,' mutters Mac.

'Back to work?' says Louise with sarcastic enthusiasm.

Mac doesn't answer, or say goodbye. He just turns away and plods towards the door. *His leather-coated back looks like a rock face*, thinks Louise.

george and marina

While Caris walks back home through the ghostly Vale, George
lies on the sofa in the pink drawing room and feels the contours
of his mouth, the hair growing on his upper lip, the edge of his
hard chin. In another room, his mother, Marina, is screaming
his name, again and again. Like all sounds in this cavernous house,
her voice is isolated, as if it has nothing to bounce off. Lately
George has stopped speaking to his mother. His closed mouth
powers her incessant, tinny prattle. She is full of schemes. She
wants to send George to Uncle Lucas in Arizona to help on his
cattle ranch, or to see a famous psychiatrist in London who she's
found out about on the Internet, or perhaps a remote 'cramming'
college in Shropshire where they program you to pass exams. Lord
knows, she tries, but George doesn't respond. Sometimes she would
like to see him conscripted into an army, and made to carry a gun.
She wants to launder him, iron him, straighten him, but most of
all she wants George to speak to her. But he won't. He stalks the
stairs and corridors and arranged rooms of the house, leaving his
mark everywhere he goes: cigarette ends floating in the toilet bowl,
spittle sliming up the sides of basins, empty cigarette packets
thrown into the bushes in the driveway, mud on the cream carpet
in the hall, dirty underpants slipping off the banisters. He
smells high, like an animal leaving its scent, of wood smoke and
alcohol.

   She never goes to his room. She pretends it doesn't exist. Marina doesn't know why George is the way he is and when it began. At night she drinks herself into a dark-green well of guilt, anger and remorse, and wakes up feeling sick.

George doesn't know either. He sometimes feels as if his interior is unlit, or not charged like other people's. That's what he likes about Caris – her energy, the light behind her eyes, the translucence of her skin, her vigour.

He hasn't seen her now for three days, and it seems as if his life has darkened in that time. But now she's waiting for him. He enjoys knowing that she waits, and has no desire to hurry towards her.

George pulls himself up and looks into a mirror at a spot on the side of his nose. His mother appears behind him, breathless from shouting.

'Didn't you hear me, George?' she shrieks.

'No.'

'Some of my shoes are missing.'

'You've got enough pairs, haven't you?'

'Have you been in my room?'

'No.'

'Are you sure?'

'I said no.'

'At least ten or twelve pairs have gone. It's not funny.'

'Sorry,' says George, 'but it's got nothing to do with me.'

'What about that girl you bring here?'

Marina's glimpsed the girl in the driveway, and once she saw her on the stairs on her way to George's room. Caris had looked at her rudely, not saying hallo.

Marina had thought that Caris looked cheap and dim.

'Caris? Why would she want your shoes?' George snorts with grim laughter.

'I can't bear it,' groans Marina.

She reaches out and touches George's shoulder and he twists away from her.

'What's the matter with you?' she asks, her voice wavering.

'I love you, Mum,' says George, seeing the words work, like a

173

spell, as her eyes loosen and she peers at him in the mirror, afraid, but full of longing.

'Do you, George?'

'Of course. You know I do.'

And then he turns to see the real flesh and blood of her, but can't meet her darting eyes, so he sidles away, and runs up to his room, leaving her to brush at the pink sofa with her frantic hands, where cigarette ash has marked the upholstery.

stella, margaret and layla

'Where's your fucking sister?'

Stella looks up from a poem by Sylvia Plath. She's sitting in her favourite place in the library, a soft chair by the window. She has just written the word 'narcissism' in her notebook. School has finished and there is a hum of polishers from the corridor outside, and the smell of disinfectant covering the stale stench of a thousand armpits, urine and school cooking.

Layla Tumility's voice is out of place in the library. She sounds like a dog barking in a church. Behind her Margaret stands like a steamed pudding, looking suspiciously at the bookshelves as if they might fall on her.

'Why do you want to know?' whispers Stella, closing her book carefully.

'She's been off for ages,' says Layla. 'We just wondered. Is she sick?'

Stella doesn't feel like talking to Layla. She dislikes her. She is sure that Caris isn't keen on her either.

'She's having some time off,' she says quickly.

'Is your mum out of prison yet?' chirrups Margaret.

Stella sits up straight. She considers Margaret, with her plump calves and dreary hair.

'It's none of your business,' she says.

Margaret sniggers, and Layla sucks in her cheeks.

No one talks to Stella about Louise. She has successfully erected an invisible fence around herself that does not allow intimate questions. Even her friends don't talk about her. They sense that this is forbidden territory. Margaret might just as well have thrown herself into the middle of a minefield. Stella feels her palms itching. She stares at Margaret, who steps back, aware of a cold draft blowing in her direction. Stella's eyes glint.

The librarian, sensing an atmosphere, calls over from the corner by the photocopier. 'Nearly time to close!'

'Come on, Mags,' says Layla. 'Let's go to the supermarket.'

Stella stands up.

'Are you in Caris's form?' she asks.

'Yeah,' says Layla.

'I don't like you,' says Stella. 'I don't like the way you speak to me.'

'We were only asking.'

'I'm telling you, I don't like it.'

'Sorry,' says Margaret, aware of Stella's power. 'We're going anyway.'

'Wait,' snaps Stella, 'I haven't finished.'

'We've got to go,' Layla tosses her hair back.

'If you go anywhere near my sister again, I'll have you.'

'What do you mean?' Layla's eyes widen.

Stella senses the character of Lady Macbeth rising in her veins. She practically spits as she says, 'Let's just say, I wouldn't want to be in your shoes if you so much as speak to Caris again. D'you hear me?'

Margaret nods. She knows that Stella has both power and influence. Layla sulks. The two girls turn and lope out of the library, breaking into a run when they reach the door.

Now the quiet room is soured by them. Stella wonders what they did to Caris. For the first time since their mother went to prison, Stella feels sorry for her sister.

Caris doesn't have words for things, Stella thinks, as she pulls on her coat. *She has tantrums because she can't say what she means.* She considers all the letters that she writes to Louise, when Caris hasn't written one thing down on paper. *I've got words*, thinks Stella, *and she hasn't, and girls like Layla know she hasn't.*

Stella carries this heavy thought all the way home, lugging it into her bedroom with her bags of books, placing it carefully in the drawer of her desk.

mac goes shopping

Mac has a plan. He drives into the town centre, parking by the
football ground. Black-and-white-shirted fans with bare goose-
pimpled arms gather in loose crowds for the afternoon match,
drifting into the middle of streets, holding cans of lager, hands in
pockets. He walks past the Dragon House Chinese restaurant where
he proposed to Louise over dim sum. He'd just started driving
taxis, and was thinking about starting a business, farming snails
for the French market with his brother from Ashington. He'd told
Louise this and she'd thought it was funny. She'd got a bit tiddly
and kept on saying, 'A snail farmer!' in a loud voice. There were
no daughters then. Nothing was fixed. Newcastle was full of derelict
buildings and there were long queues in the unemployment offices.
There was no new bridge, no mobile phones, and nobody had a
computer. Louise was petite and quick. She wore thick black
eyeliner, and her hair hung down to her waist in a dark rope. He
didn't think she'd agree to marry him. He was slimmer then, but
often couldn't think of much to say.

Mac never goes shopping these days. It's just not something he
does. Louise buys birthday and Christmas presents, even for
herself. He walks down Gallowgate, hunched in his jacket, feeling
anxious, and past Eldon Square, a dull green surrounded by a
modern shopping centre, where flocks of middle-class Goths hang
out, their faces over-painted, their clothes dingy. *You wouldn't
catch Caris here*, he thinks.

He stops outside a mobile-phone shop and examines the gadgets in the window. None of it makes any sense to him. Louise bought him his mobile the Christmas before. Now it looks ancient. He doesn't see why some phones cost hundreds of pounds, and some are only nine ninety-nine. A young man with a plucked moustache hovers at the doorway looking helpful and Mac drifts into the bright shop with phones displayed behind glass. The young man treats him courteously, as if he has been trained to be interested. Mac asks him questions, knowing that he sounds out of date and illiterate. He distrusts salesmen. He feels too big for the shop, too old, and the phones the young man displays before him on the counter are tiny, like toys.

He ends up buying two in a lavish gesture, one for Caris, one for Stella, with used notes pulled from his back pocket, notes that look dirty in this dustless place. 'For my daughters,' he says, as the salesman counts out the notes. 'At least I'll know where they are.'

The salesman makes a sympathetic noise as he places the phones in boxes and then carrier bags.

'A lot of parents say that,' he confides. 'Soon they'll be inserting microchips into their children, have a map stuck up in their houses with a light bleeping. It's all possible.'

Mac laughs, but it doesn't seem at all funny. *What's happening?* he thinks.

He feels guilty that he hasn't bought Caris a phone before. He sees all the other schoolchildren talking into them on the way to school. *Now,* he thinks, *we will all be wired up. We'll link up in cyberspace,* he thinks, liking the phrase.

Outside, the football crowds are thickening, their rough voices filling the street with anarchic growls and yelps.

'Are you going to watch the match, sir?' asks the shop assistant as he hands him the bags, and suddenly that's all Mac wants to do. He practically runs from the shop, and zig-zags through streets to a backstreet where there is a pub with a huge screen. He relaxes into a scrum of men, all holding pints, staring upwards at a bright-green square at one end of the pub.

I'll go home after the match, thinks Mac, leaning against a fruit machine. *I'll go home and give Caris and Stella their mobiles, and I'll get us all an Indian, and tell Nana Price to go home.*

park management

Spring is everywhere now. Green shoots force their way through
dead leaves. Cats sharpen their claws and hold night conferences
on the killing of baby birds. Impatient daffodils burst out in clumps
through the wet grass. Council gardeners are working overtime
to tidy the place up, hoping to win a place in the Cities in Bloom
competition.

There is a new strategy for dealing with dog dirt and vandalism.
Bins are being nailed at regular intervals along the woodland paths
behind the ornamental gardens to encourage dog owners to be
responsible. There are notices everywhere warning of fines and
surveillance cameras are being erected throughout the long park.

Two workmen, Maurice and Ned, have been told to take ladders
down to the clearing where, it has been noted, someone has been
hanging shoes in a tree without permission. Maurice, who is a bit
of an artist himself, is grumbling to Ned.

'They wouldn't take it down if someone from fucking London
had done it,' he says waspishly.

Ned doesn't answer. He likes his job, although he prefers planting
shrubs and bright borders to climbing trees.

'What's wrong with it?' demands Maurice, as they lumber
through the park, each at the end of a long metal ladder. 'I like it.
Do you like it, Ned?'

Ned hasn't thought about it much.

'They should have got permission,' he barks.

'It's organic,' says Maurice. 'It comes from the people.'

'The people are pigs,' grunts Ned, who prefers plants to human beings.

'I don't want to do it.'

'You've got to do it,' says Ned, 'or someone else will.'

They arrive at the tree. Crocuses are growing beneath it. It stands there, its branches relaxed and contented, carrying its harvest of shoes.

Maurice looks at it. 'It's brilliant,' he says.

Ned places the ladder against the tree trunk. He notices a couple of empty lager cans, and pile of blackened twigs and ashes at the base of the tree. *Fires aren't allowed, either*, he thinks. He climbs up, with Maurice holding the ladder steady at the bottom.

'Someone's put a lot of work into this,' shouts Maurice. 'They're going to be disappointed.'

But there is no stopping Ned. Like a fruit picker he pulls the shoes from the branches, letting them fall to the ground with a thud, and Maurice picks them up one by one: metallic-green strappy platforms, kitten heels, suede lace-ups, slingbacks, sensible sandals, walking boots, a pair of red Wellingtons, some denim mules, gnarled old-lady shoes, men's brogues, some silver evening shoes, red patent-leather slippers, a pair of black high-heeled boots, tennis shoes, espadrilles, grubby trainers. It takes them all morning to load the shoes into a wheelbarrow and take them to the dump, leaving the tree stripped of everything but a few misshapen buds.

the doctor's house

George is late. Caris has waited outside the house for nearly half an hour. She pretends she isn't bothered. She's watching two chaffinches flying back and forth from a nest with pieces of grass in their beaks.

George's shoulders are hunched and he looks bad-tempered. He sits on a wall next to Caris in silence, until she says, 'What took you so long?' and then he doesn't answer.

The street is deserted. *It's as if everyone's asleep*, thinks Caris, watching George light a cigarette.

'That house, there,' she says.

The two of them survey the house that lounges in between trees. It seems nervous, its mullion windows glinting with fear.

'Has it got an alarm?' mutters George.

Caris hasn't seen one.

George hasn't even kissed her.

'Have you looked in the rubbish bin?' asks George. Caris shakes her head.

He jumps down from the wall and creeps into the driveway, beckoning to Caris as if she's a pet. She feels annoyed, then, and moves slowly, not wanting to show her anxiety.

'Wait for me,' she says, and George puts his finger to his lips.

She follows him, her shoes sinking into the gravel driveway, her hands in her pockets, through a wooden gate at the side of the house, with a sign on it that says 'BEWARE OF THE DOG'. There is a short path next to the house that opens into a roomy back garden with wooden furniture carefully covered with tarpaulins on a well-kept lawn. The garden is hidden from the neighbours, with high trellises either side. There's a pond, carefully landscaped in the middle of the lawn. George prowls around the back of the house, pressing his face to the windows and pushing at doors. Caris gazes at the garden, wondering what sort of people live there, imagining a family, sitting on the patio, calling out to each other across the grass; a father with a lawn mower, or garden shears, a mother drinking tea, flicking through a magazine. There might be a dog, too, a great shaggy Labrador that lies panting on the grass, and some kids, kicking a ball about. She starts to feel angry and turns to the house, trying a door handle, even though George has already found it locked. Inside there is a sun lounge with lazy wicker chairs and dangling spider plants.

Then she hears the sound of smashing glass and she stiffens, waiting for the scream of a burglar alarm, but there's nothing, just the flap of crows in the trees. Then George is in the sun room, smiling, unbolting the back door and letting her in. He stands aside, as if it's his house, and he's the host, ushering her into a castle.

Caris is struck by the soft, lonely atmosphere of the family's absence. The place smells of dry dishcloths and furniture polish. She follows George into the innards of the house, into a carpeted sitting room lined with books, like a picture in a magazine. George is searching drawers and cupboards, leaving them hanging open. Caris has an urge to close them, to preserve the order of the house. She studies the book titles on the shelves; medicine mostly, and classic novels like *Oliver Twist*.

A doctor, then, she thinks, *a doctor and his wife*. On a shining grand piano in the corner of the room there are gilt-edged photographs of goofy schoolchildren of various ages. She traces the lives of two children, a boy and a girl, from baby photographs to shining, white-toothed university graduates.

The mother and father are distracted yet concerned, like doctors often look, with faraway looks in their eyes. They stare back at

Caris with chins cupped in palms, or with hair blown about on some country holiday, dark glasses in their hands, wearing stripy sweaters and sheepskin jackets.

George calls her from another room, and Caris kicks off her shoes and finds him in a kitchen, taking Tupperware boxes from a freezer. She has never seen such a big kitchen, with a heavy oak table, and a shining oven.

'What are you doing?' she whispers.

George laughs loudly. 'Let's have lunch!' he shouts, unafraid now.

'What?'

George looks at the label on the box in his hands and reads the words 'Boeuf Bourgignon'.

'What the hell is that?'

'Stew,' says George. 'Beef stew.'

Caris is suddenly happy. She's hungry, too. George is pleased. He likes it when he makes her light up. It's an odd feeling, like a spring bubbling up in a desert. She hasn't laughed much lately.

'I love you, Caris,' he says, recalling his mother's desperate face when he said the same thing.

Caris giggles. She grabs the cold plastic box from him and shoves it into a microwave. Soon the kitchen is filled with the smells of cooking meat, and Caris has pulled a starched white tablecloth from a pine dresser and let it fall on to the polished table. She grabs silver forks and knives, and crystal glasses. She gets a candlestick from another room and places it in the centre of the table. George finds a cupboard full of wine, neatly stored and labelled.

'Nice here,' says George, twisting a corkscrew. 'I could live here with you.'

Caris spoons the rich brown stew on to the best plates and places them on the table. She lights the candles, and draws the curtains, and tells George to sit at one end, while she sits at the other. They raise glasses, toasting each other.

'Let's take our clothes off!' yells Caris.

'Here?'

'Go on, take everything off!' she giggles, peeling off her top.

Soon all their clothes are scattered around the floor, and they are sitting at the table naked, spooning brown gravy into their mouths, splashing drops on to the white tablecloth.

These people, who live here, they must always feel like this, she thinks; *full of gravy.*

'Where are they, do you think?' asks Caris.

George shrugs. He looks at Caris's breasts, which are more beautiful than anything in this expensive house. Her cheeks are flushed from the wine.

'Put on some music!' says Caris. George nods, pulling compact discs from a shelf, so that they fall in a clattering heap on the floor. He puts on some Bach. Caris groans, but then she changes her mind. The music makes her feel glorious, assertive, and euphoric. She gets up and starts to dance, stamping her feet on the maple floor, and George leans back in his chair watching her, clapping.

Then Caris runs out of the room and up the stairs, darting from room to room, turning on taps in the bathroom, patting her bare shoulders with a powder puff, jumping on beds.

In the front bedroom there's a vast bed piled high with cushions. Caris hurls herself on to it, face down, smelling money. When she lifts her face up, George stands at the door grinning, and she chucks cushions at him. George fends them off with his elbows and opens a wardrobe, pulling out clothes, swathed in clear plastic. Caris pulls on an evening gown that is far too big for her. She looks like a child dressing up in her mother's clothes. George puts on a man's silk shirt, and a velvet skirt. They howl and giggle, tearing the clothes as they stumble about on the bed.

Then George pulls Caris towards him, and, wrestling, they fall down together on to the bed. She wriggles and snorts as George kisses her with his hard lips. She feels his body beneath the silk shirt, and wraps her young legs round his back, letting his hair fall over her skin. She imagines that George is a prince. She pictures him as she first saw him, standing beneath the tree, looking up at her with blue eyes, and she desires him again.

Later they lie in a weak pool of sunlight just before dark, while a grandfather clock strikes four o'clock downstairs.

'I'm happy,' says George. 'Do you know that? You make me happy.'

'Me too,' says Caris.

'I never felt like this before,' says George.

'Poor George,' says Caris.

after the match

Newcastle lost. Mac is filled with fury and disappointment. He is surrounded by unsatisfied men; men with faces like jam, eyes red from beer and emotion, men with mouths full of spit.

Outside the bar the light is fading and Saturday shoppers plod around the square with carrier bags and unbuttoned coats. Mac thinks about Degna, of the clean smell of her that contrasts so completely with this brown and grey afternoon, and the bar with its soggy beer mats and dark, swirling carpet.

What am I doing here? thinks Mac. He gets up to leave as a group of men lurch into the centre of the room watching a replay of Newcastle's only goal.

Mac walks back through the messy afternoon of buskers crooning down precincts, starlings huddling together on the ledges, children breaking loose from family groups with mothers calling after them, the rubbish swirling down the street, groups of teenagers hanging about in identical clothing. He finds his car, with leaflets behind the windscreen wipers advertising 'WEIGHT-LOSS NOW'. Remnants of the lost game are everywhere, in abandoned chip papers and heartbroken supporters swaying vacantly outside the doorways of bars.

I must go home, thinks Mac. *I must go home.*

In the car he starts the engine urgently, pushing the nose of the car through the crowds of pedestrians.

When he drives down his street it looks sleepy and secure after the frantic atmosphere of town. A boy happily hits a tree with a stick, while a loose dog sits on the pavement with its tongue hanging out. Mac picks up some rubbish from the front garden, peering through the window into the sitting room, and noticing that Nana Price isn't there. He feels relieved.

Then he's standing at the bottom of the stairs calling the names of his two daughters.

His voice echoes through the empty rooms. He climbs the stairs.

The door to Caris's room is wide open. The floor is covered with clothes, and broken beads, and pots of make-up with no lids. Mac pulls out an over-filled drawer and sees a mess of torn denim, rumpled scarves and skinny skirts. In the corner of the room there's a framed photograph of Louise lying tangled in a muddle of fairy-lights and tinsel. On the floor he finds a necklace that he gave Louise. He turns and runs his hands over the dressing-table, taking the tops off boxes and jars, glancing inside for something, a clue of the woman that Caris is becoming. He reaches under the bed, where old soft toys hang their heads. He finds empty cider bottles there, too, and a full ashtray. He rummages in the pockets of jackets and coats, pulling out half-eaten bars of chocolate, a letter from the school saying that if Caris doesn't hand in her art coursework she will not be entered for her art GCSE, and then, at last, a photograph of Caris with a boy. Mac smoothes it out and peers at the two faces. The boy has a pierced nose. He looks young and arrogant. Caris's expression is out of focus, and preoccupied. Mac doesn't like the way he holds Caris's neck, as if he owns her, as if she's not important. Mac stuffs the photograph into his wallet. He knows who he's looking for now.

falling

Caris is drunk on expensive wine. Her limbs feel like rivers. She's staggering behind George as they move through the Vale, carrying a bag full of doctor's shoes. It's getting dark now, and George is just a black shape ahead of her, slinking between trees. The path confuses her, and she keeps bumping into branches, falling, and stinging her hands on nettles.

Her memory of home is like something seen down a long telescope; a minute circle of light where fictional figures watch *Emmerdale* on television. She wants to reach them, but can't.

By the time she reaches the tree George is already in its branches, but something is wrong. The tree is undressed, empty. Someone has taken all the shoes away. Caris stands beneath him, holding the bag, blinking up at him.

George calls down, 'The bastards!'

'What's happened?' Caris cries. 'Where have all the shoes gone?' She starts to climb up towards George. The sky above her is heavy and oppressive, and her fingers slip as she tries to grab familiar hand and footholds. The carrier bag pulls at her wrist and some of the shoes fall out on to the ground. At last she reaches the sitting place, where George already crouches, his long legs dangling, a bottle of wine in his hand.

'Give us that bag,' says George.

Caris thinks she might be sick.

'What's the point of it?' she asks George. 'Someone will take them down.'

She lets the bag slide from her sore fingers and watches it tumble to the ground, its contents spilling out, so that the earth around them is littered with shoes, like rotting fruit.

She thinks of Mr Fortoba, his little eyes watching her as she walks into the classroom. She imagines telling him about the tree, and wonders what he would say. Then she thinks about the ground, and all its hard surfaces, its earthiness, and the roots of the tree reaching down into the deep earth. Vaguely, she wonders if the shoes lying beneath them will take root and grow into saplings with midget shoes blossoming from their branches. She turns to speak to George, but his expression is cloudy. He rolls a cigarette.

'I mean, what are we doing this for?' she mumbles eventually.

'Because we're special,' says George without looking at her. 'Because we do things that no one else does.'

'But it's all spoilt,' she says.

'We'll start again,' mutters George.

'My mum,' she slurs. 'My mum's in prison.'

'You're all right,' says George. 'You're doing fine. You don't need her.'

'I want to see her,' says Caris. 'I haven't seen her for ages.'

'I'm sick of the sight of my mother,' says George, spitting.

Caris thinks she might cry. She pictures Louise handing her a piece of toast with jam spread over it, saying, 'Eat up, love,' and then she thinks of the last time she was sick, and Louise bending over her, both of them staring down into a toilet bowl, and the feeling of her hand on her back.

Caris leans forward, to put her face into her hands. She hears George shout, and then she's falling, down and down, and there's nothing to stop her. Like falling down an endless well.

waiting for caris

Stella looks down at her father snoring on the settee. His jaw sags, and the skin on his face is creased against the cushion. She holds a copy of a video of *Pride and Prejudice* in her hands. She's been round at Elli's house watching it. Elli's mother, a woman with cushion breasts and thick cardigans, made macaroni cheese and brought it through on a tray. Then they had fruit salad and custard, and talked about Mr Darcy.

Now Stella isn't sure if she should wake Mac or not. She looks at the broad tundra of his body, his arm hanging over the arm of the settee. She turns and closes the curtains, switches on the fire. She looks around her helplessly. Her current life bears no resemblance to the world she aspires to.

'Dad,' she says. 'Dad, it's me.'

Mac hears her voice through the undergrowth of a dream. In it he's rowing a boat down a narrow canal with high brick walls either side, and his passenger is Louise, but then it's Degna, and in the distance there is the sound of roaring water that he knows will drown them all.

Stella's voice comes from high above the canal, like a rescuer. He starts awake and blinks at his daughter as if he isn't quite sure who she is.

'It's me, Stella,' she says. 'I didn't think you'd be home.'

'Stella,' says Mac, sitting up and rubbing his eyes. 'You all right, pet? Where's Caris?'

Stella shrugs. She wishes people would stop asking her about Caris. She hasn't had a discussion with Caris for days. 'How should I know?' she answers, sulkily.

'I've bought you a present,' says Mac in a groggy voice, reaching into a carrier bag on the floor. He hands her one of the mobile phones. Stella is pleased. She gently takes the phone from its box and holds it to her ear as if it's a new friend.

'Thanks, Dad,' she says.

'I was going to clear up,' says Mac, trying to sound authoritative. 'Let's get this place straight.'

Stella eagerly helps him to wash up a sinkful of abandoned cups and saucers, marked with Nana's lipstick.

Mac goes round to Abdul's corner shop to buy cheese, tea, bread and milk. The shop is always open, a beacon on the corner of a busy street with cars accelerating past all night. The shelves are piled high with tins and biscuits, toilet rolls and washing powders, some well past their sell-by date, some strangely labelled, as if they have arrived on a ship late at night from a foreign land. Abdul keeps an eye on the neighbourhood. He has noted how Stella buys Polo mints each morning, and an unusual amount of bleach for a girl of her age. He sees how her skin is tight around her mouth and eyes. He knows about the mother, Louise. He read about it in the paper and the matter has been discussed at length in the shop. *The father looks weak*, thinks Abdul, watching Mac with half an eye as he patiently stands in a queue behind some toothy teenage girls carrying a bottle of pop. *It's the red-headed daughter he needs to watch out for*, thinks Abdul. *She's going right off the tracks, that one, with her boyfriend with the credit card, always buying wine and cigarettes. He's leading her up the garden path.* Abdul loves these English phrases. He sees the girl following the evil prince up the rose-lined path, not knowing that at the end of the garden there is barbed wire and thistles. Abdul is watching a romantic Indian film. He doesn't take his eyes off the small screen beneath the counter as he serves Mac, and the whole transaction is accompanied by a shrill Indian love song.

'Your Caris is smoking,' he murmurs as Mac puts sliced bread into a thin blue carrier bag. Mac turns crimson. He glances around him, glimpsing himself on the security camera. Abdul hands him three bronze pound coins.

'Oh,' says Mac. 'Have you seen her tonight?'

Abdul shakes his head sadly.

'I'm just telling you so you know,' mutters Abdul, distracted by a flurry of saris on the film. 'That lad she hangs round with buys the fags, so I can't refuse. But I've seen her smoking them.'

'Do you know who he is?' says Mac, guiltily imagining Caris, seen through Abdul's eyes, as a neglected child.

'The one with the blue eyes, lives over the Vale,' says Abdul. 'He's called George. Hang on.' Abdul opens the till and looks through the credit-card receipts. 'George Farrish.'

Abdul shows him the name. Mac copies it out on the corner of a white paper bag.

'Thanks, Abdul,' he says, but Abdul is drawn back to the plaintive voices on the television. Mac says the name 'Farrish' to himself. It's familiar, but he can't think where from. He hears so many names every day. *It must be a fare*, he thinks.

Back home Stella is washing the windows. The house stands to attention, as if woken from a long sleep. Mac cleans the kitchen, wiping down the ring-marked surfaces, squirting Vim into the sink, his sleeves rolled up.

Stella comes into the kitchen, and Mac feels her black wet eyes on his back.

'I don't know what to do about Caris, Stel,' he says, drying his hands. 'What shall I do?'

'You've got to stop working so much. Go up the school again,' says Stella. 'See Mr Fortoba. He's always asking about her.'

'Yeah,' says Mac. 'Yeah, I will.'

'No one does anything,' says Stella. 'It's like no one cares.'

'I'm sorry, love,' says Mac, and turns and puts his arms round Stella, who begins to sob into her father's broad shoulder.

'I'm sick of her too,' says Stella. 'She's just a pain in the arse.'

'Come on, love,' mutters Mac. 'Let's get your phone working.'

So they sit down together with the phone and the instructions, playing with ringing tones and smiley faces. The room is warm and clean, and Stella wishes that it could always be like this; her and her father, alone, and safe.

They make cheese on toast, and watch other families crumbling on soaps. During the adverts Stella tells Mac about her life. She shows him her art project, with its neat examples of textile patterns in the last century. She tells him about the poem that she read aloud in assembly, and the A-star she got for her history essay on the Russian Revolution. Mac tells her how proud he is, and feels relieved. *We must have done something right*, he thinks, as he admires Stella's careful handwriting, *to have produced this shining girl. Maybe*, he thinks, *Caris is just bad. A bad apple.*

But as the evening goes on Caris's absence creeps in like a tide. Mac is restless. He stands at the window, looking out at the empty street, willing his daughter to come home, wanting to make things right with her, and Stella knows she is losing him again.

At Stella's suggestion he phones Margaret's house to hear the superior tones of Margaret's mother saying that Caris hasn't been round there for some time now. In fact, she thinks that Caris and Margaret have fallen out. 'Margaret spends most of her time with a girl called Layla,' says the mother. 'I'm not very happy about it,' she goes on, even though Mac is trying to get off the phone. 'I think Margaret is being led astray.' Her voice becomes bleating and Mac practically hangs up on her.

At nine o'clock, Mac phones the police, but the policeman he speaks to answers in measured tones and tells Mac that his officers will keep their eyes open, but it's still early, and she's probably just out with friends. Mac's hand leaves a sweaty print on the telephone receiver.

At ten o'clock, Mac stands at the front door, waiting for the sound of footsteps, fingering the folded white paper bag in his pocket with George's name printed on it, willing Caris to appear, while Stella goes up to her room, and writes in a diary about how much she hates her sister, and wishes that she had never been born.

bingo

Nana Price is at bingo with her friend Mona. They sit smoking in a long ochre room that was once a theatre, but now the stage is a flashing screen of numbers fronted by a lectern. The atmosphere is hostile, as groups of women with crumbling teeth and dappled eyes listen with wooden, desperate faces to the numbers being called. The caller is a man with only one arm, who announces each number in a sing-song voice. Stewards in blue and white suits wander up and down between the fixed plastic tables. Nana Price is reminded of the prison visiting room.

Lately she has found that the numbers seem to come from a long way off, and she has to work harder to keep up. Also, she is tired of losing, and of the strangled yelps of winners who jump to their feet when she has hardly started filling in her card. Mona has won ten pounds and Nana Price feels jealous. Mona's family are more considerate than hers have ever been. They take her out for tea in the country, and bring her breakfast in bed in the mornings. And Nana is older than Mona, although, in her opinion, better preserved.

By the time they get to the national-link game, with a twenty-thousand-pound prize, Nana is in quite a temper. She taps her hard nails on the tabletop, her legs ache, her feet feel like unwatered roots. She stubs out her cigarette and wonders why she hasn't died of lung cancer yet. Around her, everyone in the room looks as if they are dying, with yellow, nicotine-stained hair and sallow skin. There is a background wheeze of bronchitis and asthma.

Nana's valiant cells charge round her body like flanks of miners' wives. Her tinny heart beats under her vest like a marble rattling in a box. She ticks off the numbers in a trembling rhythm, trying to make herself believe that winning is still possible.

But when a player in Scunthorpe wins the twenty-thousand-pound jackpot Nana gathers her handbag in her twig fingers and announces that she can't be bothered to carry on. Mona looks at her with heavy-lidded eyes, and says she hasn't finished playing yet.

'I'll go home by meself,' says Nana, knowing that Mona will take the huff, and not caring. 'I don't feel well. I've got haemorrhoids.'

'Please yourself,' says Mona in a nasal voice.

So Nana walks along the inky streets to her bus stop, thinking about the home she hasn't got. Mac, Caris and Stella don't seem to appreciate her attempts to help. They are usually out, and she is forced to cook for herself, and to deal with teachers coming round. Somewhere in Nana's silvery, sinewed body is a fear that sometimes surfaces as a twitching eyelid, or palpitations which she quickly dispatches with a sweet sherry, but tonight, as she steps on to the lonely bus and sits at the back with only an acned boy with a Walkman and a lardy girl with hamster cheeks for company, she feels afraid. She thinks about Caris, as the bus heaves itself along city streets. *Caris is going to the dogs*, thinks Nana. *What she needs is a good hiding.* All of her feelings of resentment land on Mac, with his irritating silence. *He neglects his kids. If he was a woman they would get social services in. He doesn't listen to a word I say,* she fumes.

Two Chinese people get on the bus, and proceed to talk fast and furiously. Nana can't think. Their words sound like high-pitched squeaks.

'Will you just shut up!' she shouts abruptly, and they turn and look at her with shocked faces.

'Speak friggin' English!' barks Nana, as they resume their conversation, but in whispers.

Nowhere is home any more, thinks Nana. *No one wants me.*

broken

A beetle nestles in Caris's hair, as she lies under the tree. Her body lies on the damp earth, supported by the roots of the oak. A predatory cat sniffs her hand then jerks away, afraid of her breathing. She's lying in an underworld, caught in the shadowy arms of the Vale, her arms stretched out, her white face still, her lips blue. 'That's the end of her,' mutters George, who looks down at her from above. He stares at her moonlit skin, her not-there-ness. He feels nothing. *It's not my fucking fault*, he thinks.

Eventually, he clambers down from the tree and puts his hand to her head. There's a splash of blood on her forehead. George thinks she's dead; broken, like so many things he has had and lost. *It's not fair*, he thinks. *I didn't even push her, but I'll probably get blamed*. He doesn't scream or shout. He knows he should panic, but he never does. He remembers looking down at Wilson, as he lay on the ground beneath the window, and feeling just like this, numb, almost peaceful.

He reaches for Caris's arm and lifts it, then lets it fall. Above him leaves rustle in the branches of the oak tree. George sighs, as if he is facing an insurmountable task. He lifts Caris up, into his arms, her head lolling back, her long hair nearly touching the ground, and carries her along the uneven path, breathing heavily. They get to the park gate and the back road that curves through the Vale. Opposite there's a pub, the Snowdrop Inn, snuggled into the bottom of a hill. It's a local place, where a few men sit staring into pint

198

glasses trying to see their futures. It's the kind of pub that should be done up with pine tables, and serve tapas, but which isn't and doesn't.

Tonight, Maurice, the council workman, is talking to no one in particular about the Tree of Shoes. He tells the people in the bar that it's a work of art, and that it shows how the community longs for ritual now that religion is dead. Maurice has got himself so worked up about the tree that he'll have an argument with his supervisor the following day and leave his job. He'll end up working on an irrigation project in Mexico, and falling in love with a woman called Selina, but he doesn't know this yet.

Outside, George carries Caris to the door and lays her down on a bench outside. He tidies up her limbs, so that she looks like a corpse. As he does this he feels rather saintly, as if he's done the right thing for once. He leans over and kisses her cold lips, takes one last look at her and then evaporates into the darkness, away down the muddy paths that skirt the river, back to where his mother sits drinking gin on the pink sofa, talking about George to her dull-eyed husband who blames her for everything.

And so Caris lies, only five minutes away from where Mac and Stella sit side by side on the settee looking at Stella's art, until Maurice emerges from the public bar to find a young girl lying unconscious on a bench. He runs back into the pub, and wakes up everyone by telling them there's a body there. It's the most exciting thing that's happened in the Snowdrop Inn for some time, and most people stand up, rubbing their eyes, as if they've been woken from a deep sleep, and come to the door to look at Caris, lying there. It isn't long before an ambulance swerves down the steep hill, and, watched by an obese landlady, a drunken darts team with slabby, astonished faces, and the rest of the patrons of the public and lounge bars, Caris is loaded on to a stretcher, and lifted into the green interior of the ambulance.

She dimly senses the wild screeching of a siren, and feels the close scratching of a waterproof coat near her face, and then sinks again into unconsciousness.

louise wakes up

Carol snores in the bunk above Louise, who can't sleep. The moon is full, and its light casts a shadow across the confined space. Louise listens to the endless rattling of the prison which is always full of sighs, footsteps and bad dreams, and longs to hold Caris and to comb her red hair, to tease out the tangles, and for Caris to be a girl again who climbs on to her knee and plays with the rings on Louise's fingers, and chatters about nothing in particular.

She aches for both her daughters, but she knows that she and Caris are similar, both desiring something they don't even have words for. They would read stories together, of princesses and castles, and delight in the details, the fine leather gloves, the four-poster bed made of goose feathers, the chests full of golden coins. Caris was a child who loved to dress up in high-heeled shoes and long dresses; a child who lived as much in her imagination as in the world, and Louise had encouraged her, admired her, been proud of her beautiful daughter.

Louise had always had a sensation of waiting for someone to take her away. She had liked Mac in his car with the comfortable seats. For years she had believed that they would, one day, drive north, south, east or west.

'It's no good,' Louise says out loud in the darkness. 'It's not going to happen.'

She sees herself and Mac, each absorbed in fantasies of escape, and wonders if Mac is really going to leave her. She considers life alone, sitting in a room with no trace of Mac. *It's like losing a piece of furniture I'd got used to*, she thinks sadly. *I don't even know who he is any more.*

Carol grunts in her sleep, turning over and making the mattress springs squeal, and Louise shuts her eyes again and tries to sleep, but keeps seeing her youngest daughter, calling to her, as if she's trapped somewhere.

When I get out of here, Louise tells herself, *I'm going to make things happen. I won't go to that dream world. It doesn't do any good. There are no such things as free wishes.*

parents

Mac can't bear it any more. He looks up 'Farrish' in the phone book, and there it is, an address. He knows the street. He's taken fares there, a famous footballer, and a television presenter. He drives impatiently. It only takes about five minutes, but even the air is different on the other side of the Vale. It's a foreign country. He feels like a taxi driver picking up a fare, but this time he isn't. He's a father searching for his daughter, angry and upset.

As he drives there he says the name Farrish over and over again, trying to think how he knows it. It's only when he arrives at the house that he remembers it as the place where Louise once worked and how she had come back one day and said she wasn't going there again. She'd said they were mean, rude people. For a second Mac sees Louise's face, looking hurt and confused. He wishes that he'd asked her more about it at the time. He'd been lying on his back, reciting the names of lettuces. Louise had told him she hated cleaning, that it was demeaning.

Now Mac walks into the neat driveway. There are lights on in the house. It reminds him of a doll's house he once saw in a museum, with miniature people propped up in various rooms; the cook in the kitchen, the master in the study, the lady in her powder room. He can see a man in a brown suit standing by an ornamental mantelpiece, talking down to someone sitting on a chair. He stands at the front door, ringing an old-fashioned bell which makes a slow clanging sound that seems to echo throughout the bowels of the grand house. No one answers for ages, but finally the door opens and a girl with protruding eyes and worried hands wearing a green housecoat peers out at him.

'Is George Farrish there?' he asks.

'George. I don't know. What is it, please?'

'I want to speak to him, or his parents.'

'Shall I get Mr Farrish?'

'Yes.'

She doesn't invite him in. He stands there like a delivery boy. Mac can hear voices clashing against each other in a room off the hallway. There's a man's gravel tones, speaking in short sentences, and a woman, her sentences trickling like rivers around the man's terse words. Then Mr Farrish appears. He looks suspicious, and peers at Mac with a wrinkled nose. Mac strokes his cut, shaved head.

'Can I help you?' says the man.

'I'm looking for Caris.'

'Caris?'

'She's been hanging around with your George.'

'George?'

'Your son.'

'Marina, is George here?' calls the man, and a woman with permed, silvery hair and a powdered nose appears.

'Who's there?' she says, frowning at Mac as if he's a stray that has wandered into the garden.

'Where is George?' repeats the man slowly, as if Marina is stupid and can't hear him.

'George?' she repeats.

Mac is feeling irritated.

'My daughter is missing,' he blurts.

'I see. We'll see if he's upstairs. Helena, could you please go and call George.'

The girl scampers up the staircase.

'Come in,' says the man at last, standing back from the door.

203

His eyes are like two little black pins, thinks Mac. The woman fiddles with a loose bracelet on her skinny wrist.

'We haven't really met your daughter,' she says. 'The teenagers go upstairs.' She shrugs helplessly. 'George is going through a bit of a phase like that. You know.' She giggles suddenly, putting her hand to her mouth. Mac feels affronted. *Caris could be in danger*, he thinks, *and all she can do is laugh*. The thought seems to pass from him to the mother, who abruptly stops laughing and presses her lips back into a straight line.

'Come through,' says the man officiously, as if he is used to dealing with unsavoury situations. Mac follows him into a lavender-coloured room with two rearing china horses on the mantelpiece. There is a family photograph above the fireplace with a young George between the two of them. They both have a hand on his shoulders, and George has a head of golden curls and a winning, lopsided smile.

The woman goes and pours herself a drink, staggering slightly.

'Can I get you something?' she asks, holding a decanter.

Mac shakes his head. He is afraid he might mark the furniture if he sits down, so he stands awkwardly by the fire, his hands in the pockets of his leather jacket. He pictures Louise dusting their mantelpiece, wiping the china horses' hooves. He wonders if they remember her at all. Then he thinks that Degna would know how to behave in this room. She would slip off her coat and sit down on the long leather sofa and lean back against the cushions.

There is a long silence, broken only by the sounds of ice chinking against glass, of a piece of coal crackling in the grate.

'What do you do?' asks the woman eventually.

'I'm a taxi driver,' says Mac.

'Ah,' says Mr Farrish, 'how useful.'

George appears at the door. Mac looks up, relieved. He sees a boy with unwashed blond hair and blue eyes, who looks as uncomfortable and inappropriate to the room as Mac does himself. He hasn't got any shoes on and his feet are dirty. George slides on to the sofa and sits cross-legged.

'Are you George?' Mac asks.

George smiles politely.

'You must be Caris's father,' he says in a clear, friendly voice.

'Yes. We can't find her.'

'Oh dear,' says George. 'I hope she's all right. I haven't seen her today.'

'Are you sure?' says the mother.

'Yes.'

The parents turn to Mac as if to suggest that there is nothing else to say or do. Mac ignores them and steps towards George.

'I'm worried about her,' he says to George.

'She was fine when I saw her.'

'She doesn't go to school. She stays off with you. Do you go to school?'

'He's between schools,' cuts in the mother.

The father laughs as if someone has just made a joke. Mac suddenly feels that he's in a play, in which everyone has lines that they will inevitably say.

'How well do you know this Caris?' asks the father.

'She's just a friend. We met in the Vale.'

'I don't think you can blame our son for your daughter's truancy. Really!'

'I'd like him to leave her alone,' says Mac, not caring now.

'I haven't done anything,' says George with wide eyes. 'Honestly. I really like Caris.'

Mrs Farrish sits down and puts her arm around George.

'He hasn't done anything. Anyway, he's going soon, aren't you, George, to work at his uncle's ranch in Arizona.'

'Is he?' says the father.

'Yes, and then he'll forget all about your daughter.'

'No I won't,' says George. 'And I don't want to go to Arizona.'

'We'll talk about this later,' growls the father.

'I don't care where he's going, as long as he stays away from Caris. D'you hear me?' says Mac too loudly. The oppressive peace of the room trembles.

They wish they hadn't let him in.

The father extends his arm towards the door.

'That's fair enough,' he says. 'You can go now, George.'

'Nice to meet you,' says George meekly, and reaches out to shake Mac's hand. Mac ignores the gesture.

The mother flutters to Mac's side and says shakily, 'It's got nothing to do with us, Mr . . .'

Mac is herded to the door by the father, who looks as if he is afraid that Mac might bolt up the stairs, or steal something.

'If we hear anything we will, of course, let you know.'

'Good,' says Mac. He glimpses the young woman who opened the door looking down from the upper banister at the group in the hallway.

'My wife worked here once,' he says casually.

'Really?' Mr Farrish says.

'Louise.'

'Oh, yes,' chimes Mrs Farrish, looking confused. 'Louise.'

There is a pause.

'How is she?' asks Mrs Farrish nervously.

'Very well,' Mac says.

'Goodbye,' says the father briskly, practically pushing Mac out of the front door and closing it firmly. Mac stands there in the dark, listening. He can hear a series of rough barks followed by a torrent of sharp retorts, then the sound of someone running up the broad stairs. Mac turns and gets back into the taxi, feeling even more afraid for his lost daughter.

finding caris

Nana Price arrives home, filled with a sense of injustice and loss. She has decided to pack up and go back to her bungalow, seeing as no one wants her. But when she opens the front door she smells worry. Nana Price peers round the living-room door to see her son-in-law staring fiercely at a blank television screen.

Mac jumps to his feet with an expression of joy, and then realises that it's only Nana in her raincoat, shaking an umbrella. His face fills with disappointment and he drops down again, without speaking.

'So you're in, then!' she snaps, righteously.

Mac doesn't speak.

'What's going on?' asks Nana, crossly, in a coarse metal voice that she usually saves for complaints. Stella comes into the room and slumps into a chair.

'We can't find Caris,' she says.

'What's new?' snorts Nana. 'Since when?'

'No one's seen her since this morning.'

'Eeeh,' moans Nana. 'That girl!'

'I'm going to phone the hospital!' announces Mac.

'The hospital?' echoes Nana. 'Surely not.'

'It's worth a try, isn't it?'

Mac stands in the hall, spelling out Caris's name. Nana shivers and doesn't take off her coat. She looks over at Stella and sees that she's crying, not even wiping the tears from her cheeks.

'Oh, pet lamb!' growls Nana, relenting, and she stumbles over to Stella, wrapping her in a smelly embrace that Stella stiffens against, pushing her grandmother back.

'Everything's shit!' gulps Stella. 'It's all terrible.'

'It will be all right, love,' soothes Nana, her old voice trembling like the string of a double bass. 'She'll turn up.'

'What then?' moans Stella. 'What then?'

Mac runs into the room. His eyes are wide and fearful.

'She's in the RVI!' he stammers. 'She's bloody unconscious.'

All the anger in the room drains away, leaving only a raw mess of love as the family run for the door, and the three of them leap into the taxi, hurtling down the terraced streets towards the hospital.

'What happened? What did they say?' says Stella.

'She's hurt, somehow, they don't know how. They found her lying outside the Snowdrop.'

'What, drunk?' queries Nana.

'I don't know. She was just lying there. She'd hurt her head.'

Mac parks badly on double yellow lines and together they run through ornate Victorian doors, and down endless polished linoleum corridors, past porters who push trolleys on soundless wheels, glimpsing other darkened wards. Mac wants to shout out Caris's name.

When they reach the ward it's quiet and dimly lit. The three of them gallop up to a spectacled nurse in a maroon uniform like hungry horses.

'Where is she?' pants Mac. 'My daughter.'

The nurse quietens them as if she's a conductor stilling an allegro. She answers in a stage whisper.

'She's all right. Sleeping,' she adds. 'She's got concussion, that's all. They did an X-ray and nothing's broken. They're like rubber, young people.'

'We want to see her,' pipes Nana.

'Please,' adds Stella.

The nurse nods and leads them down the corridor, past the

uneven wheezing shapes of sleeping patients on beds with monotonous staccato drips. She shows them into a windowless room, where Caris lies on a high bed, lit only by the light from the corridor. She lies on her back peacefully, a large plaster stuck incongruously to her head. Her face is calm, her lips red.

Her family surround the bed nervously, afraid to touch her. She's wearing a torn hospital nightgown.

'You're sure she's all right?' mouths Nana loudly to the hovering nurse.

'She's had a fall. She'd been drinking. The doctor will want to see her in the morning.'

The nurse closes her mouth in a disapproving expression. She's sick of young people like Caris taking up beds just because they've drunk too much or taken something.

Stella walks round the bed, looking at her sister's limp hands on the yellow bedcover, at the way her mouth is a perfect shape, her long eyelashes. She looks like a tragedy, like something off the television. Stella begins to feel uncomfortable. The hospital is not as clean as she might have hoped. There's a ball of dust next to the skirting board, and some dead flowers in a vase on the windowsill.

'Can I stay?' asks Mac.

'I suppose so. There's only room for one, though,' says the nurse.

'What about us?' says Stella.

'I'll drive you home, then I'll come back,' says Mac.

To his relief Nana doesn't argue. She pats Caris's limp arm, and meekly follows Mac back to the taxi.

'I'll tell Mum,' says Stella in the stillness of the car, sitting with her back straight, her long hair falling round her thin face.

'Caris is alive,' says Nana. 'That's the main thing, isn't it?'

stella's hands

At home Nana falls asleep on her camp-bed like a child, clutching
a pink hot-water bottle in her bony hands, making small sucking
sounds with her mouth, and Stella is alone, with her father gone.
She feels as if she is on a ship with no sails.

She lies in her bed in the dark, but can't sleep, so she gets up and
goes downstairs. She starts to clean the kitchen. At first she washes
up the mugs and dries them and puts them in the cupboard with
the handles all facing in the same direction. Then she scours the sink
with Vim, and then she boils the dishcloths in a pan, so that the
house smells starchy, like a laundry. She wipes each knife, fork
and spoon in the cutlery drawer, and then she rubs the kitchen
window-pane with vinegar. She fills a bucket with boiling soapy
water and mops the floor, so that steam rises from it. She gets out
the hoover and attacks the front room, pushing the nozzle into
the corners and down the backs of the chairs, but then it seems as
if the air is full of dust and cells and mites, so she hoovers the air,
waving the vacuum around her head. She hoovers the lampshade
and the curtains. She notices that the cushions are grimy, and that
strands of her grandmother's grey-blonde hair are all over the settee,
so she strips off the covers and puts them into the washing machine,
but then realises that she has left footprints on the linoleum, so she
must wipe it again with the boiled dishcloths, and then she must
boil them again. She scrubs around the gas fire with a Brillo pad,
until the green tiles shine, and she takes each ornament and

photograph from the mantelpiece and wipes them all over and replaces them neatly, so that they stand in a line.

Now the washing machine is whirring and making a high-pitched screaming sound. Stella pulls down the curtains in the sitting room, wrenching them from their hooks, and bundles them into the sink, splashing hot water all over them. The more she cleans the more dirty the rooms seems. Stella feels the dust in her hair and in the pores of her skin. She runs to the bathroom. The toothpaste tube is covered with fingerprints, the basin splattered with spit. Stella doesn't know what to do first. She starts to wash her hands, and sees that her hands are raw and that her finger is bleeding a river of thin red down the plughole. Stella sobs. She sits down on the toilet holding a towel around her hands and wails.

Nana hears the sound in her dreams, like a siren calling through a fog. She's confused. She thinks it's a ship coming in, filled with sailors, purring up the Tyne. She sits up, her arms stretched out, like the figurehead of a ship, and sees only the landing carpet. She crawls from her bed, blindly feeling in the darkness for her slippers, and staggers towards the sound. There is a strong smell of burning material, and washing powder. Nana is afraid that they have been robbed. She tiptoes downstairs, one stair at a time, holding on to the banister with both hands. In the sitting room the curtains have been ripped from the rails and everything looks upturned.

Nana calls out for Stella, wandering slowly back upstairs, afraid.

When Nana opens the bathroom door she sees her granddaughter, stick-thin, half-naked, sitting with a bloody towel round her hands. *Oh, Christ, a miscarriage*, she thinks. She puts her wasted arms around the girl, tutting and shushing, and Stella wants to push her away, with her germy hair and dirty hands.

But Stella is exhausted and can't even find the energy to argue. So she sinks her head into her grandmother's neck and cries as if she will never stop, and lets herself be tucked up in her parents' bed, falling asleep at last to the lulling scratchy sound of her Nana singing 'All Things Bright and Beautiful'.

seeing the doctor

Caris sleeps in a place that smells of leaves and mud. She lies in a cushion of ferns and stretches out her arms and legs. She senses light flickering on her face; she opens her eyes expecting to see the sky, but instead there are grey ceiling tiles and a smoke alarm. She calls out for George, but then, hearing the percussion of a tea trolley coming down the corridor, she sits up and looks around her with disbelief. She touches the plaster on her head and pushes back the bedcover to see that her knees are both red and swollen, like overcooked beetroots.

A cow-like nurse charges into the room, shaking her head. Caris stares at her, not able to speak.

'She's awake,' says the nurse to no one in particular. 'I'll get her dad.'

The word 'dad' frightens Caris. She wonders if Mac has been in an accident and is also in hospital, but the nurse has gone again and there's no one to ask.

She tries to remember where she was before and recalls a bag of shoes bumping against her leg, and the sight of George climbing up a tree.

'What's happening?' she moans. 'Where's the tree? The shoes have all gone.'

The nurse reappears and abruptly smiles, as if she has just remembered that smiles have their uses.

'You're in hospital, dear. You had an accident.'

'What accident?' asks Caris.

'You fell over.' The nurse starts to methodically move around Caris's bed, straightening the covers then grasping Caris's wrist and feeling for her pulse, and writing something down on a sheet of paper.

'You haven't broken anything. I expect you need the toilet.'

She sticks a needle into Caris's arm and pulls out a vial's worth of bright-red blood. Caris winces.

'Is my dad here?'

'He's just coming now.'

Caris hears footsteps in the corridor. She wants to hide under the blankets. Mac comes into the room looking ashen and unshaven.

'You're awake,' he says. 'Thank Christ for that.'

'I don't know what's going on,' says Caris, as the nurse noisily changes her water jug.

'They found you outside a pub.'

'What pub?'

'The Snowdrop.'

'What was I doing there?'

'I don't know, love.'

Mac sits down on the bed. Now that Caris is awake, he can't think of anything to say. It's too early for a lecture. He pats her arm.

'When can I go home?' says Caris.

'When you've seen the doctor,' says the nurse. 'You'd better get yourself to the bathroom and have a wash.'

Mac helps Caris disentangle herself from the blankets and tries to hold her arm, but she pushes him away, and, shaking, staggers to the bathroom. Once inside she locks the door and stares at herself in the mirror. Her lips and teeth are stained with red wine, and her hair is matted and gritty. As she wipes her face with a piece of sodden toilet paper she remembers the house they broke into, the photographs on the piano, the tidy lawn, and wonders if anyone knows what she's done. She wants to know where George is, but doesn't dare ask. Then she remembers the tree, and its empty branches, and seeing George looking at her with his white face, saying, 'The bastards'.

Mac is waiting for his daughter. Now she's awake and not dead he feels angry again. He sits on Caris's bed, wondering what to do next. He gets up and glances out of the window to see where his taxi is parked. He longs to be in it, driving away, up the coast road.

Caris creeps back into the room.

'Where's my clothes?' she says.

Mac opens the locker and pulls out a damp top and jeans. He throws them down on the bed, and Caris stares at them.

'Eugh,' she says.

'What have you been up to, Caris?' says Mac.

'I was with a friend.'

'George?'

Caris shrugs.

'I know George,' says Mac.

'No you don't.'

'Yes I do.'

Mac feels superior. He knows something that Caris doesn't.

'I don't want you seeing that George again,' he tells her. 'I've been round. I've told his parents.'

'What are you talking about?' sneers Caris.

'I told you. I've been to his house.'

'What did you do that for?'

The idea of Mac at George's house is so horrible that Caris bursts into tears.

'Why don't you leave me alone?' she sobs. 'I don't want you messing about in my life.'

'You can't look after yourself,' shouts Mac. 'Look at you!'

The nurse trots in and gives them a housewifely look. They both look at the floor. She writes something on Caris's notes then clips out again.

'My head hurts,' says Caris, pulling on her jeans.

'Whose fault is that?' Mac's voice seems to come from a long way off.

214

'Oh, shut up.'

'You can't disappear like that.'

'Why not?' says Caris in a wrung-out way. 'You were going to chuck us out yesterday.'

'I don't know what to do, Caris.'

'Don't do anything, then.'

'Did you fall over?'

'I don't know.'

'Had you been at school?'

'No.'

Caris wishes that Mac would stop talking. She wants to sleep.

'Look at you,' says Mac. 'You look terrible.'

'Can't I leave school?' asks Caris, looking up at Mac.

'Why?'

'I don't like it there. I've never liked it. You don't know what it's like.'

'You liked it before.'

Caris is pulling on her socks now. She thinks about before, about how she once plodded into school every day, and sat and doodled in the margins of exercise books, and gave in homework, and hung around with Margaret at lunchtimes on the edges of the playing field, or sometimes ambled down to the supermarket to buy a sandwich or a milkshake and sucked from bendy straws. It never occurred to her not to go. The future appeared like a Roman road, straight and uncomplicated. She feels as if she has woken from a deep sleep, and that George is the one who has kissed her awake, and that now things are quite different. Everything has a depth that wasn't there before. In this new, resonant world there isn't time for school. It seems immaterial, something that stupid kids do.

'I thought I did, but I don't really.'

'You're not special, Caris,' says Mac. 'You've got to earn a living like anyone else.'

'Why are we alive?' asks Caris.

Mac doesn't know what to say.

'You won't be alive much longer, the way you're carrying on,' he replies helplessly.

215

Caris stands up. *She looks like one of those girls in a documentary about prostitutes*, thinks Mac. There are black rings round her eyes. Her fingers are stained with nicotine. *She was such a pretty girl, she was always washing and putting stuff on her spots*, he thinks.

'I don't care,' says Caris. 'What's the point of being alive if you just have to go to school, and then go to work, and then die. I'd rather die now and get it over with.'

'You've got a family, Caris. You've got people who care about you. That's what you're alive for.'

Caris looks bored. She slumps on to the bed.

The nurse appears, followed by a doctor with notes in his hand and his head cocked to one side. *He looks like a big bird*, thinks Caris. Mac turns to him with desperate eyes. He wants someone to tell him what to do. He needs an expert. The doctor takes in the two of them, the large, embarrassed man, and the thin, angry daughter, and sits delicately on the bed, next to Caris.

'How are you feeling, Caris?' he asks gently.

'How do you know my name?'

'It's on your notes.'

'Just tell him how you feel, Caris,' grunts Mac.

'All right,' says Caris. 'My head aches.'

'Did someone hurt you?' asks the doctor.

'D'you think someone did that to her?' interrupts Mac. 'I'll kill him.'

There is a pause. Mac is embarrassed. It occurs to him that the doctor might think he did it, that Caris comes from a violent home.

'Perhaps you'd like to talk to someone?' asks the doctor, carefully, his beak-like nose pecking the air.

'What for?'

'Well, you've obviously been drinking quite heavily.'

'What would I talk about?'

'I mean some kind of counsellor.'

'What, a psychiatrist?' says Mac, startled.

'No, just someone who might help.'

216

Mac feels suspicious. Isn't this how your kids end up being taken off you?

'I don't want to,' says Caris, and Mac is relieved.

'I think I'll just get her home and sort things out,' says Mac.

'Yeah, I just want to go home,' echoes Caris.

But the doctor isn't letting go yet. 'Let's have a look at you,' he says, and makes Caris lie down on the bed, while he shines a torch into the caves of her eyes.

'Is she concussed, like?' asks Mac nervously.

'You should keep an eye on her,' says the doctor, standing up, flapping his white-coated arms. 'Do you know what happened, Caris?' he says.

'I dunno,' says Caris.

'What's the last thing you remember?'

'Walking along,' lies Caris, 'down the Vale.'

'Had you had a drink somewhere?'

'Just a bit of wine with some friends,' she says.

'What friends?' growls Mac.

'Kids. There's always kids down the Vale, drinking,' says Caris.

'You're not going there again.'

'All right, all right,' yawns Caris. 'Can I go now?'

'Thank you, Doctor,' mumbles Mac in a meek voice. *She's showing me up*, he's thinking. *She's making me look stupid.*

Caris smirks.

'Come on, Dad,' she says.

The doctor writes something down on his notes, raises his eyebrows and leaves the room. The nurse whispers, 'I'll get you some dressings for her head', and waddles off, returning with a white paper bag that she hands to Mac.

'Look after yourself, young lady,' she says to Caris in a grim voice. 'Don't go getting drunk again.'

Caris scowls, and lopes off down the long corridor, with Mac trudging after her.

Outside the hospital he phones the prison and leaves a message for Louise, while Caris sits scowling in the taxi. He knows how much the word 'accident' will hurt Louise, and hurries to tell the officious woman at the other end that everything is all right, and to tell his wife not to worry. Then he drives his daughter home, her head lolling to one side, her eyes puffy, and wonders what on earth to do.

replenishment

The park is moist with disappointment. The ravaged tree looks empty and uncared for, and passers-by feel let down. Maurice the council workman has hardly slept, thinking about the shoeless tree, and the half-dead girl outside the Snowdrop. He goes back to the dump, where there is still a pile of decomposing shoes, and reclaims several pairs, which he hurls back into the branches of the oak, before finding his supervisor and telling him he can stuff his job up his arse.

Then a young tasselled woman with a moon-faced baby comes by, meaning to show her child the tree, and finds a mess of shoes littered all over the ground, wet with dew, so she spends hours throwing them back up while her baby gurgles and points with delight.

A violinist in a long green mackintosh who walks his four ancient spaniels morning and evening comes by and notices that the tree looks a little empty. On his evening walk he brings a selection of stiff brown leather shoes that he wore as a young man. He tells his friend Harry in the fruit shop, who goes on to tell a stream of customers that the Shoe Tree is under attack.

The shoe racks in Cancer Care and Oxfam are strangely bare. By teatime the tree is completely replenished, each branch filled with an array of footwear – slippers, platforms, mules, desert boots, cowboy boots, dancing shoes, riding shoes, shoes with diamanté buckles and ridiculous heels.

219

Caris sits at home with her swollen knees and aching head, idly playing with her new mobile phone, thinking that everything is spoilt, and George lies in his room with the curtains closed, listening to music so loud that it envelops him in sound, ignorant of the fact that he has given pleasure to so many people, that he has woken up something in them that they weren't even aware of.

taxis

After the accident Caris lies glass-eyed on the settee for two days watching daytime television with Nana Price, who is inept as a guard with her baggy eyes half closing. Stella goes to school, locking her room, her sore hands in woollen gloves. Mac is back in his taxi, circling the streets of Newcastle, drumming his fingers on the steering wheel with Jeannie whining over the radio.

Today he hardly speaks to his passengers. He lugs their bags and their shopping, opens doors for them, waits for them to finish their meetings and their conversations, but can't be bothered to be pleasant. His friendliness has been squeezed out of him. He craves silence as they prattle on about the possibility of rain, and their holiday destinations. He loathes their urgency and the way that they think that their lives are important when they're not.

An Australian woman with flat horsy teeth and a vast suitcase covered in boastful stickers from all over the world gibbers on about the weather as if it's the most important thing in her life. 'It started off nice, but it's getting damp now,' she prattles, as if only she has been a witness to the state of the day. 'I think it might fog up this afternoon,' she goes on, leaning back in her seat. 'Or there might even be a storm. What do you think?'

Mac shrugs, knowing that he's not fitting into the image of the warm northerner.

'It's difficult to know what to wear,' she prattles. 'You need an umbrella with you, that's for sure. It's looking murky over there.'

She points at a corner of the sky. Mac rudely turns on the radio, hoping to shut her up, but an enthusiastic weather forecaster just excites her even more. 'He thinks it's going to rain!' she whoops. 'Did you hear that? Thundery showers and sheet lightning!'

He watches the windscreen wipers scraping back and forth, and waits in an endless traffic queue outside Central station, finally depositing her, just as a dark grey deluge of rain reaches a crescendo, and she righteously puts up her umbrella and wheels her suitcase into a throng of raincoated travellers.

The next one is a wincing man with a shock of grey hair, who eases himself into the taxi as if afraid that his bones might break. He clutches his briefcase on his lap as if it's the Crown Jewels.

'Busy?' he asks.

Mac wonders why passengers are so interested in whether he is busy or not.

'Aye,' Mac grunts.

'What time did you start?' asks the man, as if this information is vital.

'Not long ago,' mutters Mac automatically, fiddling with his mirror.

'Traffic bad?' The passenger peers through the wall of water falling on to the windscreen.

Mac doesn't respond. He sees Caris, with her bruised face, saying, 'Why are we alive?' The passenger shuts up, then, breathing loudly. He smells of some kind of cheap hotel soap, and Mac longs for him to get out of his car so that he can be alone again. When the man reaches out with one of his long fingers and touches Louise's photograph and says, 'Is that your wife?' Mac wants to hit him. He nods sharply, his eyes hard.

'Lovely, like a film star,' murmurs the man, 'with her long hair. I like long hair.'

A traffic light blinks to red. Mac can hardly breathe.

'This is it, second door on the right. Just drop us off here, thanks.'

After he's got out Mac wipes the side of Louise's photograph.

Jeannie cackles over the radio. 'Quayside. Someone called Degna.

She says she only wants you. She's going up to Jesmond. You've got a date there, Mac!'

Mac speeds up, cutting down a backstreet behind the castle, driving along a bus lane, and then left into a narrow curving street under the railway bridge to the quayside. The rain has stopped now and the city is monochrome and shining wet and black. It takes hours to get through the quayside traffic. Mac sweats inside the overheated taxi. There's a lorry transporting a bronze sculpture of a large banana that moves inch by inch along the street, escorted by drenched policemen on motorbikes, and the hold-up stretches in all directions. Mac worries that Degna will give up and walk. He rolls down his window and shouts at taxi drivers coming in the other direction. They lean towards him, saluting.

'More bloody art!' calls Steady Eddy, a driver who works for a rival firm. 'How you doing, Mac?'

'Champion,' he lies.

Eventually he arrives outside the restaurant. Mac glances at himself in the car mirror. *Look at me*, he thinks. *I'm an ugly bastard*.

He climbs out of the car and goes to the door. Inside it's full of chewing people, with forks halfway to their mouths and plates piled high with brightly coloured Mediterranean food. It sounds as if they're speaking in a foreign language. Mac goes up to a polished bar, where a waiter in an apricot-coloured shirt is pulling a cork from a bottle.

'I'm here for Degna,' Mac says, enjoying the sound of her name.

The man grimaces.

'You took your time,' he snarls.

'Traffic's bad,' Mac mutters mechanically, knowing that he won't be believed.

'Wait there.' He disappears through a door. Mac glimpses a flurry of cooks, dashing between pans. He hears the man shout, 'Your taxi's here, Degna. Do you want it or not?'

The man returns and says rudely, 'Wait outside. She'll be out in a minute.'

A woman calls from one of the tables, 'We've been waiting for a tagliatelle for half an hour!' and the waiter rushes off to serve her. Something falls and smashes in the kitchen. A male voice shouts inaudibly, a series of sharp barks.

Mac returns to his car, turning on the radio to hear more forecasts of terrible weather. Whole towns are flooded and Northumberland is full of drowning sheep. He picks up his mobile and phones home. After a while Nana picks up the receiver.

'Oh, it's you,' she gripes.

'How's Caris?'

'Sleeping,' she tells him. 'We watched that film about the shark.'

'I'll be home soon,' says Mac, thinking that he'll drop off Degna then get back.

'Louise rang,' says Nana, bristling. 'She spoke to Caris.'

'Oh.'

Nana abruptly puts the phone down, cutting him off. Mac looks up to see Degna coming out of the restaurant door. She's crying, a handkerchief held to her face, mascara running down her cheek.

'It's all right,' says Mac valiantly as she climbs into the car. 'I'm here. It's all right.'

louise

Stella has already written to Louise. She writes to her every day, her letters forming a kind of diary that Louise keeps carefully under her pillow.

Dear Mum,
I thought I should write and tell you more about Caris, and the
accident. Don't worry, she's all right. They found her unconscious
outside a pub. We don't really know what happened. She went to
hospital and Dad stayed with her, but she's come home now. She
hasn't broken anything. She had concussion, but that's gone now,
and she's got plasters on her knees. Dad's grounded her, but I don't
think she'll listen to him. I wish he would go to the school. He says
he will, but then he doesn't.
*   I just got an A-star for my English essay about* Pride and Prejudice.
I had to read it out in front of the class. Also I'm being a
representative for the school at a science conference next month. I'll
take a camera so I can show you the pictures. I hope you're doing
all right. It's not long now. Write soon. Love and hugs,
*   Stella*

Lately Louise has been dreaming that she has no arms. She keeps forgetting and tries to reach for things, only to realise that her sleeves are empty and everything is drifting past her. She knows why she dreams these things. She feels powerless about Caris, like she's being forced to watch a horrible film with a sad ending, when all she wants to do is run out of the cinema and pull her life back together. She's even stopped going to the art class; the tutor's enthusiasm was getting her down. She prefers to stuff teabags into packets in the prison factory with the radio drowning out any conversation.

Mac hasn't been in for over a week.

Every day a queue of women forms by the pay phone in their section. The phone is halfway down the corridor, so that everyone can hear what you're saying. Tonight Louise stands behind a woman who cries for twenty minutes to her boyfriend. When Louise finally gets the plastic receiver in her hand she prays that someone will be in, counting the rings as the women behind her shuffle and tap their feet. When Caris answers she nearly bursts into tears herself.

'Are you all right, love?' she asks in a shaking voice.

'Yeah, I'm all right,' says Caris.

'What's going on there? Is your dad in?'

'He's working.'

'Shouldn't he be at home with you?'

'Nana's here. We're watching *Jaws*.'

'What happened? Stella wrote and said you'd had an accident.'

Caris doesn't answer for ages. Louise pushes herself into a corner of the booth, hearing her daughter's small breaths down the phone.

'I just drank too much, that's all.'

'Can't you remember?'

'No.'

'Are you hurt?'

Caris stands in the hall, listening to Louise's questions. She bites her nails, and picks at the wallpaper, tearing off a small rose. She notices a spider scuttling over the pile of junk mail in the corner of the porch.

'Mum,' she says.

'Yes, Caris?'

'I've been putting shoes in a tree.'

Louise doesn't know what Caris is on about.

'Have you!' she exclaims 'What for?'

'For fun.'

'Sounds like a spell or something,' says Louise. 'Shoes in a tree.'

'But they took them down,' says Caris.

'Who?'

'The council, I expect.'

Louise's heart aches. She tries to control her voice, to keep Caris talking.

'That's a shame,' says Louise. 'What about school?'

'Everything's crap.'

'Why's that?'

'No one likes me.'

'What do you mean? At school?'

'Anywhere.'

Louise can hardly hear Caris above the noise in the corridor. She is pressing the receiver to her ear so hard that it hurts. She turns to the queue behind her and yells, 'Will you shut the fuck up!' They stop and stare at her, shocked to hear Louise swearing.

'I love you, Caris,' shouts Louise.

'But you're not here, are you?'

'No, but I will be.'

'They want me to go back to school, but I hate it.'

'Have you told your dad?'

'He won't listen.'

'Look, Caris, I'll be home soon. Just hang on. If you can't talk to your dad, tell the teacher you're unhappy.'

'What, Mr Fortoba?'

'Don't be like me, Caris. Don't get into trouble.'

Caris feels like crying. The sensation makes her angry. She hangs up. It feels as if she is closing a book.

Back on the settee, Caris returns to the television where children are happily swimming in a calm sunlit sea. Nana Price laughs in her sleep, showing the inside of her yellowing teeth, her decaying fillings, her wrinkled neck thrown back. Caris looks around her, at the small stuffy room and the steamed-up window. Mac's told her she's got to stay put until he gets home from work.

She slowly picks up her new mobile phone and looks at the smiley face on the small screen and carefully dials George's number.

george

On the other side of the city George is going to see a doctor with his mother. The hospital is set back from the road, surrounded by flint walls. The car park is leafy and spacious and full of expensive cars. The hospital specialises in mental health, and offers a discreet private service for depressives, alcoholics, and those with drug problems. The walls are National Trust green and there are copies of *Horse & Hound* and *Tatler* on the low mahogany table in the waiting room. Marina waits for George, drinking black coffee while a doctor asks him questions about his feelings. George answers him in a tight, dismissive voice. The doctor feels uncomfortable. He wouldn't like to spend too much time with this young man, he decides. He dislikes him, even though he doesn't let it show. The doctor doodles in the corner of his notes, drawing a picture of a worm. He prescribes antidepressants and suggests psychoanalysis. George shrugs as if he's being offered a meal that he doesn't much fancy. The sessions will cost hundreds of pounds. Privately, the doctor wonders if it might be better to drive George to the middle of a dark forest and leave him there.

Afterwards, his mother, exhausted with George's moroseness, decides to go for a facial, leaving him to look through the prospectuses of some colleges in Europe. She lies with her eyes closed in a room with whales singing, breathing in the scent of

229

orange blossom and ylang-ylang, trying to visualise happiness and success.

At home George stands in his room playing his electric guitar, closing his blue eyes, repeating the same howling guitar phrase over and over again. Everyone around him is worried. Even Helena, the cleaning lady, scuttles out of the way when he comes into rooms. His father shouts at him, as if George is in the army. George hardly hears him. His words slip away like water down a plughole. George is bored. Caris has gone. He feels as if he has lost something interesting. Something that filled up the endless, dingy days. He is even bored with his own body. George thinks that he would like to go somewhere different. To start moving. He sees himself standing with his thumb out, hitching north or south. *I could go anywhere*, he thinks.

He would like to drift and see where he ended up. To disappear.

Then the phone rings, miles away, calling through the orderly rooms. He ignores it, but then he hears footsteps through the din, and the cleaning lady's voice telling him there is a call for him, so he unplugs the guitar and bounds downstairs.

Caris's voice is shrill and accusing. For a moment George is uncertain, wary. He looks into the mouth of the receiver, as if it's trying to trick him.

'George,' says Caris, 'are you there?'

'Is it really you?' George wants to laugh.

'Of course it's me.'

'Christ,' says George. 'I thought you were dead!'

'Well, I'm not.'

'You looked dead.'

'It's not funny. I've been in hospital,' she says. 'Where have you been?'

George pauses for a moment.

'Here. Are you all right?' he says. 'I was worried.'

'I had concussion,' says Caris. 'What happened?'

'You fell out of the tree. You were drunk,' says George. 'I took you to a pub.'

'What, and left me there?'

'I was frightened,' says George. 'I thought I'd get into trouble.'

He can hear Caris's hot angry breaths down the line.

'You should have looked after me,' she says. 'Everyone saw me. Men in the pub. They were all looking at me. My dad came up to the hospital.'

'I told you, I was scared,' says George. 'Where are you?' he asks.

'Stuck at home,' she tells him. 'I've got a bandage on my head. I haven't been out for ages.'

George grins.

'Come over,' he says. 'We'll do something.'

'Now?'

'Yeah.'

While Caris creeps along the path through the trees towards George, he rifles through his mother's room until he finds some money and a credit card. He whistles as he grabs a few things – cigarettes, a lighter, a coat – and then slips out of the house, into the sound of birds singing and the muffled late afternoon, and waits for her to come to him. When she appears she looks needy and waifish. There's a bruise on her forehead that's half covered by a plaster, and her face is pinched, like a beggar's. The light in her eyes is dim, and her face is pale. She stops when she sees George and waits for him to come to her.

He walks up to her. 'Hallo,' he says.

'I don't want to go home,' says Caris. 'I don't know where to go.'

'What happened?' asks George.

'My dad said I can't go anywhere. I'm sick of it. He'll make me go back to school. Let's leave,' she says, sticking out her chin.

'What, now?'

'Yeah.'

George pushes his hair out of his face.

'Good,' he says.

Caris stands there shivering. She feels drained, and wishes that George had hugged her, or said something loving. Suddenly, more

231

than anything, she wants to lie down and sleep, and forget everything.

'Where shall we go?' says George.

'I dunno,' Caris says. 'London?'

It's nearly dark now. Caris doesn't want to go to London. She doesn't know what she wants.

'It's too late. We could go to a hotel.'

Caris has never stayed in a hotel. She looks at George suspiciously.

'What hotel?' she asks.

'We'll find one. A posh one,' says George, 'with a minibar.'

'A minibar,' repeats Caris.

'We'll stay one night, then we'll get a train or a plane somewhere.'

'Won't they think it's a bit strange, us staying in a hotel?'

'Who?'

'People that work there.'

'Fuck them,' says George. He pulls Caris's arm, and walks her away from the house, afraid that his mother might return and see them. Caris walks slowly, her head spinning, feeling sick. She imagines her father coming home, seeing Nana Price asleep on the sofa, and shouting, the whole house filled with his roaring voice, and Stella crying, and Nana lighting her cigarette and inhaling guilt. Caris hesitates, wondering if she should turn back. George turns to look at her from the corner.

'Are you coming or not?' he shouts. *His body is a hard stick*, she thinks. *He doesn't give a shit about anyone. I don't even fancy him.*

As if he's heard her thoughts, George shouts, 'I care about you, Caris!' When he says this George does care. He feels reprieved, as if Caris coming back has given him another chance.

'Do you?' she asks hopefully, taking a few footsteps towards him.

'Oh, God,' he whispers, through the quietness, 'you know I do.'

taking degna home

Degna slumps into the passenger seat. She's wearing a white blouse
with a yellow stain down the front. Her hair is wet with sweat
and tears, and is plastered to her forehead. She sits next to Mac
and sobs. Mac doesn't know if he should put his arm round her
or not. He starts to drive, not knowing how to behave, while she
shudders and snuffles beside him, eventually quietening and
blowing her nose like a man into a tissue. Then she stares bleakly
ahead, without speaking.

'Where to?' he asks her, mechanically.

'I don't know,' says Degna. 'I've given in my notice. Fucking
bastards.'

'Was it him in the orange shirt?' asks Mac.

'Yes, him and the chef. Bullies, that's what they are.'

Mac says, 'Oh. You're better off out of it, then.'

'Telling me. Northern bullies! They think they know everything.'

Mac doesn't like her voice. It sounds harsher, colder. He clears
his throat and changes gear.

'Do you fancy going somewhere?' she says.

'What for?' asks Mac.

'I just don't want to go home.'

'I can't,' he says. 'I haven't got long. Caris hurt herself.'

Degna sighs and says, 'Take me home, then', in a resigned voice.

'I'll come in with you for a bit,' says Mac, nervously, 'if you like.'

She nods, as he slowly drives up Dean Street. She doesn't speak, just stares out of the window at the people passing on the pavements. Then, as if she has only just heard what Mac said, she repeats, 'Hurt herself? Is she all right?'

'I think so,' says Mac. 'She was drunk.'

Degna shakes her head, as if getting drunk is a familiar activity.

When they arrive at her house she waits for him to gather together his phone and bag of loose change.

'You don't have to come in if you don't want to,' she says. 'I'll be all right.'

'I want to,' says Mac, getting out of the car and walking round to open her door. He doesn't want to talk about Caris, or Louise. Degna looks herself again. Calm and assured. He wants to breathe her in, to treasure her like something precious. Degna takes out her keys and unlocks the door, and he follows her into a creamy downstairs flat with a bookshelf with clean-looking books on it, a small television, a vase of white flowers on a glass table.

'Do you want a drink?' she asks.

'Go on, then,' says Mac, and leans back on the white sofa, trying to appear relaxed.

'What now?' asks Mac as Degna clinks about in the kitchen.

She brings him a can of beer and a glass.

'God knows.'

'You'll get another job,' he tells her, trying to open the beer soundlessly.

'I suppose I will.'

Degna sips a glass of red wine and stares at Mac as if she's waiting for him to do something.

'I shouldn't be sitting here with you,' he says eventually.

'Why not?'

'Your neighbours might talk!' says Mac foolishly.

'Who cares.' Degna edges closer to him. 'I don't know who my neighbours are.'

Mac wipes a film of sweat from his neck with a handkerchief. He puts his beer on the table, and stuffs the hanky back into his pocket.

Degna lets her shoes fall from her feet. 'I might set up my own business,' she tells him.

'I wanted to do that. Luxury lettuce.'

'That's a good idea.' Degna folds her feet beneath her on the sofa, staring at Mac.

'Do you think?' asks Mac.

'Why not?'

'I like you a lot,' says Mac.

'I know,' she says. 'I like you too.'

Degna reaches out, then, and touches his hand. He sees her cool fingers against his own calloused, driver's hands, and then thinks of Louise's fingernails, which are bitten down. He feels guilty, but doesn't take his hand away. Degna leans into him, her head resting on his chest. Mac smells her hair, smoothing it with his hand. She tilts her head up and Mac kisses her on the lips, tasting parsley, or maybe wine. Degna feels different; stronger and heavier than Louise. She starts to unbutton his shirt. Mac is pressed into the corner of the sofa. He doesn't want Degna to see his belly. He wishes he could draw the curtains and turn out the lamp. His stomach swells over the top of his trousers. He tries to breathe in. He didn't have a shower that morning. Degna is tugging at the lower buttons now, wrenching the shirt over his shoulders.

'Wait a minute,' gasps Mac. 'Let me up a minute.'

Mac struggles to his feet, breathless. He clumsily undresses, and then bends down and unlaces his shoes, hoping that his feet don't smell, embarrassed about a hole in one of his socks. Degna stares from the sofa. Mac smiles back at her with what he hopes is a sexy expression. She pulls him back down.

'Is this what you want?' she whispers, as she leans forward again, her unfamiliar mouth kissing his ear.

'Mmmm,' he mumbles. Her hair sticks to his mouth. He inhales her perfume as he fumbles beneath her blouse, feeling for the hooks of her bra. He tugs and presses, but can't seem to find the trick. Degna reaches behind her back to help him, undoing the bra in one practised movement, so that her breasts tumble towards Mac, with the bra moving upwards underneath her shirt.

It feels as if they are entangled by clothes, throttling and confusing them both. Mac glances up at the window to see a Chinese man walking past. He pushes Degna away, and jumps up, aware that she can see his bare hairy back as he wrenches the curtains across, turning to see Degna peeling off her white blouse, and escaping from her bra, so that, like him, she is naked from the waist up. Mac thinks he might faint. Things are moving too fast. He rushes forward, feeling his way blindly in the near dark, grabs Degna's hand and clasps it in his, kneeling on the floor in front of her.

'What are you doing?' she asks.

'I don't know.'

'I expect you're thinking about your wife?'

'Of course not.' But then he does. When Mac thinks of Louise he feels relieved. He imagines her smell, the warm touch of her fingers rubbing his back, the way she feels close up, like soft material. In a burst of light he suddenly thinks how unimportant Louise's crime is. How he wouldn't care if she'd stolen all the diamonds in Newcastle; he would still love that smell of her.

Degna strokes his head with her fingers. It makes him shudder.

'What's the matter?' she asks him.

'I don't feel right,' he stammers.

'Do you feel guilty?'

'A bit,' lies Mac, who is immersed in a deep ocean of guilt.

'She's not here, is she? I mean, she's not going to know. I won't tell her.' Degna sounds practical and businesslike now. She lets go of Mac and gulps some red wine.

'That's not the point,' says Mac, standing up again and moving away, knocking over the bottle of beer. He turns the light on. The room looks chaotic. A dark puddle of beer soaks into the carpet.

'Oh, Christ,' he says, blinking.

'I'll clear that up. Don't worry about it.'

Mac is red now. He picks his shirt up from the floor and pulls it back on, feeling like a foolish boy.

'I shouldn't be here,' he says. 'It's not right.'

'Don't worry,' soothes Degna, putting on her white shirt. 'It doesn't matter. I always fancy faithful men. It's my downfall,

236

really.' She smiles a twisted smile, then runs out of the room, returning in a loose jersey, carrying a cloth, then mopping up the spilt beer.

'I've never been unfaithful,' he says. 'It's just not what I do.'

'I know your type,' says Degna, straightening her hair. 'You don't have to explain.'

'I'm so sorry,' splutters Mac.

Degna looks exhausted. She stands up, comes right up close to Mac so that her eyes are level with his. 'You know something?' she says.

'What?' says Mac, hating the way he can't look away.

'Men like you don't like lying to their wives, but they still treat them like shit.'

Mac gulps.

'I bet you sit at home eating your tea, and you hardly speak to what's-her-name.'

'Louise.'

'She was probably bored out of her skull living with you. I mean, look at you.'

'What do you mean?'

'You don't *do* anything, do you?'

'That's not true,' says Mac. 'I look after my family.'

'Oh, sure,' says Degna.

She smirks, but then her face falls, and she looks as if she might cry.

'I'm leaving anyway,' she tells him. 'I'm going back to London. I thought it would be a new start here, but I'm just lonely.'

Mac is backing towards the door now.

'You're right. I've not been a good father,' he says. 'I've made an arse of everything.'

'What is a good father?' asks Degna philosophically, pulling a pack of cigarettes from her bag and lighting one in a careless movement.

'I should be there with them. I should be at home with Caris.'

'Off you go, then!'

237

'Everything's gone out of control,' he mumbles. 'It was all, you know, ordinary, and now it's not.'

'You'd better get back,' urges Degna, despising him.

'I've been stupid.'

She makes a face, wrinkling up her nose, and goes out of the room. Mac thinks of other taxi drivers laughing at him. Here he was, shut away with a beautiful woman, with D-cup breasts, unbuttoning his shirt, and he couldn't go through with it.

Degna is in the bathroom, wiping her nose. Later she will remember this moment as the bottom of a large pit. She'll say to a group of women friends in a bar in Islington, 'Do you know, after I walked out from that bloody job in Newcastle, I was so lonely that I even tried to seduce a taxi driver, and, wait for it, *he turned me down*!' and they will howl with laughter. But now it's not at all funny. It's horrible.

In the hallway Mac is pulling his coat back on and gathering together his things.

'Goodbye, Degna,' he calls. 'Give us a ring if you need a lift anywhere.'

He waits.

'I'm going!' he says.

'That's all right,' comes the muffled reply. 'Just go.'

'I'm your friend,' he adds. 'Remember that. I'm your friend.'

'Thanks,' she whispers, turning on the bath water to hide the sound of her sobs.

Outside, in his taxi, Jeannie is calling to him like an aged seabird trying to track down her young.

Mac climbs back into the taxi. He turns off Jeannie's voice and drives down into the nearby Vale, where he sits in a lay-by with his head in his hands, praying for guidance.

runaways

The two teenagers stand outside a modern hotel by the river,
watching the comings and goings of breathless, hurrying
businessmen and -women with leather briefcases.

'I'm not going in there,' says Caris. 'I'll feel stupid.'

'Why?' asks George. 'We can pay.'

'People'll stare at us,' says Caris. 'They'll want to know our
names.'

George spits into a gutter. He despises fear in people. He sulks.

'Let's go somewhere else,' says Caris, 'where we can be alone.'

'Where?' says George. 'It's bloody freezing.'

'We'll find another empty house,' says Caris desperately.

'Where?' repeats George crossly, thinking of minibars and room
service.

'I don't know.'

'Come on, we'll walk along the river,' snaps George. 'We can
come back here later.'

They drift along silently, aware of each other's bad moods. The
river next to them is flat as black glass. Sparkly dressed women
totter past them as if their shoes don't fit properly, wearing tight
skirts and off-the-shoulder tops on their way to bars along the
quayside. George and Caris dawdle by Italian restaurants and bars,
with fairy-lights outside, reflected in the shining water, smelling
of melted cheese and garlic. Then George sees a steep alley of steps

leading away from the riverfront, like an incision in between buildings, and starts to sprint up it. Caris's legs are stiff and sore, and her head aches. She is too tired to argue. She limps after George, stopping every few steps to catch her breath.

At the top of the steps there's a residential square, with grand stone houses flanking a mossy green with flowerbeds and laurel bushes. George circles the square, ranging about like a dog looking for a rat. Caris leans wearily against a lamp-post, waiting. George whistles from a front garden, and she goes to find him. He points at a house built of flat grey stone with blank, shuttered windows and a look of abandonment. There is a stone eagle with a broken wing on the gatepost. Caris notices a silver plate nailed to the high wooden gate: number three.

'That's the one,' says George. 'That's it.'

Caris squints at the polished door-knocker, the smokeless chimneys, the lightless rooms, and nods. George slinks down to a basement door and Caris can hear him trying the handle. Then she hears the muffled crash of splintering glass, and goes to find George, who is pushing out broken splinters from a small window-frame with his fist wrapped in his jacket.

'It's too small,' mutters George. 'We can't get in there.'

Caris puts her small white hand through the jagged hole and feels her way to the door catch, trying to pull at a freezing bolt, but it won't shift.

'I'll try the back,' says George, and creeps back out into the street to the back alley.

Caris crouches on the dank basement steps. She feels giddy, unsure of what's she's doing there. It's hard to believe that she is in the same city that she grew up in. Her childhood city was filled with encouraging faces, lifting her up, handing her lollipops, knowing her name. In Caris's world, you didn't go to places on your own. You stayed where you knew people, and now here she was, like a stranger on her own patch. She touches the mobile in her pocket. It still feels warm. She wonders where Mac is now, and if he's looking for her.

George is calling her through the letterbox of the imposing front door. Caris is about to scuttle up the steps when she sees a couple walking hand in hand around the corner, chatting loudly, and she shrinks back into the shadows, waiting for them to pass, like a criminal.

When they've gone she runs up to the slightly open door and slips into a hallway that smells of damp cloths. George crouches at the bottom of a wide flight of carpeted stairs, undoing his shoes.

'Take your shoes off,' he says. 'Leave them by the door.'

Caris walks into the living room, aware of a vast shining table, with candlesticks at either end, surrounded by high-backed chairs that in the darkness look like silent guests. There are glass-fronted cupboards, filled with blue and white china, soup tureens and sugar bowls, and heavy drapes hanging either side of a long window.

'It's creepy,' says Caris. 'It's full of old junk.'

She senses George behind her, his breath on her neck.

Caris turns and faces him, seeing the thin lines of his face in the shadows.

'I don't like it here,' she whispers.

'That's too bad,' George says.

'Let's go.'

'Why are you whispering?' George raises his voice. 'No one can hear you.' And he takes Caris's hand and pulls her back to the stairs.

'I want to eat something,' says Caris. 'I'm hungry.' She steps away from George and wanders down the spidery black hallway to where she expects to find a kitchen, but the first door she opens reveals another heavily wallpapered room, with armchairs placed round an ornate Victorian fireplace, and a pile of dusty flowers in a glass case in the corner. Caris thinks she can hear breathing. It's as if the house is asleep. She begins to panic, and runs out of the room and further into the depths of the house, through a longer hallway filled with paintings that appear like black squares against the walls. At last she finds a kitchen, smelling of old food and the paraphernalia of cookery. It's an old-fashioned room with a high ceiling and a long white table in the middle, and white cupboards. Caris doesn't find it comforting. She feels her way across the room to a fridge door and opens it to reveal a stark white interior that lights up the whole room with a cold glow. Inside there's a plate of food, covered with cling-film, that must have been recently prepared. A pint of milk, too, and a little old-lady dish of butter, and the remains of a shepherd's pie.

Someone's here, thinks Caris. *There's someone asleep upstairs.*

George has gone exploring in another direction. She can hear him moving around, opening doors and making floorboards creak.

Then she hears a quavering voice from somewhere in the labyrinth of the house; an old voice revving up like a rusty engine that has sparked alive.

'Who is it?' it croaks. 'Who are you?'

Caris cries out, shutting the door of the fridge and retreating to a corner of the kitchen, where she hides among brooms and mops. There's the sound of something falling over upstairs, and then silence.

She stands there trembling for what seems like hours and then hears footsteps coming down the hall stairs, and George shouting her name.

'What?' whispers Caris in a hoarse voice, as George comes into the room.

'There's an old lady up there,' says George in a calm, cold voice. 'She's in bed.'

'Let's go,' says Caris. 'Let's go now.'

'We can't,' says George briskly, turning on the kitchen light and pulling open a drawer. 'She's seen me.'

stella makes a wish

When Stella comes in Nana is fretting, pulling back the curtain and peering out into the street. Caris has gone.

'She was here,' says Nana, her mouth drooping into a limp downward line. 'Then she went.'

'Where?' asks Stella, standing there in her raincoat, wishing she had never come home.

'I fell asleep, and when I woke up she'd gone,' says Nana. 'She's done a runner,' she moans sadly.

'You were supposed to be looking after her,' Stella tells her.

'I'm not a bloody prison warder, Stella,' protests Nana.

'What will Dad say?' says Stella.

'I couldn't help it, pet,' says Nana, and she folds back into the chair. *She looks like an old sack*, thinks Stella.

'We should phone him,' she says quietly.

'He won't know what to do,' mutters Nana.

'We can't just do nothing,' says Stella. 'She might be in trouble.'

'This whole family is in trouble,' says Nana slowly, and then Stella realises that she's drunk again, that her lips move in slow motion over her yellow teeth. 'Let her go,' growls Nana. 'It's all you can do. Let her go.'

Stella feels useless. She puts her bag down, and sits next to her grandmother. The two of them stare at the silent television screen. A man with a gun edges round a doorway, his forehead glistening with sweat. Stella keeps her gloves on. She's worn them all day, ashamed of her hands.

'I was like Caris,' says Nana. 'I was the same. I didn't listen to no one. Look where it got me.'

Stella can't be bothered with her grandmother's negativity. She pulls her new mobile out of its bag, and dials Mac's number. It rings and rings and no one answers. Stella watches her Nana smoking a cigarette, the blue ash falling down her front as she slowly inhales, with a rigid expression on her face.

'I wish you wouldn't smoke,' she says. 'It's filthy.'

Nana looks defiant for a moment, but then stubs out the cigarette.

'I'm going out to look for her,' Stella tells her.

'It's no use, pet lamb,' rasps Nana. 'Let her go.'

'I can't sit here,' says Stella. 'I'll go round the streets and see if anyone's seen her. I'll go to Abdul's.'

Nana has descended into a place where nothing will ever get better, where she will never win at bingo, where she will get older and older until she is one of those carcasses in old-people's homes, gasping in an armchair with stick-thin arms reaching out towards the tea trolley.

'Don't leave me, pet,' she pleads, turning her befuddled head to Stella.

'You wait here for Caris. She might come back.'

'She won't be back,' says Nana pessimistically. 'She's gone. She doesn't care about us.'

Stella wants to scream. She picks up her coat and runs out of the room, slamming the door behind her, and sprints down the empty street. She wants to get hold of Caris and shake her until she cries. She walks up to the small shop on the corner of the hill, where Abdul sits counting silver behind an array of confectionery.

'Yes?' he says in a preoccupied voice.

'Have you seen Caris?' she asks him.

'She's all over the place, that girl,' says Abdul. 'She'll be taking drugs an' that down the Vale.'

'Has she been in here?'

244

'No, not tonight. How's your mother doing?' he asks. 'Does she get out soon?'

Stella doesn't answer. She turns on her heels and runs out of the shop, and down towards the Vale, too angry to be frightened of the lonely path that leads her down to the park gates. She remembers Louise telling her and Caris never to walk there at night. For them the word 'strangers' and 'the Vale' were always intertwined.

Above her the moon is a buttery yellow ball in the sky, half wrapped in clouds. She calls out Caris's name in the darkness, her voice hardly penetrating the gloom.

'Caris,' she yells, 'come here. Damn you!'

When she reaches a clearing the clouds open up and the moon lights up the landscape, throwing light on the trees. Stella stands in front of the tree that is filled with shoes, and looks up. The shoes turn in the breeze, glinting in the moonlight. Stella calls Caris again, searching for a shape among the branches, but no one calls back.

Without really thinking why, Stella takes off her sensible school shoes and ties the straps together and hurls them upwards, so that they catch on the highest branches. Then she wishes out loud, her voice as clear as a bell ringing across the lonely park. 'Please,' she pleads, 'I've changed my mind. Give me back my family. Please. Let Caris come home. Bring them all home.'

Then she stands there, shivering, feeling mud between her toes, waiting for a sign that someone or something has heard her, but there is nothing, just the call of an owl across the valley, the ever-present wail of a distant police car.

making a decision

When Mac lifts his heavy sorrowful head from his hands he knows what he must do. He looks at the dashboard of his taxi, the familiar sight of his speedometer and his petrol gauge. He strokes the gear stick, and the hand brake. He looks lovingly at the well-polished windscreen; he circles the parameter of the worn steering wheel with his fingers; and reaches out and pats the head of the ornamental Dalmatian that has nodded for years. Then he drives to the taxi rank, where a line of unemployed taxi drivers wait for rides; where Jeannie sits lazily answering the oily telephone and overseeing the network of cars that twist and accelerate around the city.

As he pulls up the other drivers salute him. He's like an old soldier in the ranks, a well-liked driver who has always been there.

Inside, the small room is filthy and dented, with a couple of girls standing with their heads pressed against the glass screen asking for a cheap fare in lean, whining voices. He can hear Jeannie telling them to walk home and to stop wasting her time. In the corner there's an ancient coffee machine, scarred with the kicks of a thousand drunks. *It's horrible here*, thinks Mac. *I never liked it*.

He knocks on the reinforced door that contains the cramped taxi office, and waits for it to be unbolted. Inside, Jeannie sits like a prisoner at the cheap desk, staring dismally at a thumb-marked screen and a telephone.

'I'm packing it in,' says Mac.

Jeannie looks at him as if he's told her that he's won the pools.

'What?' she says.

'I'm leaving.'

'Bloody hell!' she says admiringly. 'Why now?'

Mac glances around the room, as if to say, 'Look at this.' Jeannie nods.

'You'll have to see Tony,' she says.

'You tell him.'

Jeannie speaks into the microphone just under her chin.

'Mac's leaving,' she tells the throngs of drivers all over the city, and there is a frisson of astonishment running through the veins of Newcastle, as other drivers think of Big Mac, who somehow embodied the spirit of the rank. Some of them feel envy at the news.

'Is it family?' she asks Mac.

Mac nods, but he isn't going to discuss it with Jeannie, who now talks in a monotone into the receiver, her eyes still on Mac. He turns and leaves the room, and walks out of the scuffed building, and breathes in great gulps of fresh air.

The other, idle taxi drivers burst into spontaneous applause as he climbs into his car. Mac hoots his horn as he drives away, feeling their eyes on the back of his head.

When Mac arrives home he finds Nana Price packing a haphazard suitcase, the sitting room filled with her stuff: bags of dirty cosmetics, vests, a pile of romantic novels, a few tattered ornaments.

'What are you doing?' he says. 'What's going on?'

'I'm going home,' she says in a blurred voice, her hands full of thermal underwear. 'I've had enough.'

'Where's Caris? Where's Stella?'

'I can't keep them in. Caris has gone again. She waited until me back was turned and then she left. So then Stella goes. No one listens to anything I say!'

Nana stumbles and falls sideways on to the armchair, looking ridiculous as she struggles to stand up, her legs sticking up in the air.

'Come on, Nana,' says Mac. 'Come on.' Then he reaches out and helps her sit up straight, smelling the alcohol on her breath. She looks at him with her giddy eyes.

'I only wanted to help,' she whispers in a little-girl voice.

'I know, Irene,' says Mac softly. 'Let's make you a cup of tea.'

Nana falls back into the cushions, amazed as Mac boils a kettle and then brings her a mug of tea, which she takes from him with trembling hands.

'No one's going anywhere,' he says, closing her half-filled suitcase. 'Calm down.'

He gets out his mobile and sees that it's switched off, and dials Stella's number. Her breathy voice answers the phone.

'I can't find her, Dad.'

'Come on home, Stella.'

'I am nearly home. Dad, I've got no shoes.'

Mac sighs. He feels calm. He knows what he wants. He rings Caris, but this time no one answers.

nightmare

George takes a carving knife from the drawer. Caris can't speak. Her throat is tight and her body shakes. She stands there, in a stranger's kitchen, looking at the dull silver blade and the wooden handle in George's thin fingers. *How did I end up here?* she thinks. *I'm going mad.*

She sees herself in a black-and-white film, playing a bit part, her eyes shining in the gloom, her mouth open.

'Are you coming up, or what?' asks George, as if he's asking Caris if she wants to go for a walk. Caris can't speak. She feels sick. She looks at George's slitted, hard eyes, and the fine hair on his upper lip, the way he sniffs at the air like a rat.

'You should cover your face,' he says, feeling the blade. 'Just in case.'

He grabs a tea towel and throws it at Caris. She catches it gratefully, covering up her mouth, breathing in a sour, unwashed smell.

'Say something,' says George irritably.

She shakes her head. She is afraid of what she might say.

In the distance a clock strikes, a tinny flat sound that makes them both jump.

'Let's go,' whispers Caris. 'Please.'

'It's too late,' snaps George.

'What are you going to do?' she croaks.

'Sort things out,' says George. 'I'd better cut the phone line.'

George stuffs the knife under his coat and goes back towards the stairs. Caris hears him scuttling about in the hallway, pulling out wires, growling to himself.

'Come on!' he shouts. 'She could be doing anything up there!'

'I'm coming,' she calls back, feeling in her pocket for her mobile.

She looks at the phone in her hand, thinking of her father and how he must have chosen it for her. She turns it on, and a round smiling face appears on the small screen. With sweating fingers she looks for the word 'DAD' and steps back into a broom cupboard and presses the call button. When Mac answers she whispers to him like a child lost in the night.

'Dad, it's me. It's Caris.'

'I'm here,' he calls. 'Where are you?'

'I need you.' Caris sobs silently. Her voice is stuck somewhere in her chest. She squeezes the phone.

'Are you still there?' cries Mac.

'I don't know what to do,' Caris tells him. 'I'm sorry, Dad.'

'Where are you?'

'It's a square, near the quayside. It's got stone houses in it. Grass in the middle. It's number three. You've got to come. Something awful is going to happen.'

George snarls from upstairs: 'What are you doing down there?' and she switches off the phone, stuffing it into her coat pocket.

'I'm coming,' shouts Caris, winding the tea towel around her face, walking back through the ghostly parlours and smells of old polish and lace. As she climbs up the stairs she grips the banister, her knees aching. When she reaches the landing there's a passage full of doors, one of which has a thin slit of light beneath it, and Caris hears a sound, a kind of squealing, that is more horrible than anything she can imagine. George opens the door, standing there lit by a dim light. He's breathing heavily.

'What took you so long?' he asks her.

'I was looking for the toilet.'

'Did you find it?' he asks suspiciously.

'No,' she tells him.

'It's probably down there.' Then he shouts over his shoulder, 'Will you just shut up!'

Caris walks past him, tensing as she glimpses something moving in the room behind him.

She feels her way to the end of the corridor, opening doors as she goes, finding a room with furniture covered in sheets, and then another room with a single bed covered with a patchwork quilt. At last she opens a door and sees a cold, tiled bathroom. She switches on the light, smelling lavender soap and bleach, and sits on the toilet with her head in her hands, staring at her feet on the linoleum floor, and praying that Mac will come and rescue her. There's a pair of red velvet slippers on the floor that make her want to cry. They remind her of Nana Price. She dreads to think what George might be doing and forces herself to move, to pull the ancient chain, making a gurgling rattling sound as water flushes through the antique pipes.

She stumbles back to the room and forces herself to step inside, wrapping the towel around her face again.

The first thing she sees is the old woman's eyes, huge and glittering and terrified. She's hunched up on the bed, her face lit by a dim night light, and her face seems to be all bone. She has a long grey plait that is coming undone. She looks reptilian, her wrinkled neck emerging from a white nightdress. Caris blinks, unable to believe what she's seeing. George has tied a black scarf around the woman's mouth, so that she can't speak, and can only squeal. Her hands are tied in front of her in a knot of brown stockings. The knife lies on the floor, and George is pulling open the drawers of a mahogany chest, dragging out handfuls of clothes and throwing them on to the carpet.

Caris is aware of closed velvet curtains, an ornate dressing-table with a large blotchy mirror, and an immense wardrobe.

'I need some help here,' George says angrily. 'She won't keep still.'

Caris makes herself look again at the woman.

'Who is she?' she gasps.

251

'I don't know her name, if that's what you mean. I just wish she'd shut up.'

George is holding a long silk scarf in his hands. 'We ought to tie up her legs,' he says. 'You any good at knots?'

The old woman thrashes about, wriggling and kicking. Caris walks to the bedside and reaches out to her, trying to calm her down. Their eyes meet, both edged with fear. 'Sssh,' moans Caris. The old lady points to the gag around her mouth and Caris leans forward to loosen it.

'What the fuck are you doing?' shouts George. 'That took forever. She bloody bit me. Look!' He shows Caris a mark on his lower arm.

'You've got to stop this,' Caris sobs. 'You're hurting her. She's old.'

'Exactly,' growls George. 'Too old. She's nearly dead anyway.'

He strides over to the bed and pushes the old woman back so that she lies motionless.

'Hold her legs!' he commands, testing the strength of the scarf.

'I can't.'

'Yes you can.'

'I don't want to.'

'You're useless. I have to do everything round here,' says George, grabbing the old woman's leg in his hand as if it's a stray branch that needs tying down.

'Please stop!' screams Caris.

'Shut up!'

Caris looks on powerlessly as George ties the scarf round the woman's ankles. She feels helpless. The woman has stopped struggling now. Caris walks over to the window and pulls back the heavy curtains, looking down on the dismally empty square.

'Come away from there,' George says. 'Someone might see you.'

He follows her to the window and grabs her wrist, pulling her back into the room.

'Let me go!' cries Caris.

'Go and sit on the bed with her,' says George. 'Just sit still.'

Caris does what he says. George picks up the knife and

contemplates it, as if it's his only ally. He looks at himself in the mirror, pushing his hair back from his eyes. Caris watches him in the glass, seeing herself and the old woman reflected there behind him, both shaking. She reaches under the covers and touches the woman's bony elbow, trying to impart hope with one small touch. Downstairs the tinny clock chimes again, reminding Caris that time is running out.

George starts to clean his fingernails with the knife, glancing up slyly at Caris and the old woman. Caris remembers the first time she saw him, standing innocently beneath the tree, and how blue his eyes were, how entranced she was by him. Now she hates the sight of him.

'I wish you'd speak,' he says, sulking. 'It will start getting light soon. We'll have to leave.'

'Where will we go?' asks Caris.

'Anywhere we like.'

'I don't feel very well,' she tells him.

'Take an aspirin,' he grunts.

'I want to go home,' Caris pleads. George doesn't answer. He opens the wardrobe door and peers inside at a row of gloomy coats. He kneels down and pulls out some shoes.

'It stinks in here,' he mutters. 'It's bloody old, like everything. Like her.'

The woman tenses next to Caris.

'Why don't we get some sleep?' suggests Caris. George ignores her. He opens a hat box and pulls out a mossy green hat, which he places on his head.

'What do you think?' he asks Caris, who tries to answer, but her voice comes out more like a sob.

Caris wonders where Mac is, and why he's taking so long. She strains to hear the sound of his taxi turning the corner, the familiar tones of gears changing, doors opening and slamming shut, but there's nothing, only the urgent gasps of the woman huddled next to her on the bed. George is putting on a fur coat now, turning this way and that to admire himself in the mirror. He looks bizarre, like an animal in human clothes.

253

She must have worn that hat and coat, thinks Caris, *to a wedding, or a funeral, or a day out. She chose it in a shop. It must have cost a lot of money, and now George is spoiling it. She'll never wear it again after this.* The room is a mess now, strewn with shoes and underwear. Caris turns to the woman and mouths the words, 'I'm sorry.'

Mac, Stella and Nana Price are all in the taxi, driving up and down narrow streets looking for Caris. It's after midnight, and drunks keep on stepping out into the road, with flailing arms, trying to flag down a ride. Mac tries to phone Caris again, but the phone is switched off. He keeps on repeating her words to himself. 'You've got to come. Something awful is going to happen.'

They find a square, but the houses are built of red brick and there are no gateposts, just trim hedges and wrought-iron gates. Nana and Stella sit in the back. Stella studies an *A to Z*, holding it close, tracing her finger over the intricate black-and-white grid of streets. Mac feels desperate. He thought he knew every part of Newcastle, and now his knowledge is failing him. He's dizzy, driving down cul-de-sacs, then reversing backwards, cursing. At last they turn into a side street that Mac has never seen and find themselves surrounded by gloomy stone buildings in a secluded square.

'I can't see this place on the map. Look!' Stella jabs at the *A to Z*.

'This is it,' announces Mac. 'This must be it.'

'Creepy,' mutters Stella.

'What's Caris doing here?' mumbles Nana Price, who is wrapped in a tartan blanket and looks like a bewildered refugee.

Mac stops the taxi. A cat runs out of the darkness and is caught in the headlights. It looks affronted, paralysed for a second, before slithering underneath a hedge.

'I've never been here in my life,' says Nana. 'Funny how you can miss somewhere.'

Mac climbs out of the car. Most of the windows are dark. The square feels oppressive, as if it doesn't welcome strangers. Mac glances back at the taxi, seeing his daughter and mother-in-law lit up in the back seat, both looking unsure and worried. He walks down the pavement, counting the house numbers, until he reaches number three. In an upstairs window there is the faintest glimmer of light.

George is sitting on the edge of the bed now, still wearing his ludicrous hat, holding the knife. He slices at the air, enjoying the way that Caris and the woman flinch. He knows that he's lost Caris. She's sided with the old lady. They huddle together like old friends, watching him with frightened eyes. Their fear makes him feel superior. He likes the taste of it in his mouth. He leans over and pulls the old woman's long grey plait.

'What are you doing?' whispers Caris, horrified as George holds the plait in his hand like a dead snake. The old woman curls against Caris, whimpering.

George grimaces, and hacks at the plait with the knife. Caris watches in horror as it frays like a rope, until George holds it above his head like a trophy.

'How long did it take you to grow that?' he sneers, throwing it across the room. 'You should have cut it off years ago. It's unhygienic, isn't it, Caris?'

Caris hears a car purring along the street outside. It stops and the engine is turned off. She holds her breath. She prays. She can hear footsteps outside, and speaks to cover the sound.

'Have you got a cigarette?'

George turns to her with his eyebrows raised.

'So you *can* speak!' he mocks.

'There's some wine downstairs in the fridge,' she tells him. George looks at her coldly.

'Go and get it, then,' he rasps.

But Caris is afraid to leave George alone with the old woman. She tries to smile at him, but the thought doesn't reach her mouth.

'My legs hurt,' she tells him.

Grudgingly George reaches inside his pocket for the packet of cigarettes. He lights one and passes it to Caris. Her hands shake as she puts it to her lips and inhales. George ambles to the door of the room, turning to look at her with a warning expression.

255

'Don't do anything,' he says, 'or I'll kill you.'

Caris nods. She listens to George padding downstairs. She furtively loosens the gag around the woman's mouth.

'Are you all right?' she asks.

'Who on earth *are* you?' croaks the woman. Her voice is Scottish, and much sweeter than Caris had imagined.

'Caris.'

'What will he do?'

Caris doesn't know what to say; already she can hear George bounding back up the stairs. 'Someone will come,' she whispers. She puts the gag back in place, but the brief conversation has cheered both of them, and Caris is suddenly braver, and angrier. The door opens and George appears carrying a bottle of wine and a long-stemmed wine glass. He pours some wine into it and sips at it, as if he's tasting wine in a restaurant. The clock downstairs strikes one and George frowns, as if he has important things to do. He drains the glass, then throws it at the fireplace where it shatters.

Outside Mac is pushing at the locked front door. Stella and Nana hover by the gate now, nervously watching. Mac shrugs, not knowing what he should do next. He rings the doorbell, hearing a deep ring reverberate through the old house. He waits. Nothing happens. Stella tiptoes up to join him.

'Perhaps she can't answer the door,' says Stella. 'We should go round the back.'

'It might be the wrong house,' says Mac.

'We've got to make sure.' Stella strides back out to the street and Mac pushes at the doorbell one last time before joining her, leaving Nana Price flapping her tartan arms under a street lamp. They find an alley running between two houses, which leads to the back lane. Behind the houses there's a regiment of green rubbish bins, each one numbered. The back of number three has a redbrick wall with broken glass glinting along the top, but when Stella pushes at the door it opens easily. They find themselves in an enclosed back yard, filled with ragged plants in terracotta pots. There's a glass porch, and a pane has been smashed. Shards of glass lie on the ground. The door is slightly open.

They step inside, afraid now.

'Wait,' whispers Stella. 'I think we should call the police. Just in case.'

'In case of what?' mumbles Mac.

'I don't know.'

'Who's ringing the fucking doorbell?' rages George, trying to look down from the window. Caris has her arms wrapped around the old woman now. She feels like a bag of bones.

'I don't know!' she lies.

He grabs the old woman by the shoulders and shakes her.

'Who is it?' he says.

The woman dumbly shakes her head.

'It was you, wasn't it?' growls George, turning to Caris. 'You stupid little cow.'

'I don't know what you're talking about,' Caris tells him.

'Oh, Christ,' George is white underneath his wide hat. 'I think there's someone down there.'

Caris can hear creaking steps on the stairs now. George runs to the door, holding the knife. Suddenly Caris is afraid for Mac. She jumps from the bed and faces George.

'It's my dad,' she cries. 'He's come to get me!'

The door opens. Mac stands there in his leather jacket with an expression of disbelief on his face. Behind him Caris can see Stella, her white hands held to her cheeks in horror. The old woman begins to wriggle and squeal again. Caris sees Mac taking in the chaotic room, the gagged woman, the strange sight of George in a green hat and fur coat. With a surge of exploding energy, she leaps on to George's back, pushing her face under the fur collar to bite into his smooth neck with sharp teeth, digging her nails into his face and eyes, so that he screams with pain, and falls backwards, the knife clattering to the floor. She's struggling in a scrum of fur and elbow, kicking and yelping, until suddenly George is yanked away and she sits up to see Mac, shaking his head, holding George by the scruff of his neck, like he's a dog.

Caris is aware of Stella behind her, untying the old woman, murmuring kind words to her. She looks at George, standing there, bedraggled and defeated. He stares back at her, a thread of blood dripping from his nose, a raw scratch across his cheek.

Then he opens his mouth and screams, a high-pitched scream that echoes through the house, rattling the chandeliers. He stamps his foot and rages, like a child having a tantrum. Mac and the three women look at him in amazement. George looks like an apparition, like a goblin who might disappear in a cloud of sulphur, with his glittering, bloodshot eyes, his mouth an awful screaming hole.

At last George stops screaming, snot dripping from his nose, his head hanging down.

'Well, Caris!' says the old woman in a loud and annoyed voice, 'you're well rid of that lunatic!'

Then, abruptly, Caris starts to snigger, her laughter gathering momentum. Mac shocks himself by joining in. Caris points at George and guffaws, and even Stella and the old woman giggle from the bed. The laughter becomes a wave of hilarity, filling the room. George, hearing their laughter, steps backwards. He panics, his wild expression coming undone, and turns and runs from the room, scarpering down the stairs, their laughter burning him like flames, straight into the wide blue arms of an overweight policeman, who stands on the front step, thinking he's been called out on a wild-goose chase.

dawn

Mac knows everything now. He has sat on the hard chairs of interview rooms and listened to Caris tell her story. Mrs McPhee, for that was her name, has been taken to hospital and is also telling her story, in which Caris features as a heroine. George has been ushered away to a police cell, while his parents sit uneasily on opposite sides of the reception room in buttoned-up clothes with an expensive lawyer standing between them who has a sharp nose and a cashmere scarf knotted round his neck.

Mac and Caris walk past them, ignoring their frozen expressions, arm in arm. They climb into the familiar warmth of the taxi, but now it's silent, with no Jeannie to interrupt the peace.

'I didn't tell you, I gave up my job,' says Mac.

'What?' Caris says.

'I've left my job.'

'For ever?'

'Yes.'

'Oh,' replies Caris. 'Good.'

They drive in silence, exhausted. Caris looks out of the window as they crawl along by the Vale. Then she suddenly sits up and shouts, '*Stop!*' by a white bridge. Mac nearly jumps out of his skin, but he does what Caris says, turning the engine off. They sit side by side, both aware that something has changed.

Nothing feels urgent any more.

It's barely dawn and the park is laced with an ethereal mist that floats between the trees. There's a loud dawn chorus of waking birds. Caris opens the car door and tells Mac to come with her, and he steps from the car and stretches his arms into the air, yawning.

'What now?' he asks her.

'I want to show you something,' she tells him, and disappears through an arched gate and up a winding path into the woods. Mac follows her. He feels as if nothing will ever be the same. Caris calls back to him through the trees. She sounds like a small girl. Mac climbs after her towards the clearing where the Tree of Shoes stands dripping with dew.

'This is how it started, me and George,' she tells him.

She looks and sees that the tree is filled with shoes again, as if by magic.

'I thought it was spoilt,' she says, 'but it isn't. Look, Dad.'

She climbs up into the tree and looks down at him.

Mac stares up at his daughter. She reminds him of something from a story book.

'A tree of shoes,' he repeats.

'Do you like it?' asks Caris.

'I don't know. What does it mean?' asks Mac, noticing his brown brogues dangling above him.

'I don't know,' says Caris. 'It was just something I did, with George.'

'Is that the end of it?' asks Mac.

'I think so,' she says, patting the bark with her palm.

'Will you go back to school now?'

Caris looks young and sad. She turns to Mac without answering, and he suddenly doesn't care if she goes to school or not.

'Let's go home, love,' he says, holding out his hands, guiding her back to the ground.

release

Caris stands in the driveway of the prison, feet apart, eyes bright, waiting for her mother. It seems like hours before the heavy door creaks opens and Louise steps out, squinting, into fresh air. Caris gasps. Her mother looks completely different, more defined, older. She looks like the last survivor of a battle.

Louise is wearing her old court clothes but they no longer fit her. She holds her handbag uncomfortably in her fingers, as if it's an accessory that's been forced on her. And all her hair has been cut off, revealing a thin, strong face, like drawing the curtains back in a darkened room so that everything is suddenly very clear.

Caris feels as if her heart is wrapped in tight elastic bands that keep snapping apart. She doesn't know what to do. She smiles hopefully, as Louise approaches her.

'Who cut your hair?' she blurts.

'Carol did it in hair-and-beauty skills,' says Louise. 'Do you like it?'

Mac stands behind Caris in a loose green jersey, looking nervous, his hair grown to a dark shadow on his head, and his face is expectant and afraid. Louise thinks of the word 'divorce' and nods at him politely, bravely. She wonders if he's spoken to Caris and Stella about it. She raises her eyebrows, and Mac walks up to her and takes her handbag, as if it's too heavy for her.

Louise holds up her wrist and shows him her watch. 'It stopped,' she tells him, 'months ago.'

'I'll wind it up for you,' says Mac, 'later.'

Their eyes meet. Mac touches her hand, squeezing it. *Something's changed*, she thinks. *It's not over yet.*

Stella runs up, wearing tight jeans. She has plasters on her fingers, and she looks taut and eager. She takes Louise's arm, and Caris takes the other. Nana Price totters towards her happily, wearing a silvery tracksuit, sucking a toffee. She's holding a bunch of ragged carnations and grinning wildly. *She's not smoking*, thinks Louise, who gave up in prison, and was dreading the temptation of her mother's Embassy Regals. Nana starts waving the flowers, some of the flower heads dropping on to the tarmac.

'Where's the taxi?' asks Louise.

Caris giggles.

'I sold it,' says Mac.

'Sold it?' repeats Louise, confused.

'Just like that,' says Stella.

'I decided we didn't need it,' adds Mac.

'He's given up his job as well,' cuts in Caris.

'Caris got in trouble,' interrupts Stella. 'Big trouble.'

'Sssh,' Mac holds his fingers to his lips. 'It's all right now.'

Nana thrusts the flowers against Louise's chest.

'It's over,' she whoops. 'You're out!'

'How are we supposed to get home?' Louise is puzzled.

'Public transport,' says Mac cheerfully.

'What?' Louise has never seen Mac on a bus or a train. It's just not something he does.

'We'll get the bus,' says Mac, and starts to walk along the prison driveway, his feet crunching on the gravel, his daughters hobbling after him, shivering in the cold.

'The bus?' repeats Louise again.

'He's turned over a new leaf.' Caris turns back to speak to her mother.

Louise thinks of lettuce. In her bag she has the rolled-up painting that was in the exhibition. *Maybe I'll show them later, when we get home*, she thinks. Nana toddles behind them, wheezing, and Caris puts her head on her mother's shoulder.

'Are you all right, Caris?' asks Louise.

Caris wipes her cheek and nods. She wants to whoop and giggle, to run about like a yelping puppy, but she wants to cry as well.

'Caris is going to change schools,' whispers Stella.

Louise hands Caris a handkerchief that she finds screwed up in the bottom of her handbag, filled with tears from months ago. Old tears.

The group reach the end of the prison driveway. There's a long, tree-lined road with banks of daffodils stretching in either direction. Louise looks around helplessly for a bus stop. She can't recall a time when the family rode together on public transport. She's not even sure there is a bus from there to Newcastle.

Then Mac turns to her with an expansive expression, his arms flung in the air, like that time when he started singing hymns.

'*Surprise!*' he shouts.

Louise is confused. She squints at Mac.

'I'm not sitting near the sink,' says Caris. 'It smells of egg.'

'Well, you needn't think I am,' Stella snaps.

Louise sees a rather dilapidated blue and white camper van with checked curtains and white leather seats.

'Is that thing yours?' she asks Mac.

'It's ours. Get in.' Mac looks smug.

'I'll sit in the smelly seat,' says Nana nobly.

The doors open with a rusty squeak.

Louise stares at the van.

'Has it got an MOT?'

'Of course,' says Mac.

'Wait,' says Louise.

Everyone stops and looks at her.

'I'm not sitting in the back.'

'Why not?' Mac sounds hurt.

'I want to drive,' she says.

A look of panic crosses Mac's face.

'Can you drive, Mum?' whispers Caris.

'Of course I can drive.' Louise holds out her hand, waiting. Mac drops a set of car keys into her palm. Then she strides round to the driver's seat, climbs in and fiddles with the ignition. Caris is impressed. She gets in next to Louise, watching her mother moving the gear stick and checking out the indicator. Mac climbs in next to her with Caris squashed in the middle. She feels their hot bodies pressed against her and squirms.

Louise turns on the ignition and the van shudders to life.

'Where to?' says Louise, glancing backwards and then into the mirror, pressing her foot down on the accelerator.

'Just drive, Mum,' says Caris.

So Louise indicates and swerves out into the road, following a sign that says 'ALL TRAFFIC'.